James H. Graff, Archibald C. Gunter, William H. C. Russell, C. P.
Morgan

Running the Blockade

James H. Graff, Archibald C. Gunter, William H. C. Russell, C. P. Morgan

Running the Blockade

ISBN/EAN: 9783337383428

Printed in Europe, USA, Canada, Australia, Japan

Cover: Foto ©Andreas Hilbeck / pixelio.de

More available books at **www.hansebooks.com**

RUNNING THE BLOCKADE.

BY

LIEUT. WARNEFORD, R.N.,

AUTHOR OF "THE PHANTOM CRUISER," ETC.

LONDON:

WARD, LOCK, AND TYLER, WARWICK HOUSE,

PATERNOSTER ROW.

CONTENTS.

RUNNING THE BLOCKADE.

——

THE "NORTH STAR."

THE British public read from time to time in the newspapers that an English vessel, endeavouring to run the blockade of the Southern States, has been captured by a Yankee cruiser, and taken to Key West, or some other American station, where, if there be only a plausible pretence for doing so, it is sure to be pronounced a lawful prize. So loose, however, is the blockade, that running pays uncommonly well on the average. The capital employed in the trade, already enormous—there never being less than contraband of war to the value of two millions sterling at Nassau alone, ready for shipment—is rapidly increasing, and our seamen like the business immensely. The excitement inseparable from such enterprises,—the high wages paid,—an instinctive contempt and dislike of the bragging Yankees—attract them to, and retain them in the service; and there appears to be little doubt that, should the suicidal war continue many

months longer, a new and formidable brotherhood of
the coast will have been created, who will practically
nullify the blockade, careless of the cobwebs spun by
Vattel and other adepts in international law.   I
myself once heard the eloquent member for Birmingham observe, at a public meeting, in reply to the
objection that the blockade not being effective, was for
that reason invalid,—that it was only too effective,
forasmuch that no cotton could be brought away from
the blockaded coast. This blunder of Mr. Bright's
was loudly cheered by his admirers. The vessels
which run the blockade with cargoes of military munitions could with equal success bring away cotton,
if the Southerners would but sell it—at a paying
price, the risk being reckoned. This, however, they
will not do: from no ill-will towards the English
nation—very far indeed from that ; but because they
believe that the cotton famine must ultimately, and
at no very distant day, compel the British Government to interfere and terminate the disastrous conflict.
They know very well, heedless of anything Parlia-
mentary and platform orators may say to the contrary,
that were the essential conditions of the war changed,
by the opening of the Southern and shutting up of the
Northern ports, by the British fleets, the most frantic
Northerner would see that the game was up, and
nothing to be done but to make the best terms possible
with the South.   This, at all events, is the conviction
of every officer of the ships engaged in this popular

contraband commerce with whom I have spoken upon the subject; and their opinion is surely entitled to more weight than that of stump-spouters, or the sensible gentlemen who argue that the quickest and most effectual way to quench a conflagration which threatens at any moment to set your own house in flames, is to wait, with folded arms, till it goes out of itself. I am not, however, about to write politics. That, thank God, is not my vocation. Having a large acquaintance with those officers, I have been kindly supplied by them with materials for these sea-stories—the only condition imposed being that nothing shall slip from my pen (my friends being, with one exception, still engaged in the traffic) that may too closely identify them, or afford " the enemy" a hint he might take advantage of.

I start, then, with the *North Star*, a sailing clipper-brig of large tonnage, commanded by my old friend Samuel Rowley, one of the first vessels that left England for the express purpose of running the blockade. She cleared for Nassau in the Bahamas; but would, if opportunity favoured, slip into Norfolk, Charleston, or other port north of the Florida peninsula; and, failing in that, touch at Nassau, and wait for a favourable chance of trying her luck at one of the ports in the Gulf. As I had this narrative mainly from Rowley's own lips, I shall relate it in the first person, and as faithfully as memory, *ad memoranda*, will serve, in the stern old salt's own words. To excuse the bitterness with which he speaks of Yankees, I have only to mention that a son of his—a wild slip, but his only son—ran from his perhaps too sternly disciplined home, though all was done in love, and worked his passage out to America, possessed as he was of all the elements, and a portion of the experience, which make up an English seaman, and there regularly engaged in the American Mercantile Marine. He had his reward, poor young man. He accepted a berth in the *Constellation*, bound from New York to Liverpool, with a cargo of bread-stuffs, the officers of which ship appear to have been the most unmitigated ruffians that ever trod even an American vessel's deck. Young Rowley in some way incurred the animosity of the chief mate, who, with the tacit concurrence of his equally brutal brother officers, so maltreated and scourged the helpless English youth, with knuckle-dusters, cat-o'-nine-tails, belaying-pins, and like weapons of masterful cowardice, that John Rowley died a few days after the Liverpool police took him out of the *Constellation*, and placed the murdered lad in hospital. The case was heard at the police court; but, as the wounds which caused death had been inflicted upon the high seas, beyond British jurisdiction, the matter was referred to the American Consul, which, as hundreds of examples testify, invariably means impunity to the assassins. Cotton— the exigency of Lancashire—has hitherto almost compelled the British Government to wink at such atrocities; and one of the immense benefits—largely

compensating for present suffering—sure to result from
the American Civil War, compelling us to enthrone
King Cotton in our own dependencies, will be to
enable the English Minister to take prompt and stern
action in such cases. There is no maxim of international law more firmly established than this : That
if the authorities of a country cannot, or will not,
punish outrages upon the persons or properties of
foreigners temporarily subject to their jurisdiction, the
sovereign power to which the victim or victims owe
allegiance has a right to fulfil that duty for them.
The cotton incubus removed, England will be free to
use the sword with such effect that " *Civis Anglicanus
sum*" shall cease to be a mockery on board a Yankee
ship.

" I was stranded, Warneford," said Captain Rowley,
" as I thought for life, and not much caring how soon
that life came to an end, when the American row
broke out. John, as you know, had been murdered
about a year before. The boy's death had killed his
mother ; so I had been a childless widower about
seven months. I had plenty of property, and wanted
for nothing, except a chance of blowing that villain
Chidley's brains out (Chidley was the chief mate of the
Constellation). No such luck as that was, in the natural
course of things, to be hoped for ; but the idea got
fixed hold of me that I should like to kill a few
Yankees—in fair fight, you know ; not with knuckle-

dusters and iron belaying-pins. I was afraid, for a time, that the braggadocio scoundrels wouldn't fight. They did, however, after a fashion, at Bullies' Run——"

"Bull Run."

"Bullies' run, it ought to be, if it isn't. Well, time went on ; but it seemed that I should never get my idea into ship-shape working order. I tried, you remember, I and Wilford, to get up a company, limited for the purchase and fitting-out of a fast, well-armed, well-manned steamer, to sail under the Palmetto flag, and prey upon the Yankee commerce. Twenty thousand pounds, at least, would have been required, and it being generally thought that Samuel Rowley would go heart and soul at the work, and wouldn't be likely to bungle it, we should have got the money, and, lawful or unlawful, have fitted her out in Liverpool, and got clear off to sea but for one thing, which upset tho whole scheme—we should nowhere be able to dispose of our prizes ! That was a settler ; so I tried to console myself with the accounts in the newspapers, showing that Yankeedom was going to the devil as fast as could reasonably be hoped or expected.

"That blessed thought was warmer at my heart than usual one afternoon, when Tater Roberts, as they call him — (Tater Roberts was the popular sobriquet of the wealthy shipowner, Mr. Edward Roberts, who gave a female servant in charge to the police for the crime of bestowing a few cold potatoes in charity upon a beggar)—when Tater Roberts, as they call him,

dropped in, as if he hadn't meant to—had called about
nothing particular. You know the man—a wide-
awake gentleman, that. Can steer full and by as
cleverly as any man in Lancashire. I couldn't persuade
him to put his name down for a guinea in the priva-
teering project. It was an immoral enterprise, objected the hoary sinner. So, after chatting about a
score of things he did not care a pin for, out at last
comes what was really working like yeast in his knowing noddle—not freely, all at once, but like liquor out
of a bottle, into which the cork has been pushed instead
of pulled out. His clipper-brig, *North Star*, a fine
roomy ship, which, though about 500 tons register,
could stow away between 600 and 700 tons without
lessening her speed, had just finished shipping a full
cargo, consisting of Enfield rifles, gunpowder, and
seven Whitworth cannon, destined for the Confederates. I had been skipper, you may recollect, of the
North Star during two trips to St. Petersburg, and
knew that no canvas vessel sailed the seas better
fitted to run the American blockade than she. From
being so out-and-out fast upon a taut bowline—
only a steamer could keep to windward of her.

" 'If,' said Tater Roberts, 'we succeed in landing
those military stores at a Southern port the profit will
be considerable.'

" 'I should think it would,' says I; 'a little fortune
—and not so very little either.'

" He wanted me to command her, don't you see,

because he well knew I would sooner sink her with every soul on board than let the Yankees get her. That suited his game first-rate, the brig's cargo being insured 'special' against total loss ; but not against capture, the premium being too exorbitant.

" 'If,' he goes on, in his oily, coaxing way, as if I wanted oiling and coaxing to go at the Yankees ; 'if, my brave Samuel, you succeed in placing the rifle-cannon with the gunpowder safe in the hands of the Southerners, they'll be the means of sending a whole army of Yankees to kingdom come. With respect to terms, you must be moderate, as there are several prime seamen——'

" 'D—n terms,' said I, jumping up ; 'if you've cleared the brig, and got the right sort of crew shipped, I'll drop down the Mersey this very night.'

" I must not dwell upon these minor matters, or the yarn will spin out to an unconscionable length. Enough that the crew were of the right sort, with arms and ammunition in plenty. I had also insisted upon shipping a swivel forty-two pounder, which we could mount amidships, should there be a necessity to do so, in a very short time. So we sailed in good spirits for the Bahamas. I know that coast so well that I almost fancy I could feel my way without the use of eyes through its tortuous channels. Absurd, of course—quite so. I need not tell you what baffling weather we meet with in those horse latitudes. I used, when in command of the *Dolphin*—trading between Liverpool and Charleston, sometimes calling at the Bahamas for sea-island cotton—to adopt the old-fashioned plan of getting well to the south'ard, and drifting back with the Gulf Stream, and found it answer. That of course was not to be thought of upon the actual occasion. I intended, if no better chance offered, to sail direct for Nassau, and wait there for a sneezer from the east or north-east. It would be March when we arrived out, and were not therefore likely to be humbugged and baffled by the westerly or south-westerly winds, which in autumn blow steadily off the American coast. You don't want to take lessons in navigation ?—No excuses needed ? That was what you looked.—All right!

"Well, we arrived out, as I may say, in about eight weeks from the day of departure from Liverpool. We had seen only one vessel of the blockading squadron, a steam-sloop, but at a great distance off, who did not see, or at all events did not suspect the *North Star* to have the wicked intention of running the blockade. We were then in Chesapeake Bay, keeping a good offing, but intending soon to stand boldly in for my old port—Charleston. Whilst the Yankee steamer was in sight, certain suspicions which I and Wilford (who I had insisted should be engaged as chief-mate) entertained of one of the crew, a cute-looking chap, John Adams by name, were confirmed. He had the inconceivable audacity, careless wantonness, or stupidity, to let fly the fore-sheet, the brig being close-hauled. We at once concluded that this was intended as a signal to the steamer, probably one of a number arranged to be given by the American spies, shipping themselves for that purpose on board 'contraband' British ships. It had fortunately not been seen, but it was necessary to stop that game at all hazards. I sent for John Adams; he was death pale, and trembled very much when he entered the cabin. Addressing him in my sternest manner, I said, 'You shipped in the name of John Adams, and declared yourself a native of Devonshire—both lies I have no doubt. Your hatchet, lanthorn-jawed Yankee phiz, disgusted me directly I saw it, which did not happen till we were four or five days at sea. And now, mark me attentively, John Adams. You are, I doubt not, a very clever fellow, and far too much in a general way for any Britisher. It so happens, however, upon this particular occasion, you have placed yourself in a very awkward fix—an infernally awkward fix—which I wish you clearly to realize. Spare your breath, John Adams. Nothing you could say would alter the situation, which I am desirous you should thoroughly realize, in the least. It is this: if by any chance—through no fault whatever of yours—the *North Star* should be overhauled by a Yankee cruiser, I myself, or should I be otherwise busy, Mr. Wilford—half a dozen others whom I have instructed —will, first blowing your head off, then pitch you into the sea. You understand. Now go to your duty.

"The very next day, at about two bells p.m., another

steam cruiser was descried. The weather had been thick since the dawn, and suddenly clearing up showed us the sloop-of-war, with the stars and stripes at the main, only about two leagues away to windward. She proved to be the *Tuscarora* that lately had the impudence to pretend keeping guard over the *Nashville*, in the Southampton waters. Fortunately, she did not sight us so soon as we did her, and as she no doubt would see us in a few minutes, more or less, and escape being out of the question, I immediately ordered the helm to be put down in order to bear up directly towards the cruiser. The Jack, upside down, was run up as a signal of distress. I noticed that John Adams was uncommon fidgety and dreadfully scared, not knowing what to be at. So I thought I'd just give him a 'refresher,' as the bewigged and be d——d lawyers, in that cause I had against the lord of the manor, used to call an extra pull at my purse.

"'John Adams, lad,' said I, 'you wont forget that little conversation we had yesterday. I don't think we shall be nabbed by the smoker yonder; but if we are *very likely* to be, I shall keep the pleasant promise I made you. Be quite sure.'"

"I thought that dodge of the Federal Government feeing one or more sailors shipped in vessels suspected of an intention to run the blockade, to signal the American cruisers, easily enough done in a hundred ways, was quite a recent Yankee notion."

"As recent as the beginning of their brutish *un-*

civil war. The cunning, if anything but wise Washington people, are equal to that sort of sea-strategy. Well, the sails of the *North Star*, close hauled, and steering to meet the steamer, had hardly begun to draw when the *Tuscarora* spied us, stopped her engine, and waited to hear what we wanted. The brig kept on till within hailing distance through the trumpet. Then hove to.

"'What ship is that?'" sung out the Yankee captain.

"'*The Edinburgh Castle*,' says I, bold as brass—that vessel, as I knew, and I doubted not the American knew from his list of departures, having sailed from London a day or two before we left Liverpool.

"'*The Edinburgh Castle*,' (of course we had no name painted at the stern,) 'from London to Rio Janeiro, driven out of our course. Leaky and short of water. Want medicines. Small-pox on board. Can you lend us a surgeon?—Ours dead of the disease.'

"There was a hurried consultation on the *Tuscarora's* quarter-deck; a brief one, during which I had one eye upon her and another upon John Adams. The American captain reappeared at the steamer's side.

"'Send a boat; two if you can, for the water and medicine. We can't spare the surgeon.'

"'Thank you kindly,' said I.

"'Please ask the surgeon to write down the proper directions. Cases very severe. What our doctor called virulent.'

"Two boats were lowered and sent off. Wilford

went in one, the second mate, in whom I had equal
confidence, or nearly so, in the other. All the water
that could be spared was lowered into the boats ;—the
medicine, with directions also ; but not one of the probably infected men was permitted to go on board,
though that audacious trump, Wilford, expressed an
earnest wish to personally consult the surgeon with
respect to one very bad case, that of the second mate,
a particular friend of his. The modest request was
civilly declined, and Wilford, with grateful thanks for
the water and medicine,—an imaginary thumb the while
with continuations of outspread fan-like fingers pressing the tip of his nose —bade the men give way—and
was quickly alongside. The steamer had meantime
gone ahead, and would soon be at a comfortable distance.

" 'Not a trick that to be sneezed at,' said I,
slowly passing John Adams, ' for a beef-bellied
Britisher, eh? I was really afraid that the pearl-but-
toned pea-jacket of this young chap would by this
time have been disturbing the digestion of a shark.
His employers ought to pay him well, if only for the
fright ?'

" After that, I had no trouble with John Adams. He
was seized with diarrhœa, slipped his cable in less than
twenty-four hours, was sewed decently up in his
hammock, and with a twenty-four pound shot to assure
him a sea-sepulchre more suitable to a Christian,
though a scampish one, than the stomach of a shark,

dropped overboard. We found ample proof among his papers that he was a well-paid tool of an American agent at Liverpool. His name was, however, John Adams, and himself a native of Exeter.

"I determined, the wind having veered to east northeast, and blowing half a gale, to run direct for Charleston. The change of wind occurred during the night. The *North Star*, directly my mind was made up, was got before the wind, and we cracked on at a famous rate.

"The dawn showed us we had pressing need to do so : two Yankee steam gun-boats were lying-to scarcely a mile distant, and the instant we were seen both gave chase,—firing at first blank, next shotted guns to bring us to. The *North Star* declined the invitation ; we got more sail upon her,—somewhat too much, for we snapped two flying jib-booms, and sprung the sprit-sail yard. Spite of those mishaps, we more than held our own with the gun-boats,—the shots from which fell more and more short, and after about six hours' run, during which we managed to get ten knots an hour out of our lively craft, we were safe under shelter of the Confederate batteries. Not long afterwards the brig was snugly moored in Charleston harbour,—and met with an uproarious welcome. The supply was a most seasonable one, and as rifles, cannon, powder were found to be of first-rate quality, 'Tater Roberts's' Charleston agent realized an enormous profit for his principal.

"So far, well—capital ! But to get safely back again, and second to that, what to fill up with, was the question. I had not much fear, with such a craft as the *North Star* under our feet, of being able, taking advantage of a fair wind and dark night, to run the blockade outwards as successfully as I had inwards. My instructions were to get a cotton cargo if possible, but that I found southern policy forbade. The exportation of flour was not, however, at that time prohibited, and the agent and I were on the point of concluding a bargain for a full cargo of the article, when information reached me which turned my ideas topsy-turvy for the time. Not for very long ; they soon settled into shape, and the course to be taken lay plain and straight before me.

"This is a long yarn, Warneford," resumed the veteran with a grim smile, after refreshing himself with a caulker, " which I'm spinning for about the hundredth time, though never slick out from beginning to end to you before ; and what I'm coming to now would warm the cockles of my heart to tell if I were dying. Of course it was ordained up aloft that it should come to pass. A man must be an atheist, or, if possible, a worse fool to doubt that, which Tucker, one of Parson Raffles' deacons must be, or he would never have said I should have to answer for the villain's blood at the day of Judgment. It was the grandest, most solemn moment of my life. I knew myself to be God's chosen minister of justice, and I devoutly give Him thanks and praise

every night and morning, for having called me to the
work! Glory to His name, Amen."

"You are speaking of your encounter with Chidley, once chief mate of the *Constellation*, and its
results."

"Certainly, I am speaking of that cowardly murderer—of Henry Jefferson Chidley, born at Albany
State of New York. Mind you put his real name in
full. The whole affair was, I repeat, most providen-
tial, Rowley went on to say, as much so as that the
sun setting yonder in the west will to-morrow rise
in the east. Humanly speaking, our meeting was
brought about in this way. I and the agent, as I
have said, had nearly concluded for a cargo of flour;
were in fact walking to the seller's store, to pay a
deposit and arrange for shipping the flour without
delay, when the harbour battery thundered out a salute
of eight guns, the signal that another ship, English, no
doubt, and laden with arms, had run the blockade.
She proved to be the *Ann and Eliza,* a topsail schooner
of not more than a hundred and fifty tons register,
James Turnbull, master. She brought military stores,
and was as warmly welcomed as the *North Star* had been.
The agent and I deferred our visit to the store, precisely
why, I do not remember, so I sauntered about the
quay till the *Ann and Eliza* came in. I had known
Turnbull, a Liverpool man, for years, and of course
accosted him directly he stepped on shore. We were
both pleased at having met, and arranged to spend an

evening together at the 'Palmetto,' formerly the 'Stars and Stripes,' hotel, where I was staying.

"We chatted freely of many matters, of the war, of home, of cotton prospects, various dodges for running the blockade. Turnbull remarked that if I could succeed in reaching Nassau, I might perhaps obtain a full cargo of Sea Island cotton on freight, at a high figure. I said, that if I had not been told all the Sea Island cotton had been already shipped, I should have chanced the run to Nassau a fortnight before.

"'You will find it more difficult than you think to get away,' said Turnbull. 'One of the fastest gunboats in the Federal navy guards the entrances to Charleston harbour. The *Ann and Eliza* had a very touch-and-go escape from her, the *Alabama*, that's her name, going through the water two feet to our one, though there was a smart breeze, and right aft.'

"'I suppose,' observed I, 'that the *Alabama* was one of the gunboats that gave the *North Star* chase. If so, I shall give her the slip easily enough, never fear.'

"'No,' said Turnbull; 'the *Alabama* did not, I know, arrive off this coast till about ten days since. It's curious, Rowley,' says he, after silently finishing his pipe, refilling it, and puffing away again, all the time looking at me in a queer sort of way; 'it's curious, Rowley, but such things do sometimes happen. The *Alabama*, waiting to snap you and me up, is commanded by—by who *should* you guess now?'

2

" ' How the mischief should I guess who the *Alabama*
is commanded by ?   Some cursed Yankee, no doubt.'

"' You are right so far; an accursed Yankee, accursed
of God and man.   Well, old friend, I saw the commander of the *Alabama* at Nassau, saw him myself
more than once.   He is Henry Jefferson Chidley,
once first mate of the *Constellation*.'

" I leapt up from my chair.   My heart was in my
throat.   I felt a sensation of choking, as if my breath
was gone for ever ; and, lost to all control of myself,
seized Turnbull by the throat with fierce violence, as
if he were the hated villain Chidley.   That impulse
lasted but for half a minute ; a torrent of tears relieved
me, and I fell back into the chair, weak for the moment
as a child.

" It was not difficult to ascertain all particulars about
the *Alabama*.   She was a fast wooden gunboat, of
about ninety tons, carrying one heavy swivel 'Parrot'
gun.   Her crew might number sixty.   My measures,
based upon those facts, were soon taken.   There were
at the time four vessels, including the *North Star* and
the *Ann and Eliza*, that had successfully run the
blockade, waiting for a chance of getting safely away.
The obstacle was the *Alabama*, whose swiftness and
Parrot' gun, which would smash in their light scantling
as one crushes a walnut-shell, rendered the chance an
almost desperate one.   I began operations by assem-
bling the crew of the *North Star*, expounded my purpose and **my** plan, frankly stated that they would,

every man Jack of them, be perfectly justified in refusing to risk their lives in the venture. I gave them
two hours to consider. At the end of that time,
twenty, including the mates, all of whom were Liverpool lads, and had known my boy, volunteered to
stand by me, go in, win, or perish. Twenty against
sixty was too great odds, and with Turnbull I waited
on the naval commandant, explained what I purposed
to do, and how and why I meant to do it. He said
the venture was an extremely hazardous one. He
agreed that playing long bowls would never do. The
North Star's gun would make comparatively slight impression upon the gunboat's stout timbers, whilst her
'Parrot' would quickly make chips of a merchant
craft. My plan might succeed, and, acting in the interest of the Confederacy, he would offer no objection
to my engaging as many men as I thought proper,
willing to engage, well knowing what they were about
in the enterprise. He would do more, inform me
where the devil-may-care fellows I wanted might be
found. 'Remember,' said the Confederate officer, in
conclusion, 'that you will fight under the British flag;
that the Confederate Government, represented by me,
will not be responsible for anything that may happen;
though I guess pretty well what will happen, if you
are successful, which I much doubt. Jefferson Chidley
may be—I have no doubt he is—an execrable villain,
but he is also a daring, skilful seaman.'

"Having obtained all I required—the leave to raise

2—2

men to fight under the English flag—I left, with many
thanks, and before the morrow's noon I had got
together fifty fellows, chiefly English and Irish, who
eagerly accepted the bounty and the risk. They were
the right sort, making up, with the *North Star*, volunteers, seventy good men and true.

The *North Star* had gotten well to sea at dawn on a
fine breezy morning, the 2nd of May, steaming south-
east for the Bahamas. Not the speck of a sail was
to be seen in any quarter. Had my purpose been
simply to run the blockade, that object would have been
easily enough accomplished. Mine was another and
much more difficult task—to find one particular vessel
of the blockading squadron, attack, and overpower it.
There was no fear that I might mistake any other
gunboat for the *Alabama*. I had obtained a too
minutely accurate description of her for that. As
the day grew on, the fear that I should not meet with
her became intense ; and when twilight fell, and she
was nowhere to be seen, I was ungovernably savage—
half mad. Presently, Wilford, who had been for some
time gazing in a particular direction, placed the glass
in my hand, saying, ' There she is, sir ; or, at least, there
is a Yankee gunboat just perceptible yonder.' He
was right ; the gunboat had seen us, too, it was soon
apparent, and was putting on all her steam to make
our closer acquaintance. The moon, which was nearly
at the full, rose about an hour afterwards, and it was
for all practical purposes light as day. God was visibly

with us. We could not have escaped the *Alabama*—
it was unmistakeably her—had we wished to do so.
How wonderfully *alive* I felt, Warneford! I don't
know how else to describe the springiness of my limbs
—the flashing exultation of my thoughts.

"We crowded sail, in the vain hope of escape,
quickly seen to be vain, hopeless. The *Alabama* came
up with us hand over hand. At about ten p.m.
a shot from the 'Parrot' across the bows of the
North Star brought her to. The gunboat ranged up
abeam within two cables' length of us. Of course, only
the ordinary watch of the brig were on deck, my
supernumeraries being secretly confined below.

"'What vessel is that?' sung out Commander
Chidley.

"'The British brig *North Star*, from Liverpool to
Nassau, Rowley, master,' was the reply."

"Surely you threw away a chance by mentioning
your name," I remarked.

"No—not at all. My boy entered the Yankee service in the name of Ford, you remember. His real
name, for several reasons, was not mentioned at the
Liverpool police-court. The name of Rowley would
be no more suggestive to the miscreant than Brown,
Smith, or Robinson. A hoarse laugh responded to me,
followed by 'The *North Star*, eh? The brig that a
few weeks ago carried into Charleston arms and ammunition for the rebels! You are caught, my fine fellow.
The *North Star* has set for ever. Send a boat on board

with ' Rowley, master,' in her.   He must bring his papers.'

" Wilford, who was to act ' Rowley,' taking the brig's papers with him—and being himself, like his men, apparently unarmed, though all had concealed six-shooters about them—pushed off for the gun-boat. All this time, the brig was gradually, favoured by the stream, closing, without seeming intention of doing so, on the steamer. As I have more than once said, God's hand was visible throughout. Wilford, as Rowley, was received with supercilious civility ; the papers were glanced at, tossed upon the table, and the first-mate was informed that the *North Star* would be at once taken possession of, and sent to Key West. He himself, with his four sailors, would remain where he was, and a prize crew be immediately sent on board the *North Star.*

" Commander Chidley and ' Rowley, master,' then went on deck. The brig and the gunboat—a screw-steamer—were then so near that a biscuit might be tossed from one to the other.

" ' It is hardly worth while to lower a boat,' said Chidley. ' Lay the *Alabama* close alongside. The men can then step on board.'

" He was a low, hectoring, bully-mouthed brute in his mildest moods, and I heard every syllable he uttered. I gave certain directions, and went below. I and my merry men—we were extremely merry—feeling sure of turning the tables in a jiffy upon the swelling, strutting Yankees—heard their tramp on deck, and presently *our* signal for action.

"'Turn all the hands up. All but five, who will help to navigate the prize, must go on board the *Alabama*. Be smart, now,' added Chidley, addressing the second mate; 'get your fellows up just in no time.'

"'All hands on deck!' shouted the second mate down the forecastle; 'the gentleman's in a hurry!'

"Up we all swarmed by the companion way and the forecastle. The struggle on our own deck did not last a minute; in another we were fighting upon the deck of the *Alabama*, with the astounded, unprepared Yankees. I must do them that justice. They had not, under the circumstances, half a chance. My chief anxiety was lest Chidley should be killed in the *mêlée*, not knowing his death-giver. Happily I was spared the cruel disappointment that would have been. He was not, though he fought bravely enough, even wounded.

"The fight did not last ten minutes—the *Alabama* was ours. The crew were handcuffed and safely bestowed. Chidley was the first to recover cheerfulness. He was a fellow possessed of strong, gross animal spirits, and nothing but lack of provender and strong liquids could depress him for any length of time.

"'All right, Rowley,' said the burly ruffian, addressing Wilford—we were in the *Alabama's* cabin—'all right,

Rowley ; everything is fair in these cases ; but of course you don't mean to declare war against the United States. The *Alabama* and her crew will be liberated as soon as the *North Star* is beyond danger of capture ?'

"'I am Captain Rowley,' said I, 'and I shall, a few hours hence probably, first taking some obvious precautions, release the gunboat and her crew, with one exception—*you !*'

"'With one exception—*me !*' said the villain, considerably startled. 'What *do* you mean ?'

"'You wont have much difficulty in finding out my meaning,' said I, 'when I tell you that a running-noose, a hempen necklace, is at this moment dangling at the main yard-arm of the *Alabama*, and that I am the father of the English youth you murdered—a youth falsely called John Ford, and whose real name was John Rowley.'

Those few words seemed to take the very life out of Chidley ; his face changed to the hue of that of a corpse, his knees smote each other, and big drops of sweat stood out upon his clammy forehead. He felt he was in the presence of a man who meant what he said.

"'You cannot mean it,' he presently gasped ; 'it would be murder.'

"'Perhaps so ; but not, I shall take care, cognizable by a British Court ; and if I ever trust myself within reach of a Yankee one, I shall deserve what I should be sure to get. I take,' continued I, 'all respon-

sibility in the matter upon myself. Bind this fellow,'
I added, speaking to three or four sailors, stationed at
the doorway. That done effectively, I said, 'You are
justly, most justly, condemned to death for the brutal
murder of John Rowley on the high seas, and as sure
as there is a living, avenging God, who has delegated
this great duty to me, you, for that infernal crime, die
at sunrise. You have till then to prepare yourself.'

"He was struck dumb, overwhelmed, crushed by the
sudden horror that had fallen upon him, and in that
state he was left to himself.

"The dawn was without a cloud—the noose fitted
round the murderer's neck. As the sun's rim appeared
above the sea-horizon I waved my hand as a signal to
the men at the ropes to sway away, and before the
glorious luminary had fully circled into sight, Henry
Jefferson Chidley was swinging in the air—my son
avenged. Six weeks afterwards, the *North Star* reached
Liverpool without having met with a misadventure,
and I bade adieu to the ship and sea for ever. Counsel's opinion was taken, as you well know, by philanthropic busy-bodies and Yankee sympathisers here, as
to whether a criminal indictment would not lie against
me ; but nothing was, nor, as I believe, can be done.
I recked not of the consequences to myself of per-
forming a solemn duty, manifestly cast upon me by the
most high God himself. And you, Warneford, what
do you say? Was I justified in what I did or not?"

"Not justified, Rowley, though much may be pleaded

in extenuation of the deed. I believe, and so does
every one with whom I have spoken on the sad subject, that the murder of your son—he *was* murdered,
no question of that—followed by the death of his
broken-hearted mother, flawed your brain, rendering
you to a certain extent irresponsible for your actions."

"I have heard fools say that many a time; a sensible man never before. Good evening. Print that
villain's name in full, in your book," he added with
vivacity—'Henry Jefferson Chidley, native of Albany,
New York State, United States.'"

Less than a month from that time Captain Rowley
was the inmate of a private lunatic asylum, where he
still remains, a perfectly harmless, but confirmed madman. It is a curious circumstance in connexion with
Rowley's criminal adventure, that the temporary capture of the *Alabama,* and the death of the captain,
were not inserted in any American newspaper that I
have seen.

LOVE AND WAR.

Not longer ago than the second week in last July, I
made one of the pleasantest of pic-nic parties in Ep-
ping Forest, although—a curious fact—we had no lady
with us. Were in all seven, men and seamen. Admitted
that female ministration had much to do with creating
that pleasantness. Mrs. Warneford and granddaughters
took the supplies under their charge; and with such
judicious care had they fulfilled the self-imposed task,
that when the hampers were opened, nothing, it was
found, had been forgotten; the viands and condiments
were first-rate and abundant; wine, cigars, spirits,
capital. So complete was the success, that Mrs. Warneford's health—although seven more loyal subjects of her
Majesty could not be found within the four seas—took
precedence of the Queen's, and was, I think, more up-
roariously cheered. The truth was, that the domestic
deities had shown themselves for once remarkably propitious. Out of the seven, four were old brother salts
of mine; two, relatives of these four, and commanders
of first-class ships in the British Mercantile Marine, both
of whom had run the American blockade. They had
all come to town to see the Great Exhibition,—which

I believe, though except by yawns, and unusually frequent aspirations for a cigar or a pipe, they did not
express such a barbarian sentiment, was to them a
great weariness. What we wanted was a quiet day by
ourselves, to chat about bygone times, fight battles o'er
again, splice new yarns to old ones, with greater free-
dom than the exigencies of lady companionship permitted. Hence the pic-nic. I have expressed myself
too absolutely in saying there was no lady present. I
should have said, personally present, as I was sure Emily
Preston was not for a moment absent to the mind's eye
of the youngest of our company, Mark Dalton, the son
of an old, long before departed friend of mine, and one
of the most promising officers in the commercial sea
service of this country. He had earned, by twice running the American blockade, the right—measured by
her father's rule of right—to marry Emily Preston, and
the next day but one he and I would set off for Bristol,
where the Prestons resided, and the nuptials would be
forthwith celebrated,—myself, by special invitation, to
give the bride away. Usually one of the merriest
hearted of men, he was a very dull fellow that day,—
not in the least infectiously so, as one could see that
his silence was very far from being sadness, as his
glittering, flashing eye testified. He was thinking of
sublimer things than formed the staple of our talk ;
and, being about the best-hearted chap in the world,
was, I felt sure, mentally commiscrating us that,
unlike his fortunate self, we were not each of us going

to marry an Emily Preston before the week was out. There is no chance, thought I, of his telling us to-day, how he twice ran up the Mississippi to New Orleans and back, without giving the Yankee cruisers a chance of putting salt upon his tail. So it proved. But I had it all out of him whilst in the train on our way to Bristol. Had I missed that opportunity, I should not have been offered another. I doubt that he will ever tell the story again. Ever, it is true, is a long day, and such hurts as his, though deemed incurable when inflicted, are never, experience tells me, fatal, except to extremely feeble organizations. Of this Emily Preston business more at large presently.

We had one "running the blockade" story from Captain James Bamford, a not much older seaman than Mark Dalton. It was thus, as I remember, led up to. We had been talking of the *Trent* affair, and what a thousand pities it was the American government had backed out of the business. This brought up the Naval Reserve, and the affiliation of the officers of the Mercantile Marine to the Royal service. The *rot* spouted in the House of Peers upon the subject by Lord Hardwicke, and the noble lord himself, were freely commented upon, in a by no means complimentary spirit.

"Hardwicke, of the *Superb !* 'Genoa' Hardwicke," said Lieutenant Davis, a grey-haired, battle and weatherbeaten officer; "a cursed sight *he* knows about man-of-war qualities of Naval Reserve officers. The master of his ship brought her safely home; but I doubt that Hardwicke himself could have done it, though it was only from the Mediterranean. Oh, yes! brave! I don't say he isn't. All Englishmen that I have met with were brave, with one or two exceptions at most, and then I have always thought there must have been something wrong in the family. A Quaker, or some creature of that kind must have been violating the seventh commandment. It couldn't be else. I wonder how his lordship would have set about retaking the *Emilie St. Pierre*, if he had been in Wilson's place? Not quite so boldly and skilfully, I'll warrant, as that Naval Reserve officer did."

"Who," said Bamford, "ever supposed that a born lord would attempt such a thing? As to Hard-wicke himself, I believe you are right in the main. The second mate of the *Solway*, a first-rate seaman, as well as a chap of surprising nous, sailed with the Earl when he was going through the three years' sea service —as sea lords call pleasuring about in the Mediter-ranean in fine weather,—to qualify himself for a flag when his turn comes. Finch says that, though nothing of a seaman, his lordship is rather generous with his shiners."

"It was Finch, was it not," said Mark Dalton, descending for a moment from the empyrean to vulgar earth; "it was Finch, was it not, that rendered you such valuable assistance in running the blockade to Pensacola?"

"To Saint Augustine. We were bound for the

Gulf, but found it prudent not to venture so far. You are right, though, about Finch: but for him, the *Solway* would probably have been captured by a Federal cruiser, taken to Key West—condemned, of course, and shared amongst the vampires who there suck the blood and grind the bones of Englishmen,—not to make them bread only, but turtle-soup, canvas-back ducks, champagne—Admiral Milne looking on the fun a long way off, quite contentedly. 'We must suppose,' said he to Richard Reeves, master of the *Cambria*, captured in the Bahama channel, 'we must suppose that the American prize courts decide strictly according to the evidence before them and the maxims of maritime law.'

'Suppose be d——d,' was Reeves's comment (to me) upon the admiral's speech; 'we know they *don't* decide strictly according to the evidence before them and the maxims of maritime law, and that it's infernal humbug to pretend to suppose they do.' "

" I quite agree with Reeves," said Bamford. " We shall have a sweet score to settle with Jonathan when the war, which must come, does come."

Hearty assent followed Bamford's speech; and— " Here's wishing it may come quickly," was drunk in full bumpers.

I firmly believe that sentiment, righteous or unrighteous as it may be, pervades the British navy. The Royal fleets, from a burning desire to, once for all, put an end to the eternal crowing of the Yankees about the glorious victories in the war of 1812-13 of their Liners,—they *were* Liners,—in two or three instances over weak, half-manned English frigates.

Bamford's father was a petty officer of the *Java*, and was killed in that ship's gallant, but from the first hopeless struggle with her gigantic, immensely superior antagonist, the *Constitution*. The officers of the Mercantile Navy have griefs of their own to avenge. There is a powerful *esprit de corps* amongst these men —the first seamen in the world beyond all question —and the coarse indignities to which their unarmed, defenceless comrades are constantly subjected by commanders of American cruisers, have excited in the general body a thirst for vengeance which, should, I again repeat, the civil war long continue, with its loose, vexatious blockade, will one day burst forth with a sustained fury that *must* carry the Government with it, whoever may be Minister—whether an admirer of the North or a sympathizer with the South. This in passing.

I seized the opportunity of reminding Bamford that he had promised to favour me with the narrative of the *Solway's* run from Glasgow to St. Augustine, remarking that a more favourable occasion could not be hoped for, his hearers being friends, feeling a strong interest in the workings of the blockade. My request, echoed by every one present, was complied with, Captain Bamford delivering himself nearly as follows :—

"You won't find it to be much of a story," he

modestly began, "especially as told by one like me, who hasn't the knack of dressing the plain facts up in fine colours; nothing like the *North Star* business which friend Warneford kept us up listening to the night before last. Most of you know," continued the captain, "that when the *Royal Charter* went down, and I was flung up high enough fortunately on the beach, but very far from dry, I had scarcely a feather left to fly with. All my precious uninsured nuggets and gold-dust were gone, and I had the world to begin afresh with about six sovereigns which happened to be in my purse at the time—as far as money was concerned, I mean. My character as an honest man, my skill as a seaman—not to affect a ridiculous modesty I do not feel—with youth and health—I am still on the summer-side of thirty—were sufficient riches for a bachelor at all events. It was some time, however, before I could obtain a command. Once captain of a first or second-class ship, a man does not like descending, even by one step, the ladder the top of which he had been so lucky as to reach. A portion of the nuggets and gold-dust that went down with the *Royal Charter* were recovered; by the small share of which awarded to me I was enabled to hold on till I received an acceptable offer. Messrs. Travers and Sons applied to me; they had contracted with a Confederate agent to send a large quantity of military stores to the Southern States, and if I had no squeamish prejudices upon the subject of the American war, they would give me the

3

command of the *Solway*, then lying at Glasgow.
Well, I was quite free of squeamish prejudices. I
lived, off and on, two years in the States, and
knew perfectly well that the negro, if 'a chattel,'
in the Slave States, he is, in ninety-nine cases out of
a hundred, a kindly-treated one, and for obvious
reasons; whilst in the Free States—as they are, or
used to be called—a negro is treated like a dog
rather than a man. I was not surprised at that. Let
people preach and prophesy as they like, placing negroes
upon an equality with whites is quite impossible.
God himself—some say from the time of the first
murder, about which, not having been bred to the
Church, I say nothing—God himself, I say, has stamped
inferiority upon the negro in the qualities which distinguish men from brutes. The Almighty's decree
cannot be reversed by man. I can therefore excuse
the Northerners' cruel contempt—abhorrence of the
African. The feeling is instinctive; they cannot help
it. I had consequently no squeamish prejudices to
prevent me accepting the command of the *Solway*, at
twenty pounds per month. In fact, I fancied the employment, being in my heart favourable to the South,
for the simple reason that its people were eight or nine
against twenty. Just the same feeling that makes us
shout, 'Well done, little one!' when we see a big,
brawny bully pitching into a chap less than half his
size. So Messrs. Travers and I soon came to terms, and
I was off in a brace of shakes for Glasgow. The *Solway*

was nearly full, had a likely crew—a few hands short
only—and in a week or less we should steam out of the
Clyde. From the first I took to Finch, the second mate,
a sinewy, active man, a prime sailor, who could see a hole
through a rattlin as well as any man I have ever known.
I need not say there were Federal agents at our seaports
before Tramway Train was heard of. There was a shoal
of them at Glasgow. Two sailors applied for berths
whose fluent gab did not influence me in their favour,
and I declined to engage them. They went away growling. Finch, as soon as they were out of hearing, said a
few words which at once determined me to ship them.
They were called back, and, to their great satisfaction,
Dennis Grady and Peter Mulligan—genuine Pat-
landers who had licked the blarney-stone out of
measure—were permitted to sign articles for the
voyage out to Boston and back. It was settled
they should bring their traps next morning. They did
so. All right so far; and the next day the *Solway*
slipped her moorings and we were off for the Puritan
capital—though there are almost as many broad-brims
there as in Philadelphia."

"That's true," observed Mark Dalton, again sub-
siding into common life; "that's true; but a large and
increasing number are 'wet' Friends. A 'wet'
Quaker," added Mark, "is a son or grandson of the
genuine article, who keeps up the 'Friends'' flag and
signals—broad-brimmer, buttonless-coat, and so on—
for many reasons, but who seldom attends Meeting,

who holds the memories of Fox and Penn in about as much reverence as he does those of Johanna Southcote and Joe Smith."

"You may be right, Dalton; I can't say you are not. Quakerism is dying a natural death, which every sensible man knew must be the case sooner or later. I can understand the gospel according to Fox might prevail if all mankind were Quakers; but for one nation to adopt that, would be just to realize the story of a country where fat, ready-roasted geese run about cackling Come and eat me—come and eat me. Beg pardon, Warneford. Quakers *have* nothing to do with running the blockade. Good. Well, the *Solway*, as I have said, steamed out of the Clyde, and directly we were well at sea, steam was shut off, and the screw and funnel unshipped. This was a capital dodge, at once converting the smoker into an hermaphrodite sailing brig, which sort of vessel, I need not tell you, will hold her own, especially upon a wind, as well as any craft that swims. The next thing was to paint out her broad white stripe, and the ' *Solway*, Glasgow,' at the stern, substituting the ' *Dove*, Boston.' So transmogrified, and with stars and stripes flying at the fore, the sharks waiting for us, and who had no doubt been furnished with correct photographs of the *Solway*, would be completely nonplussed: to a dead certainty that would be the case when Grady and Mulligan were disposed of. That little matter was soon settled. We were distant about twelve miles from the nearest land,

the night was calm and clear, when those two worthies
were called upon deck, and strictly searched, to their
intense astonishment and alarm. Nothing criminatory
was found upon their persons—we had not expected
there would be—and they were ordered into a small
boat—punt, rather—alongside, which I had bought
for the purpose. In it were two sculls, a few pounds of
biscuit, and a keg of water. As soon as they saw our
little game, didn't they raise a howl, and struggle,
kick, bite, blaspheme! Of course no use. Over the
side they were bundled, the end of the painter was
shied at them with a blessing, and a request to present
my compliments to Messrs. Sharman, Federal agents
at Glasgow, and request them to get their friends
Grady and Mulligan another ship, they having found
that the *Solway* was over-manned."

"It strikes me," said I, "whether the oversight had
bad consequences or not, that you should have sent the
two scamps adrift *before* transmogrifying the ship."

"I ought to have done so; it was a stupid blunder
on my part. I unaccountably overlooked the fact that
I was to *sail* to the Gulf, unless pursuit compelled us
to make use of our steam legs, in view of which con-
tingency we had shipped coals sufficient for four days'
steaming; space for more could not be spared. Messrs.
Sharman might easily communicate by the fast line of
packet-steamers with the blockading squadron before
we arrived out. I remembered that too late. We,
Finch and I, lost no time in overhauling the Irish-

men's traps, and, as we expected, found valuable
memoranda intended for their guidance, and which
would be equally serviceable for ours.

"Four days out, we spoke the *James Adler*, Federal
frigate, or, more correctly, the *James Adler* spoke us.
Of course we were the *Dove*, hailing from Boston,
Briggs, master, from Glasgow, to the New England
capital, laden with saltpetre and other war-stores consigned to Mappin and Co. of that city—which *Dove*,
Briggs, master, serenely unconscious of their names
being so scandalously taken in vain, were at that blessed
moment, the time being daybreak, quietly reposing
upon the placid bosom of the Clyde. Quite satisfactory. And had we seen a steamer, an English steamer,
of about our tonnage, with an unusually broad white
stripe round the under-edge of her bulwarks, and a
white new jib—which bran-new jib, I might have told
the *James Adler's* captain, was, thanks to Grady and
Mulligan's memoranda, snugly stowed away below.
Yes, we had seen such a steamer, about forty-eight
hours previously; she was the *Solway*, believed to be
laden with gunpowder and rifles for the rebels. When
seen she was steering a much more southern course than
ourselves, bound, no doubt, for the Gulf. This tallied
with information previously received by the *James
Adler*. Of course it did. And we parted company
very good friends indeed.

"My 'corrected' course ran through the passage of
Cape Race, keeping as well northward of the Bergin

Rocks as the dangerous currents thereabout permitted. There the *Solway* would hardly be looked for ; and, by afterwards hugging the northern shore pretty closely, till past Cape Hatteras, we should probably reach so far without being challenged ; after that, we must trust to fortune, and our sail and steam legs. Nothing particular happened till we were off Norfolk, well eastwards, as you may suppose. Here our troubles began. First, we were terribly scared about 8 bells a.m., by a man-of-war sloop heaving in sight, and coming on, it seemed purposely to overhaul the *Dove*, like a racehorse. She carried British colours, but that might be—in all probability was—a *ruse*. So we reshipped funnels, got up steam, doubling on our course —the war sloop was coming northwards—at our best speed. Much better than that best would not have helped us. Fortunately, she was the *Rinaldo*, British man-of-war, as we afterwards knew, and passed us about a league to windwards. Of course, we put about, and cracked away under wind and steam for the Gulf. In about two hours the wind had fallen to a dead calm —the heavy, lowering calm, which, in those latitudes, precedes a hurricane. The upper currents of air moved rapidly the while, and black clouds, surcharged with tempest and electricity, gathered swiftly overhead, piling themselves upon each other in lurid masses. I had given orders to make all snug, clew up every sail, when Finch, touching my arm, directed my attention to a stream of smoke, plainly discernible through the glass,

in the distance, about three leagues off, amid the fast
thickening darkness.   The steamer—the hull of which
soon rose out of the water—must, we saw, be a swift
one : the smoke, though not a breath of air was stirring, streaming afterward as if she was sailing head
to wind in a gale.   The stars and stripes were flying
at the fore. We felt—fancied, if you like—that she was
chasing us, and knew what vessel she was chasing.   Of
course, we heaped coals upon the fires, and did our best
to drop her.   It was labour thrown away.   In less
than two hours the *San Francisco* ranged up abeam,
fired a shot across our bows, and the poor *Dove*, of
Boston, was done for.   The tempest had not yet
broken, but it was close at hand, and would be a stun-
ner when it did come.   The air was charged with electricity, and at the end of the fore mainyard a ball of
pale light glittered, called by the sailor the corposant
—a corruption, I believe, of *corpus sancti*.   It is considered a certain sign of death if the light of a corposant shine directly on a man's face——"

"Tell that to the marines !" interrupted William
Chorley, a somewhat ancient and very pock-marked
mariner ; "tell that to the marines, Bamford.   I have
had the light of the corposant shine upon my face half-
a-dozen times at least, so direct that you might have
counted every pit and seam in it, and I'm worth three
dead people yet, at a modest estimate."

"I merely said sailors have such a superstition—not
that I myself believed it; you know that to be true

enough. But don't interrupt my paying out this yarn ;
I want to come to the end of it, and have a quiet
cigar. The corposant, I say, was flitting about at
the yard-ends and mastheads when the *San Francisco's* barge pulled alongside, and between thirty and
forty marines and seamen, under the command of
Lieutenant Coxwell, took possession of the hermaphrodite sailing and steam brig.

" 'No explanation is required—no papers, real or ficti-
tious, need be produced, Captain Bamford,' said Coxwell, a very decent fellow. ' We know all about the *Solway* transformed to a *Dove*. I must tell you, too, that
those ill-used gentlemen, Dennis Brady and Peter Mulligan intend entering an action against you for breach
of articles, and assault and battery, the first time they
catch you in the tight little island again. Never mind,
captain,' added the good-humoured officer, proffering a
cigar—a real, genuine Havannah ; ' never mind, Captain Bamford,—better luck, perhaps, next time. This
little haul—we have an inventory of your cargo—is
really most acceptable just now. First quality, we
hear—both rifles and powder,—and purchased for us
by the rebels ; delightful, eh ?'

" The fellow's wonderful gift of the gab—a pleasant
fellow, I say again, was Coxwell ; the fellow's wonderful gift of the gab would have enabled him to give out
any quantity of that kind of chaff, had not a sudden
stopper been put upon his jawing-tackle by the bursting of the tempest. Bursting with the roar of a thousand thunders—with lightning that blinded one ; with

a Niagara of sheeted rain, with a tornado of wind,
that tore the sea into foaming furrows, and split the
unfurled sails of the *San Francisco* into ribbons. Coxwell and his men hurried to shelter—he himself following me to the cabin. The *Dove*, alias *Solway*, bore
the shock of the tempest very well, thanks to our having made everything very snug. The *San Francisco*
was less fortunate. Her sails, such as were set, were
torn, as I have said, to shreds; her foremast badly
wounded, as we understood, in a long-ball duel with
the *Sumter*, and perhaps as badly fished, went shortly
afterwards by the board; her main hatch having been
carelessly left open, a vast volume of water breaking
over her doused the fires, and for a considerable time
the gallant craft drifted helpless before the wind—
momently increasing her distance from the *Solway*,
which, in obedience to the order brought by Lieutenant
Coxwell, bore up, directly she was got under command,
for the west.

"This state of things, in general, was keenly conned
by Finch, whose watch it happened to be—keenly
conned, with mental finger on lip. Not a sailor or
marine of the *San Francisco*—having every man-Jack
dived below—knew what had befallen the frigate; and
when the men told off by order of Lieutenant Coxwell,
to keep armed possession of the ship, went on deck—
it being then so dark that they could scarcely see each
other—they implicitly believed Finch, who, pointing
into the thick night, remarked that the frigate was

keeping well abeam of her prize. The excellent rum with which they had been plentifully supplied no doubt helped to obfuscate their eyes and intellects, for they certainly kept very careless watch."

" Rum," interjected Chorley, a little obfuscated himself, and helping himself to a jorum of his favourite liquor,—"rum, if it is genuine old Jamaica, is often the means of doing wonderful things. I've heard a Trafalgar old salt say it won that battle, the mainbrace having been handsomely spliced therewith afore the shindy began ; and I believe it. Have you most done, Bamford ?" added the uncomplimentary veteran ; " you've had a precious long spell. All present company excepted, of course, but I should give the preference to a song."

" I shall cast anchor and clew up in a few minutes, Chorley ("Thank'e kindly, James"). The American lieutenant, as I told you, followed me to the cabin, and when the tempest had well abated, Finch and the first mate—a rather wooden chap about some things, but a skilful seaman—joined us, and we passed quite a jolly three or four hours together. I had accepted the misfortune that had befallen the *Solway*, since there was no help for it, with a sufficiently good, if growling grace ; and as one is always natural when sincere, suspicion of foul play—rather what Coxwell would have esteemed to be foul play—did not for a moment cross his mind. We drank, sang, played half a dozen rubbers of whist, the only one of the company acting a part being Finch. At about midnight, Coxwell, to my great surprise—for he had been very guarded in his potations, and certainly not taken more than four glasses of far from strong grog—grew drowsy, as if from the effect of drink—nodded now and then, recovering himself with a start, staring with half-fixed eyes, and finally sank down on a locker dead asleep.

"'He's safe!' said Finch, after passing a lighted candle closely across the speaker's closed lids; 'he's safe enough till the morning. Now then, captain, to take stock of the others. I haven't much doubt that they are as safe in the arms of Murphy as their commanding officer, or Compton (the surgeon) must have miserably mismanaged else.' I twigged Finch's little game at once. 'The *Solway's* now our own.' Of course that was about the size of it; and not much matter how. Decidedly not.

"'All fast?' said Finch, meeting Compton, who was coming to us.'

"'As blocks of wood,' says he; 'it would take half an hour to wake one of them with a cowhide. We've only to settle with the ten fellows on deck.'

"They were easily enough settled with. As soon as we were once more in possession of our own ship, Finch advised that we should lose no time in making ourselves scarce in that quarter."

"'I've overheard,' says he, 'that there's three or four smokers arter us; perhaps we sha'n't be so lucky with the next. Saint Augustine is under our lee, distant only about fifty or sixty miles : suppose we run in there ? I've a strong notion we shall come to grief, if you are obstinate, captain, in going to the Gulf.'

" I readily agreed, and at about eleven in the morning with some difficulty awoke Lieutenant Coxwell. His men had been more roughly awakened and sent ashore half an hour previously. ' Now, lieutenant, rub your eyes well open ; it's time—here we are at Key West. Come on deck.' "

" ' Devilish quick passage,' said the yawning gentleman, stretching himself, ' or else I must have had an awfully long nap. On deck, you say—to be sure. Saint Augustine, by——!' exclaimed the lieutenant, scarcely believing his eyes. ' Is it possible, Bamford, that that d——d soft sawder of yours was gammon— meant to——'

" Fact, really, lieutenant. Look, there is the famous spire of the Saint Augustine church, nearly as old as the settlement of Florida, they tell me.'

" ' Well, I'm d——d !' says he.

" ' Nonsense,' says I ; ' that I hope wont be true for thirty or forty years to come. Meanwhile, we'll take, if you please, lunch together—my lunch, your breakfast. Come, better luck next time, you know.'

" So ends my story. How did I get away ? Well, half a gale of wind from the westward, and a dirty, moonless, starless night, did that for us. We did not so much as sight a single vessel of the blockading squadron. I no longer feel,' concluded Bamford, 'the high opinion I once entertained—derived, as I now see, from bunkum boasts—of the aptitude for sea-service of the Americans—quite the contrary. The Dutch and Danes, in my opinion, are far more skilled and daring mariners."

Bamford's opinion in that respect was demurred to. The dispute which arose therefrom was happily settled by Chorley's expedient of a song, himself the singer ; "'Twas in Trafalgar Bay," with an awful chorus, in as many keys as there were choristers. But for the help of Mark Dalton, who had been sipping little else but imaginary nectar all day, I should never have got my enthusiastic friends safely home, and out of the newspapers.

" Upon my word, Robert," said my much the best half as I turned in, very tired and weary, at about three in the morning,—" upon my word, Robert, this is a pretty hour to come home from a pic-nic—of course the night air will do your rheumatism a world of good. Well, I never ! As the girls say, how ever a lot of men can go out together, gormandizing, boozing, singing, without any civilizing influence to restrain them within decent bounds, is amazing—perfectly amazing ! Even you, Warneford—who, considering what abominable wretches are most men—are, comparatively speaking —only comparatively, that is well understood—a sort of a—model—far from an unobjectionable model man, Heaven knows—have come home to-night in a

state that——There, don't 'dear love' me! Go to sleep."
No doubt I obeyed orders, as I remember nothing more
of what passed.

I was not surprised to find upon reaching the Padding-
ton platform with Mark Dalton, that he had paid for
the exclusive use of a carriage. A young man flush of
cash, desperately in love, and about to be married, is
apt, from mere gaiété de cœur, to fling sovereigns reck-
lessly about. It was, however, no concernment of mine,
except as an intimation that he meant to inflict upon
me a monologue upon the graces, virtues, and charms
in general of beautiful Ellen Preston, to be interrupted
only by the arrival of the train at Bristol, if then. I
was not mistaken. He started off before the engine
did. "Mark," said I, at once interrupting,—"I am
patient as Job upon reasonable conditions. I will cheerfully resign myself to bear with your raptures, provided
you minutely describe not only the divinity you have
won, but how you won her : a reasonable quantity of
bread to the else intolerable dose of sugary sack I am
expected to swallow, is only fair."

"Quite fair, old friend. You want to know how I, a
greenhorn as to age, contrived to bamboozle those
wonderfully 'cute Yankees. Well, I think you'll say it
was rather cleverly managed ; but of course, in a general
sense, my success was wholly attributable to Ellen.
But for the inspiration derived from the rapturous
hope that——"

"Come, come, Mark, start fair. I will give you the

proper cue. You and an amiable good-looking young girl
fell in love with each other——Don't swear, Mark,
in an express train flying along at the rate of sixty
miles an hour—You then and an angelic, transcendently
lovely young lady, fell in love with each other ; at least
you did with her, for I, you are aware, was scep-
tical as to the reciprocity—*was*, I say—not so now ;
you are a hero with heaps of money, and circumstances
alter cases——"

"Much Ellen cares about money ! Mr. Warneford,
you are becoming quite sordid in your notions."

"Perhaps so : at all events if Miss Ellen has no
idea that money means a handsomely furnished house,
servants, rich dresses, faring sumptuously every day, and
a pony-carriage, dear papa has and had ; which, in your
case comes to the same thing.   One moment—I have
not come to your cue yet.   You, having fallen over
head and ears in love with enchanting Ellen Preston,
pop the question. Referred to papa, who in the blandest
manner, assures young Mr. Dalton that he esteems him
highly, not only for his own undeniable merits, but for
his father's sake ; at the same time, begs to observe
that being unable to give his daughter a shilling of
dowry, it results, from the eternal fitness of things,
that she can only marry a man of money—a commodity
which he is grieved to know his estimable young
friend possesses only *in futuro*,—a shadowy estate that
may or may not be realized : *if* realized, he will be most
happy,—delighted,—but *till* that to be devoutly wished-

for consummation, *non possumus*—to quote his holiness the Pope. The lovely damsel placidly accepts the parental decree; the loving youth goes frantic for a time, drinks dreadfully, gloomily assents. Dalton in his calmer moments hints darkly at suicide, but in a quite sane interval consults his father's friend, Robert Warneford. That practical individual, first hinting to his patient that there are as good fish in the sea as ever came out of it, a truism which shocks and disgusts his auditor, reminds him that he has a rich relative on the maternal side long since settled at New Orleans, U S., who, having no family of his own, might possibly, upon personal application, help him in the only way help would be available. Should that hope fail, he might take service with the South, and advantageously expend his rage upon the braggart Yankees, whom his father loved so well, and with such good cause. In thus advising, Robert Warneford was chiefly influenced by a desire to send William Dalton's son to a sphere of action where stirring events were in progress, which, if they should not wholly wipe away all trivial fond records from the tablet of memory, would, at all events, gradually dim and weaken the impression. Mark Dalton caught eagerly at the suggestion; it warned the sickness at his heart more than wine. Warneford smiled to hear, because he fancied that out there Mark might, in some way or other, achieve the fortune without the unreasonably speedy attainment of which divine Ellen might be—dare I avow to

4

it ?—the bride of that plethoric son of a Bristol
banker. Again—I say, don't swear, Mark,—there was
a terrific accident not long since near the Reading
station, which we have just flown past. To wind up
my prologue: Mark Dalton sailed for New York—
managed to reach New Orleans, and was warmly welcomed by his relative, James Manvers, Esquire, a large
holder of cotton, and coloured folk held in most in-
voluntary servitude,—I rather like that expression of
Polk's. 'Warmly received,' by his relative, James
Manvers, Esquire : that is your cue. Now leave your
damnable faces and begin.

" Willingly. First, however, permit me to say, with
all deference, that, judging from your chaffing jibes,
you cannot have as yet quite recovered from the effects
of the pic-nic. But never mind about that. I did
arrive safely at New Orleans, and was heartily welcomed
by Mr. James Manvers, my mother's bachelor brother.
His residence was, and is, in the old town, amongst the
French habitants. He is very rich, but keeps as firm a
grip of his wealth as if he feared to die of destitution in
his old age,—that is to say, he wont give or loan money,
except in the way of business, to mortal man or woman.
I don't think he would have lent me, had I asked him,
a twenty-dollar note. But he will point out how you
may make money for yourself. He knew I was
a skilled seaman,—that my mother and father's son
could be no craven ; furthermore, that I was in a temper to jump into a volcano if there was the ghost of a

chance of coming out again with twenty thousand pounds, or a good deal less, in my grip. Upon that knowledge he based his plans. Mark, said he to me one day after dinner—he keeps a splendid table, as do all New Orleaners, and Southern gentlemen everywhere ;—Mark Dalton, you are uneasy in your mind —of course you must be, having no money to speak of, and feeling convinced that if you ventured to ask such a thing—which of course you wont do—I wouldn't lend you a cent. I would not—that's a fact ; it's against my religion, and I never do it. You knew that—of course you did : all New Orleans knows it. But look here, nephew mine. I'll put you in the way of making a fortune for yourself—supposing always you ain't wiped out whilst it's being done, which of course is an element in the reckoning—in a very little time. Don't interrupt—listen first,—hear what I have to say, then give tongue as long as you like, in reason. Look here, Mark—it was always ' look here' with the old cock ; I think I see him now ;—look here, Mark, says he ; I'm with the South in this war, heart and soul—that can surprise nobody,—and sha'n't die happy if I haven't seen bargee, rail-splitter Abe Lincoln tarred and feathered and then hanged as high or higher than Haman. O yes; I know ! Christian charity,—'Am I not a man and a broder?' stuff: all right in the world to come, I daresay, but don't suit this. Well, now, this is just the case : we, the South, want arms and ammunition, Armstrong or Whitworth guns,

4—2

Enfield rifles, gunpowder. Now, all these desirable
requisites are to be found in plenty at Nassau, one of
the Bahama ports, you know—at least, if you don't, I
do. I had once a narrow escape of my life in Booby
Rook Channel, in consequence of the pilot being drunk.
Well, there have been many attempts to bring these
requisites over here; but the attempters being mostly
fools, mostly failed. Yes, I positively assert, mostly
fools. The only excuse, speaking seriously, for the
North Star skipper is, that he had a tile off. What
the plague right had he to jeopardise his owners' property for the whim of hanging a Yankee on his own
private hook? I don't, however, believe that he did
hang the fellow. There'd have been the devil's own
kick-up over here if he had. What he really did—I'd
bet a thousand dollars to as many cents, if it could be
proved—was to have the Yankee dropped quietly over
the side at night when a shark or two in want of
supper were close by. That was what he did, depend
upon it.' I mentioned, when you told us the story at
length, Mr. Warneford, that this was my shrewd relative's opinion."

"You did. It doesn't alter mine. But about twice
running the blockade to New Orleans? 'tis that I am
taking note of."

"True. Well, after a good deal of circle-sailing, my
uncle explained that the cleverest dodge would not
pass current more than twice or thrice at the most.
It was essential, therefore, when one had a good game

on, to venture heavily, if profits worth while were to
be realised. He himself was so confident in this scheme
of his own concoction, that he should now hazard a
fourth at least of all he was worth upon its success.
What he meant by *now*, was *my* appearance at New
Orleans. The hitch with him had been the difficulty
of finding a skilled seaman in whom he could thoroughly confide to take the chief direction. I had
therefore turned up just in the nick of time. There
could be no doubt, he was pleased to say, about me,
considering I was his sister's son, and the fine haul I
should make if successful, the Bristol beauty inclusive.
I remember, he said, having been spooney in that way
myself a very long time ago, when the bloom was on
the rye. Now then, nephew, he went on, coming
to business,—now then, nephew, mark, learn, and inwardly digest; he is a sort of out and in Scripture
talking man,—mark, learn, and inwardly digest my
instructions. I did so to the best of my ability; and
having finally mastered all the details, been furnished
with a number of essential documents, reliable memoranda amongst them of the private signals in use by
the Yankee cruisers between themselves and in accordance with the courtesies of friendly nations when communicating with British ships of war. How these were
obtained I neither know nor care. Easily enough, I
believe, through the agency of the all-mighty dollar.
In fact, a plan was arranged by which I should be kept
well posted up in that respect. Well, I left New

Orleans, reached Canada, *via* the Mississippi and the
Lakes, and just one month after final leave-taking of
my uncle, arrived at Prince Edward's Island, in the
Gulf of Saint Lawrence. There is snug anchorage there,
good holding ground, and, unlike Halifax, Prince Edward's Island was not very closely watched by Federal
cruisers. That, however, was of no great consequence
in reference to my uncle's scheme, which had, I dare
say, been altered a dozen times during the four or five
months it had been in preparation. Let me at once
say there was no wonderful originality in my uncle's
plan. The transmogrification of a ship at sea is a very
old dodge. Bamford, as we know, and scores of others,
have had recourse to it with more or less good fortune.
There were, however, other devices to be resorted to
which were novel. The scheme required not only a
very large outlay of capital, but business forethought
to the minutest details, or ruinous failure was certain.
But those conditions realised, with audacity and luck
one might hope——"

"Tell the story right away. Never mind whether
the dodges were old or new !"

" Very well ; going direct ahead then : five days after
I arrived at Charlotte Town, Prince Edward's Island,
the *Victoria*, Captain Dalton, a fast screw steamer of
nine hundred tons burthen, weighed and stood out to
sea, bound for Nassau in the Bahamas. The *Victoria*
was in ballast, and she was going to the Bahamas in
quest of Sea-island cotton. Of course everybody felt

convinced that was all flam ; but mere surmise is not evidence, even at Key West. We had made an offing of about three leagues, when we were brought-to by the *Cyane,* American sloop of war, and boarded by a lieutenant and boat's crew. Papers being all right, not an article of contraband to be found, they left us with a volley of curses, returned, of course, with large interest. Arrived off the Bermudas, we lay-to ; and so favourable was the weather—so well had preparation been made, that barely three hours sufficed to bring off the articles we called for—sixteen quaker cannons of large calibre, and two real swivel barkers, forty-two pounders. Half of this armament was for the *Victoria,* half for the *Amazon*—a sister ship which we expected to find at Nassau. Setting to work with a will the *Victoria* was pierced for artillery, eight wooden cannon and one swivel forty-two were mounted long before daylight. No one at but a moderate distance off, could have suspected that the *Victoria* was not a genuine man-of-war. It is, you know, perfectly impossible to distinguish a well made, well painted quaker from the real article."

"That is true enough ; but why did you not ship the real article ?"

"For several reasons. First, they were not easily to be had ; secondly, the heavy cost. Then their weight would have materially diminished the ship's speed. Lastly, that if it had been determined, in case of extremity, to *force* the blockade, the extra crew required to really fight guns of such calibre, would have swallowed up more of the profits than would have suited my uncle's book. We made sail soon after daybreak. Steam had not been got up since we left Prince Edward's Island, it being advisable to keep our stock of fuel untouched, so as to avoid the delay of recoaling; promptitude, when the decisive moment came, being the chief element of success. As it was now essential we should not be overhauled by a Yankee cruiser, both the British ensign and the pennant were run up."

"That trick, if detected, would have got you into trouble with her Majesty's cruisers."

"No doubt of that. In fact there were plenty of breakers ahead, upon which at any moment the whole scheme might have been wrecked. Luck's all in such cases. Every precaution was taken, and of course the obvious one of togging myself and the two mates off in naval uniform. I liked myself amazingly in a commander's cocked hat and epauletted coat, and wished that—that—bosh! where was I?"

"In Bristol at that moment, wishing that a certain young lady there had seen you in the epaulette coat."

"Stow that stuff, Mr. Warneford, or I shall clew-up without another word. I remember now: we sighted a number of American cruisers, mostly at great distances; but not one took any notice of us. Perhaps we were not seen; our look-out, sharpened by anxiety, having been keener than theirs. At last the moment of trial came. We were within sixteen leagues of Nassau, well to westward, when the *Minnesota*, American screw frigate, suddenly loomed through the grey dawn about a mile to windward. She almost immediately fired a blank gun, and up shot the signal, technically known as 'the demand.' The reply was equally prompt. Her Britannic Majesty's ship *Triton*, Captain Bullen, last from England on a cruise, showing at the same time the appropriate number. 'All-right.' The *Minnesota* continued her course ; we ours."

" If I remember rightly, the *Minnesota* ran aground during the fight in Hampton Roads, about which such an outrageous fuss was made in this country ?"

"That was so. To continue. At evening fall of the same day, the *Victoria, not*, you may be sure, with the royal pennant flying, ran through Booby Rook channel into Nassau harbour. Now came the crisis of the game. The slightest hitch during the next twelve or fourteen hours, and it would have been lost. It was, I repeat, a happy-go-lucky business altogether. As I had been instructed would be the case, the *Amazon* was ataunt, ready for sea, her full cargo stowed, and waiting only for our cannon-dummies and a swivel forty-two pounder. These were quickly transferred, at the same time, the cargo cleverly packed ready for the *Victoria* was shipped. Such a number of hands skilled at the work were employed, that before daylight—the nights were long—both the *Victoria* and the *Amazon* were standing out to sea, the latter

flying the pennant as well as the *Victoria*. We soon
parted company, arranging to become consorts as soon
as that could be done in sight of the Yankee squadron
blockading Nassau—observing the port, they call it.
In fact, there are two blockades to run in getting
from the Bahamas to a southern port. The *Minnesota*
was reputed to be one of the fastest and most active of
the American cruisers. It would, I thought, be fortunate
if the *Minnesota* sighted us within view of her consorts. She had so recently made the speaking acquaintance of the *Triton*, that common civility would prevent
her asking impertinent questions. I was deucedly
nervous, Mr. Warneford, I can tell you. The cost
price of the two cargoes, as per English invoices, was
not much under fifty thousand pounds. The future of
my life hung upon success. The chances, I repeated
to myself again and again, were in our favour, everything having run so slick off the reel that the Yankee
spies in Nassau must—unless the devil had helped his
own at a pinch—have found it impossible to communicate with the outlying squadron. We were running
through the water at the rate of about ten knots, under
sail and steam. Then or never it was necessary to put
both legs foremost. The horizon was decidedly bright-
ening, when suddenly darkness fell. A steam sloop
of war, with the stars and stripes flying, hove in
sight at about two bells p.m. steering towards us in
so direct a course that unless we changed ours, which
was not to be thought of, we should pass—if we did

pass—within three or four cables' length of each other.
This was far too near to be pleasant, notwithstanding
the excellence of our quaker imitations. The paucity
of the crew in comparison with the complement of a
sloop of war might excite suspicion. Besides, there
are numerous trifling particulars which to a practised
eye—the swabbed, comparatively dirty deck, instead
of the white holy-stoned one, for example—would betray the *Victoria's* character if closely viewed. It
being necessary, if we would not visit Key West, not
to throw half a chance away, I ordered the swivel 42-
pounder to be loaded."

"You surely could not have meant to fight an
American sloop of war with a 42-pounder, and a crew,
I suppose, of about thirty men?"

"Not quite such a fool as that. But if the American—as was sometimes the case—should insist upon
boarding, our only chance of escape would be superior
speed, getting without the range of his guns as quickly
as possible ; and in realizing that chance a lucky shot
might help us wonderfully. I was told then, and have
been told since, that for a merchant vessel to fight or
fire at, any ship of a blockading squadron belonging to
a friendly nation, is to make 'private war,' as they call
it, and amounts to piracy. I didn't and don't believe
it. The *Emilie St. Pierre*, to wit. Captain Wilson
made 'private war'—war on his own account—if ever
a man did. But legal or not legal, was all one to me.
I did not care just then a button for the law of nations

—a far mightier law than that possessed, inspired me."

" Just so. The lust of lucre and—love !"

" As you please. On came the war-sloop, and on we stood, bold as brass in appearance, whatever secret tremors we might feel. When nearly a-beam of each other, the sloop's engine was stopped—she was a paddle-steamer—and the *Victoria* keeping on, the Yankee fired a shotted gun across the bows of her Britannic Majesty's ship *Triton*. The impudent rascal ! It was necessary to stop that game at all hazards ; and our prompt defiance came from the throat of the 42-pounder, the shot of which flew across the Yankee's stern, more closely than I had intended, the *Victoria* not for an instant slackening her speed, and a drum below beating the man-of-war's call to quarters. The unhesitating return of his shot had evidently plunged the captain of the *Saint Louis*—we afterwards knew that to be the sloop's name —into a state of great mental disquietude. He must have been perplexed in the extreme. Two opposite ideas would be struggling for mastery in his cute and conceited, but, as a rule, far from clear, logical Yankee brain."

" Speaking generally, I believe you are right."

" The double train of ideas or notions must have been these :—'That infernal Britisher—he *is* a Britisher, no doubt about that—is either a contraband or really does belong to Mrs. Victoria. But where's the crew, if she is that little lady's property? If she warn't genuine would she have dared fire that shot close across the stern of a ship carrying the immortal stars and stripes? Certainly not! And that was the drum-beat of the regular Britishers, I've heard it many a time. Wal—and now she's about out of gun-shot. 1 must report to Gideon Welles. Perhaps he'll understand it, though be cussed if I can.' Seriously, continued Dalton, though I wrote that, or something like it, in the first flush of young-manish exultation, it was, I really believe, pretty near the truth. The *Victoria* having swept on, not only regardless, but contemptuously defiant of his challenge, the Yankee sloop remained stationary, her guns silent till we were beyond effective range. Then the American captain appeared to wake up. The paddles went round, and sharply turning, it seemed that the *Saint Louis* was about to give chase—only for a minute or two, it so seemed. The responsibility of seriously engaging one of Mrs. Victoria's ships of war—which the audacious stranger *might* be—crew below at dinner, perhaps—was too great for the American captain; the *Saint Louis* resumed her course, the *Victoria* continued hers. In less than half-an-hour the sloop was hull down, and all danger as far as she was concerned had passed away. That was an occasion to splice the main brace, which was done in style.

" Early the next day we joined our 'consort.' The *Amazon* had had a very narrow escape. She had been

chased by an American corvette, who, spite of her
answering 'signals,' suspected her true character. Speed,
and the coming on of night, saved her; but not till she
had been struck twice—once by a round shot close to
the water line, an injury which it had been found very
difficult to but temporarily remedy—and once by a live
shell, which burst within frightful proximity to some
hundred barrels of gunpowder she had on board.
Evidently there was not a moment to be lost. So,
putting on a full head of steam, we calculated that if
we eluded the Philistines, we should in about ten hours
be off the mouths of the Mississippi. We did fall in
with one Philistine, but he behaved like a Christian.
We spoke the *Minnesota* in Penanscola Bay; and I
took the liberty of asking if they had seen the *Rinaldo*,
British sloop of war. He had not. 'Any News?'
'None of consequence;' with which civilities we took
cheerful leave—I can answer for self and consort—of
each other. We had no longer anything to fear, and
having excellent pilots, we stood boldly and swiftly in
for the Mississippi. The *Victoria* did the distance to
New Orleans, up the river, over a hundred miles, in
thirteen hours, gaining an hour upon the *Amazon*.

"I need not tell you that the governor was mightily
pleased; but my uncle is one of those men who, though
not born with one, somehow suck in golden spoons till
they choke themselves. He seemed to think nothing was
done whilst anything remained to do. I had been in
New Orleans but three days, when he, as I was cosily

enjoying a cigar and some first-rate champagne, brought
me up all standing with, 'Now, Mark, says he, we'll
talk business, if you please.   You've made a famous
start ; it does you credit.   You are the right sort, as
my sister's son would naturally be.   Your share will be a
thumping one, and shall be at once invested, so that
you can either take it yourself, or forward it to England without trouble or risk.   For the matter of that,
he went on—for the matter of that it will be well,
as life is uncertain, that you should leave written
directions as to whom the money should be sent to, in
case of accident—yellow fever, for instance ; though I
think I could rightly direct the envelope containing an
account that a certain thumping sum had been forwarded to Peabody and Co. by the St. Louis bank, to
the credit of the fair recipient of the letter.   I couldn't
make the artful old fellow out.   What's he heading
for now? thought I.   ' Yes, he went on, all to himself—' yes, that would be a prudent thing to do ; for
it's a goodly heap of money, though not nearly enough,
I should say, to satisfy the Bristol daughter-dealer.
Beg pardon ; but certainly not enough, though you
have been so uncommon lucky.   Always, Mark, follow
luck up sharp.   It seldom turns suddenly.   That's the
reason why I have had the *Victoria*—it seems to
me that about every other British ship is named
Victoria ; silly, that, to my mind—that's the reason, I
was saying, he goes on, that I have had the *Victoria*
got ready for another immediate run over to Nassau

and back again. There's another cargo all ready there
—can be shipped in no time ; back you come all right
—those skunks of Yankees are no use to you, that's
quite evident—and away to England with money to
buy half the girls in Bristol. Don't fly out, Mark,
he delighted to rile me upon that subject. The
Yankees can't have got scent of the *Victoria*, alias
Triton, and her consort, yet ; but they soon will. Not
an hour to be lost, my dear boy. Another bottle, and
be off. Everything ready. The *Amazon* can't go.
Will need extensive repairs. Not a lucky ship. We
shall sell her ;' and a precious lot more of the same
lingo which he paid out without a check from me, for
I'll be hanged if he hadn't taken my breath away.
However, the long and the short was I allowed
myself to be persuaded ; and in just no time the
Victoria was running down the Mississippi to again
tempt fortune. The closer I looked that second venture in the face, the uglier it showed. The Federal
spies at Nassau would to a certainty have found
means of communicating with the Federal squadron,
and in a precious rage, I could not doubt, were the
captains of the *Minnesota* and *Saint Louis*. Such
another game could never be played again with the
least chance of winning. Faint heart, however, never
won fair lady. I was in for it, and could not, would
not attempt to back out. The *Victoria* steamed out
of the Mississippi long after dark—and it was very
dark the next evening—and was well out to sea when

day broke. There again I had wonderful luck. We were steaming steadily, with the stars and stripes flying at the main, and in the distance were two large ships, both steamers; one, a corvette, evidently an American cruiser, chasing the other, which we concluded to be an English ship that had attempted, or was suspected of an intention to attempt, running the blockade. The position of the ships was such that the corvette might easily have cut off the *Victoria*, whilst the *Victoria* could, supposing her rate of sailing to be only equal to that of the corvette, more speedily overhaul the Britisher, from which the American cruiser was about three leagues distant. The chase was steering pretty nearly in the direction of the Bahamas, so, seizing the chance, I immediately got up a full head of steam, and went off like a good one in pursuit of the fleeing contraband, which we should no doubt overhaul much sooner than could the corvette. The real Yankee held on nevertheless, one motive no doubt being that if within cannon-shot of the prize, should the *Victoria* capture her, the corvette's officers and crew would be entitled to a share of the spoil. In about three hours the *Victoria* ranged up alongside the chase, fired a gun, and brought her to. A boat was immediately lowered, manned, and I went on board. The prize proved to be the *Samson*, of Liverpool, Skinner, master, with a full cargo of warlike stores, and terribly scared Captain Skinner was, till I disclosed the true state of the case, and he could believe his own ears. He was not, however, out of danger; very far indeed from being so. I, of course, would do my best to help a brother contrabandist, and after remaining a sufficient time on board the *Samson*, I returned to the *Victoria*, and the *Samson* proceeded on her course. The corvette seeing that, at once discontinued the chase, and began signalling, by which she learnt that the stranger was the *Samson*, bound from the Brazils to London, with a legitimate cargo; papers quite correct, &c., and that our noble self was the United States' cruiser *Cyane*, Captain Burbage; in return for which valuable information we were told that the corvette was the *Susquehanna*, &c. Perfectly satisfied, the *Susquehanna* steered for her regular cruising ground, and the *Victoria*, alias the *Triton*, alias the *Cyane*—risky things by sea as well as land are *aliases*—went on her way rejoicing. 'Luck! sheer luck!' said Dalton, laughing. I had no sooner signalled 'The *Cyane*, Captain Burbage,' than the stupidity of having done so caused me to heat and blush like a school-girl who fears she has committed some impropriety before company. Surely, it struck me, the Yankee captain must know that the station of the *Cyane* is hundreds of miles away from this. Fortunately, the captain of the *Susquehanna*, whose name I forget, was as great a buzzard as myself; suspected nothing, and, as I have said, gave up the chase. This yarn,' yawned Dalton, 'is pretty nearly run out, and not a bit too soon.

"Nothing further happened till we ran into Nassau,

where our reappearance created quite a sensation. The trick we had played the blockaders had transpired, and it was sorrowfully predicted that we should not see New Orleans again in a hurry, should I be mad enough to make the attempt. Nothing could persuade me *not* to run the risk. I had too much at stake to throw up the game till the last card had been played. I comprehended that I must trust this time to speed alone. The cargo was light—rifles and percussion-caps. I procured a supply of the very best coals, had the engine, boilers, screw, overhauled; and managed to careen my vessel, so as to clean her bottom. All ready at last, and opportunity favouring—a dirty, starless, moonless night, half a gale blowing, and a tremendous sea on outside. I knew we should have to run the gauntlet of three cruisers at least—my old friends, the *Minnesota, Saint Louis*, and another sloop, name unknown— as there was no question light-signals of some sort from the Yankee agents would inform them of the very moment of our departure. It was of no use shilly-shallying, so, slipping our moorings, we ran boldly out into the dark night. We were about passing the limit of distance from the British coast within which we were safe from attack, when suddenly bluelights flared up on board the three cruisers, casting a ghostly illumination over the wild sea for miles around. For a few hurried pulse-beats I half resolved to double back. I did not, fortunately, yield to the cowardly impulse. The cruisers were wide apart; the bluelights enabled us to see them much more distinctly than they could see us, and with such a sea on, first-class gunnery would be but haphazard work. In speed we could certainly beat the *Minnesota,* and, I believed, the *Saint Louis.* As to the speed of the other sloop, I could of course say nothing. That we must chance. I recalled to mind a naval anecdote, which had fired my blood when a mere lad—Sir Peter Parker successfully running the gauntlet through the midst of a large French fleet in the *Menelaus* frigate. You remember it?"

" To be sure. Who that has sailed beneath the pennant does not ?"

" Right. It struck me that I might imitate in a very humble way that grand exploit. I had no right to risk the lives of the crew : their stake at issue was a very trifling one. Mine, if I succeeded, would be the great reward ; and mine, in common justice, should be the greatest risk. The men were consequently ordered to lie down ; I, myself, took the wheel—the *Victoria* steered like a fish—and we kept swiftly, steadily on. I do not think the *Minnesota* had her full steam on : a blunder if that was so. Seeing that the *Victoria* must pass her within seven or eight cables' lengths, the American captain trusted to his guns to bring us to, or failing that, to blow us to the devil. He did, in compliance with civilized usage, fire a blank shot—at least, I supposed it was a blank shot—then waited till we should be direct a-beam to give us a settler. The

bluelights showed us the opened ports, the trained
cannon, the ready and attentive gunners, in a more
terrifying aspect than if seen by honest daylight, and
I candidly confess I felt very queer. On we swept—
were directly a-beam of our tremendous foe: the hoarse
command to fire rose above the howling wind and
raging sea, and a tremendous broadside broke in flame
from the American's guns, followed by a stunning
roar, the whizzing of shot through the air, the snapping of ropes and spars. No real harm done. ᴀ
gave a wild hurrah, more from excitement than any
other feeling, which the men on deck sprung to their
feet to fiercely ˉecho without well knowing why.
'Down, men !—down !' I shouted. Another broadside
quickly followed, flung back again as it were by our
exultant hurrahs, no damage having been done. The
Victoria flew on with unchecked speed : that was our
assurance that the fire of the *Minnesota* had been
thrownˉaway. Practically, we had got beyond reach
of the frigate, but right ahead were the two sloops
with full steam up. They were about half a mile
apart, in order, no doubt, that one or the other might
be certain to cut us off should we suddenly endeavour to change the *Victoria's* course. I determined to pass between them, having very little apprehension of their fire, though of course one unlucky
shot might cripple us. Not one touched us, though
both ships kept firing with furious energy when all
their exertions were required to keep us in sight at

least till daybreak and we neared the American coast. Their artillery having failed to stop or sink us, chase was given by the three cruisers. All *my* tactics consisted in stimulating the stokers, and if the enginery did not give way, I had no doubt of effecting our escape. The *Minnesota* we soon found had not the ghost of a chance with us; neither had the sloop the name of which I did not know. When day dawned they were nowhere, but we could not shake off the paddle-steamer *Saint Louis.* There was no fear that she herself would overhaul us, but should another cruiser appear in sight, her guns and signals calling attention to the chase would probably bring us to grief. The wind and sea had by then greatly abated. It was possible to fire with some degree of accuracy, and I was advised by the second mate -- himself a first-rate gunner—to try the chance of crippling the *Saint Louis* with our forty-two pounder. His counsel was instantly followed, and some dozen shots were fired in quick succession without effect, the sloop disdaining reply. At last the mate, whose eager glance followed the shots as they skipped over the waves, exclaimed, with a shout—'Crippled, by —— !' He was right. One of the paddles was literally shot away. Long before she could possibly have shipped another, we had dropped her, and without further chance of mishap we regained the Mississippi and New Orleans. Wonderful luck, was it not ?"

"You may call it luck, but for my part——"

" Bristol ! Bristol !"

We had reached the end of the story and our journey at almost the same moment.

What I have further to relate of Mark Dalton has, strictly speaking, no reference to running the blockade, but I may as well briefly jot down the result of our visit to Bristol. I put up at an hotel in Wine-street, where he was to join me after paying his devoirs to his lady-love and her father. I did not expect him till near midnight at earliest, and having dined, was about to write out my notes of the foregoing narrative, when, Dalton having been absent scarcely an hour, a hurried step ascended the stair, and presently my gallant young friend burst into the room, much paler, more agitated, I'll be sworn, than when exposed to the American cannon.

" What's the matter ?" I exclaimed, standing up. " Is—is Miss Preston—anybody ill ?"

" No, no ; not ill. Hand me a glass of water. I have spoken with Emily. Mr. Preston wishes to see you in the morning. Great God ! that this should be the end !" And the brave, chivalrous young seaman burst into an agony of tears, sobbing like a child. I asked no questions, got him with some difficulty to bed, administered a powerful sedative in a glass of brandy-and-water, and had the satisfaction of soon seeing him fall asleep, although a troubled, moaning, exclamative sleep, as one may say. He was still sleep-

ing, and more calmly, when I left the hotel to see Mr.
Preston. A few words explained all. Miss Preston
had been seen and admired by the only son of a wealthy
baronet, who only the day before had proposed. He
offered present riches, an eventual title, and of course
was accepted—an old, old tale !

Mr. Preston was grieved, but—— I stayed to hear
no more, and a few hours afterwards Dalton and I
were whirling back to London in the express train.
A lucky escape, say I. He will console himself, and,
should opportunity be afforded him, play a great part
as a sea-hero yet. He has certainly all the stuff in
him.

THE CASSIUS MARCELLUS CLAY.

I DO not mean, by Cassius Marcellus Clay, the stump-orator, whose mission is or was to abuse Great Britain and all which it inherits, but a Yankee brig so named after that distinguished gentleman, by an admirer of his—at least, I presume so, though for aught I know, the *dis*-United States can boast of a thousand Cassius Marcellus Clays, one of whom may have been a dear relative of Ezra Sidebotham, ship-builder of Portland, State of Maine, and owner of the brig so named in compliment to his dear relative and friend.

Ezra Sidebotham, so lately as 1861, was a highly esteemed citizen of his native town. He had prospered, was well to do, and deacon or office-bearer of some sort in a large and influential Dissenting congregation. The incidents of the story have been furnished to me by Captain Crosbie of Liverpool—verbally only and at one hearing, which will account for some gaps or short-comings in the narrative. Captain Tobias Crosbie is now, and has been for some months, absent from England, in command of the *Robert Peel*, from Liverpool to

Wellington, New Zealand. I cannot therefore refer to him, either to refresh my memory or supply inadvertent omissions of his own in the story. Crosbie has passed many years of his life in the Canadas, and the Northern States of America, Maine especially; knew Ezra Sidebotham intimately, and heard the narrative from that worthy's own lips. My friend is a serious, truth-loving man, and, except it may be for some excusable twistings and deviations by Mr. Sidebotham himself, the reader may be sure that the story runs in a straight line—is trustworthy.

As I began with saying, Mr. Ezra Sidebotham was, up to the year 1861, a prosperous, respected citizen : he was not only deacon of a church, but the father of a promising family—two boys and three girls, the last being, according to Crosbie, buds of beauty, that in a few years would disclose into radiant flowers, though no doubt transient as beautiful, like all American loveliness. The mother lived a notable thrifty woman, a real helpmate for Ezra. Once only in his life the husband rejected the wife's counsel, and by so doing brought himself and the *Cassius Marcellus Clay* to grief.

The brig so named was built by himself after his own design, and measured four hundred tons burthen. Ezra, who had passed full fifteen years of the first quarter of a century of life at sea, and knew a *likely* vessel at a glance, offered to back her for any sum in a trip to England and back, both as a clipper and a sea-boat, against any canvas vessel belonging to Portland. His challenge was not accepted, nor did he meet with a customer for the *Cassius Marcellus Clay.* The reason of this was the high price—twenty pounds per ton, when ready for sea—he asked for her ; and the reason of his asking that exorbitant figure was, that a strong desire—passion, we might almost say—had arisen in his mind, to take her himself across the Atlantic with a cargo of breadstuffs. The speculation would probably be a successful one, and in an English port it was likely he would obtain a higher price for the brig than at Portland. More than all, he had a morbid hankering to be once more at sea—in blue water.

This bent of mind was well known to Abram Dallard, a distant relative, as he said, of Mrs. Sidebotham, and one of the cutest of cute Yankees, if he himself was to be believed. Circumstances being propitious, he, a moral agriculturist of much experience, resolved to diligently cultivate that bent of mind, not doubting that he should reap, and speedily, a very profitable crop. Cute, indefatigably industrious, as he, according to his own showing, had been from his boyhood—and in 1861 the snows of fifty winters had grizzled his head—Abram Dallard was a hand-to-mouth Loafer still; his chief dependence for several years past having been Ezra Sidebotham, to help him out of the moral mire into which he was always tumbling, and set him on his shifty legs again. Yet, strange to say, practical Ezra's high opinion of Abram's business capacity suffered not the slightest diminution for all the fellow's failures and mishaps. They were all plausibly accounted for by the plausible rogue, and the shipbuilder's faith in him remained unshaken. Mrs. Sidebotham, with whom he claimed blood-relationship, never, it seems, *cottoned* to him, as the Americans say. She could not deny that he was the Abram Dallard who she remembered ran away to sea from Baltimore, where she herself was raised, when a mere boy. The letters, old letters from her own nearest relatives—one from her mother, addressed· to him, and her father's old-fashioned silver watch, which she knew had been given him as a keepsake upon the runaway's return to Baltimore a few years after she herself settled at Portland with Ezra Sidebotham— were conclusive vouchers that he *was* that scant-grace ne'er-do-weel. For all that, the shrewd woman doubted, distrusted him. He did not seem to be of her kith and kin ; she could not realize that he was; and she owned to Crosbie that her private opinion had always, since he claimed relationship with them, been that his mother, a flighty high-rope sort of woman, had been false to her husband. Her hostility to Abram Dallard was not, however, an active hostility; and believing that all the harm her husband was likely to suffer from his attachment to the fellow would be the loss of a few dollars' loan from time to time, she held her peace, and entertained him hospitably whenever—which was about every day—he inclined to avail himself of that hospitality.

In September, 1861, the *Cassius Marcellus Clay* was ready for sea, thoroughly equipped in every respect; and Ezra Sidebotham, who had finally made up his mind for a trip across the Atlantic, was negotiating for a cargo of breadstuffs, when Abram Dallard flourished a dazzling suggestion before his eyes. It was well known to Ezra Sidebotham, as to every one else, that an immense quantity of shoes, boots, saddles, and other army accoutrements, furnished by contractors to the Federal government, had been condemned as unfit for use, and were to be had in the lump dirt-cheap. Here was a magnificent opening for the exercise of Abram Dallard's commercial genius. First exacting a promise that Mrs. Sidebotham was not to be consulted in the matter, that the business on hand should not be mentioned or hinted to her, Abram Dallard bluntly proposed that his friend Ezra should take the brig in ballast, himself accompanying it, to New York, where the said condemned stores were to be obtained; purchase a full cargo thereof, clear for Vera Cruz, and by hugging the coast of the Rebel states, seize an opportunity of running the blockade, which need not be attempted till not the slightest risk of failure was to be apprehended. Now Ezra Sidebotham was a high-flying Union man, and naturally both startled and scandalized by such a proposition. Upon a closer examination, however, of the scheme—viewed by the light cast thereon by Abram Dallard's glozing comments—its obnoxious features disappeared, leaving the

attractive ones in full and bright relief. Profit and
patriotism were reconciled—embraced each other. The
profit, should they succeed—and Dallard convinced
Sidebotham that it was just impossible they
should *not* succeed—would be at least two hundred
per cent., at so low a figure were the goods to be had,
and so wofully in want of them were the Southern
armies. Yes, and those rebel Southerners would
purchase at an exorbitant figure perfectly worthless
goods. It would be a great act of patriotism, a spoil-
ing of the Egyptians, to the manifest advantage of
the great, indivisible, immortal Republic. There was
a good deal in that, thought Deacon Sidebotham, and
two hundred per cent. profit, all expenses paid, as
friend Abram reckoned, *was* a temptation. Ezra's
cash capital not required in his business did not reach
over five thousand dollars—nothing like sufficient to
freight the *Cassius Marcellus Clay* with a full cargo of
shoes, boots, and saddlery, dirt-cheap as it was said
those articles were to be had. What of that? He,
Ezra Sidebotham, was known at New York. His
banker at Portland would endorse his reputation as a
man of substance; and his bills, therefore, for whatever further sums might be required, would be easily
negotiated; and the two hundred per cent. profit
would be realized upon the borrowed as well as his
own actual capital. The bait was a tempting one, and
the Deacon gulped it, hook and all. Abram Dallard
was authorized to at once telegraph to a friend of his

at New York, instructing him to purchase as many of the condemned stores as would furnish a full cargo for a ship of four hundred tons burthen; and three days afterwards the *Cassius Marcellus Clay* sailed in ballast for the Empire City, where Mrs. Sidebotham was told breadstuffs were to be purchased upon much more advantageous terms than at Portland.

Ezra Sidebotham left the entire management of the business to his cute relative, handing over to him the drafts of the Portland bank for five thousand dollars, and blank acceptances, which said relative was to fill up as the necessities of the case required. Abram Dallard was exceedingly active, zealous, successful. The *Cassius Marcellus Clay* rapidly filled up; and, so far as Sidebotham could judge, with excellent goods. The shoes and boots, the saddles and bridles, were of English manufacture, and really seemed to be unexceptionable; but of course there must be some radical defect in them all, or they would not have been condemned—that was quite clear. The brig having, as I have said, rapidly filled up, cleared for Vera Cruz— with respect to which there was no difficulty, the authorities having satisfied themselves, by communication with Portland, that Ezra Sidebotham was one of the staunchest of Union men—and sailed for her destination in the second week in October. The very name of the brig was a certificate of her owner's loyalty. That of Joseph Train would hardly have been a more emphatic voucher.

The tremendous labours which Abram Dallard had gone through at New York so knocked up that enterprising person, that he did not leave his berth for several days; and as to furnishing his relative with an account of purchases and payments, the thing was impossible. He could, however, say that the cargo had not cost more than eight thousand dollars; and if it did not realize four times that sum, he would consent to be sold south for a white-skinned nigger. The *Cassius Marcellus Clay* was twice brought to and boarded by the Federal cruisers, but immediately released. In addition to the regularity of her papers, a certificate under the seal of the New York Customs had been obtained, which vouched for the legitimate character of the brig and the well-known loyalty of her captain and owner. Under such circumstances, Ezra Sidebotham felt it would not be in the slightest degree difficult to run the blockade. His conscience thereupon smote him rudely, but he pacified it by the comforting thought that he was really about to spoil the rebels to the tune of some forty thousand dollars; not certainly to the profit of the Washington Government, but for all that, a smart dig in the ribs to Jeff Davis and Co.

As soon as the *Cassius Marcellus Clay* opened up Chesapeake Bay, Abram Dallard made his appearance on deck in apparently vigorous health, and certainly in boisterous spirits. He was evidently well acquainted with the coast, and proposed that Charleston should be the port made for.   Ezra Sidebotham objected that the stone fleet had blocked up the entrances to Charleston.   At hearing which, Dallard laughed derisively; said he could find the way in blindfold, and that the absurd confidence of the Federal officers in the stone scheme rendered running the blockade at that point extremely facile.   It so turned out.   Arrived off James River, Abram Dallard hoisted the Palmetto flag, took the wheel himself, and ran boldly in, without accident, or the chance of one.

As the brig was nearing Charleston Harbour, Abram Dallard requested to speak with Ezra Sidebotham The purport of what he had to say was, that as Charleston was full of Federal spies, some of whom would no doubt recognise Mr. Ezra Sidebotham, of Portland, it would be prudent that the said Ezra Sidebotham should not show himself in Charleston.   He had better remain below till the *Cassius Marcellus Clay* was again at sea. The impudent manner in which this proposition was made, so different from the deferential, not to say cringing tone in which wily Abram had been accustomed to address his considerably rich relative, grated harshly upon Ezra Sidebotham's ear ; still, as the proposition itself seemed reasonable—wise—prompted by friendly forethought, Ezra Sidebotham acquiesced therein ; remarking that it was also probable he, Abram Dallard, though he had been off and on but few years in Portland, might be recognised by the Federal agents, and upon his return there be brought to book.

6

"Brought to book! interrupted the rascal, with a grin. 'Locked up for life in Sing-Sing, you mean! Why, man alive, you and I have committed treason—high treason—against the Federal Government, by running the blockade with the help of fraudulently obtained Federal certificates. What's the use of staring and staggering like that! Moonshine—make-believe! You are not a child, and must have known the tremendous risk we have run as well as I did.' I can tell you, Captain Crosbie, said Ezra Sidebotham, that I dropped down upon the locker as if I was shot, and felt as if I was going to faint away. And so I dare say I should, but for a tumbler of brandy that infernal villain handed me. As sure as I am now a living man—and how I survived it all is a miracle—the notion that I was committing high treason never once crossed my mind. It seems strange, and Esther says I must have been bewitched by that darned scoundrel. She advised me to fill up with breadstuffs in Portland, she did—and not to let that warmint Abram sail with me. He'd be sure, she said, to turn out a Jonas, and we couldn't pitch him overboard if he did. I laughed at her like a cussed fool as I was. Wal, the feller's words, Captain, was a real flash of lightning, showing me as plain as daylight the fix I was in, with Sing-Sing, or some other State prison, in the distance, and not very far off either. Wal, but, Abram, says I, as soon as I could fetch breath; Abram, says I, we're buth in the same buat.

Yar're as likely to tread the wheel for life as myself.
Not a bit of it, says he. State of Maine, nor any of the
infernal Yankee .States, don't see this child again—I
should rayther think not.   With that he leaves me
and goes on deck.—Captain, said Ezra, turning livid
with rage at the recollection of his sufferings and
wrongs ; Captain, the dictionary haven't got words
enough to describe the tortures I underwent during
the next ten days.   I durs'n't go on deck ; and my
suspicions, once aroused, were daggers.   There was
serpent Abram disposing of the cargo, pocketing forty
thousand dollars.   How many of them should I ever
see ? Then there were the blank acceptances ; to what
amount had they been filled up ? Lord, Lord ! what a
blind buzzard I must have been !   Then there was the
Cassius Marcellus Clay, how on airth was I to get her
safe back to Portland, or anywhere else ? Six thousand
pounds, to put it low, gone there ! It would be better
to sell her where she was, if I could, which was doubtful.   Captain, I was distracted, mad a'most, and took
to drinking frightful.   At last the brig was cleared
and cargo sold.   Abram Dallard, whom I had not seen
for a week, comes to me bright and smiling, and uncommon friendly.   I have concluded, says he, everything quite satisfactory.   The cargo has realized forty
three thousand dollars, which, deducting commission
for myself at ten per cent., which you can't say is
unreasonable — Certainly not, says I joyfully, and
feeling quite ashamed of having suspected my wife's

clever relation. Certainly not; let your commission
be an even five thousand dollars. You are very kind,
says he; but the bankers here have already sent off
the exact amount by a certain circumbendibus means,
well understood by them, to an agent in Wall-street,
New York, by whom it will be forwarded to Portland bank, payable to your order. By that means,
you see, Ezra Sidebotham will not be suspected of ever
having visited a Southern port. This precaution
raised me up again a little, having been cast down
considerably at hearing that the dollars had been sent
off without consulting me. And now, says Abram
—and now, he goes on—and now all we have to do
is to settle about the *Jefferson Davis.* What the
devil, says I, have I to do with settling Jefferson
Davis? Oh, says he, I forgot not having mentioned
that I had painted out *Cassius Marcellus Clay* and
rechristened the brig *Jefferson Davis.* You have!
says I; d—— your impudence, then. I used to swear
awful when a youngster, afore I was married, and
the old Adam was biling up strong and fierce as ever.
'D—— your impudence!' 'Why,' says he, as cool as
I was hot, 'why, you surely wouldn't venture to
sea in the brig! You would be snapped up by one of
Abe Lincoln's cruisers before you had been an hour
out, or there's no snakes. The fact is, I have managed
that for you as clever as the rest. The brig is sold,
she is, for twenty thousand dollars.' Twenty thousand devils! says I. What are you talking of? She's

worth forty thousand, though I don't mind, as things
stand, taking thirty.   She's sold, I tell you, Ezra, to
Cornelius Vanrynk, a first-rate merchant here, and not
one hour too soon, or she would have been confiscated
as Northern property.   The cursed robbers !   Wal,
says he, I don't know about that.   It's only tit for
tat—paying Lincoln's Confiscation Bill in his own cur-
rency.   You have led me, Abram Dallard, says I,
biling over again, into a damnable mess.   According
to that, they might have confiscated the cargo ?   Certainly, and would, too, have done it, but for a pretty
dodge of mine.   I showed by invoices the cargo was
British property, and the *Cassius Marcellus Clay*
chartered by Spence & Co., of Liverpool, to run the
blockade therewith, because likely to be more, successful than a British ship.   My head, captain, spun
round like a top, and I felt sick, actually sick, and one
moment shivering with cold, the next burning hot
from the crown of my head to the sole of my foot.
Abram, says I, if you have been acting all along as
a traitor——.   Stop, says he ; what do you mean ?
Do you take me for Beelzebub hisself ?   *I* behave
traitorously towards my own relations, that have been
so kind to me ! Ezra, you ought to be ashamed of entertaining such a vile suspicion—of me, too, who have
put nigh to thirty thousand dollars in your pocket.
That was softening, that was ; so milding down, I
asked how the brig was to be paid for.   Paid for
down, says he, by bills at sight, drawn in my favour

upon Roberts & Co., Wall-street, New York. You
know Roberts & Co.?   Everybody knows Roberts
& Co., says I, the bile rising again at the mention of
bills ; but who knows whether Master Vanrynk has
a right to draw upon them for twenty thousand dollars ?
—and why, again, are the bills to be drawn in *your*
favour, I should like to know ?   ' You are wonderful
cantankerous, Ezra, this morning,'—Captain, I have
thought over and told this damnable story so many
times that I could repeat every word in my sleep—
often do, Esther says, in parts, till she is obliged to
elbow me awake,—You are wonderful cantankerous,
Ezra, this morning.   Vanrynk & Co. are, I tell you,
first-class merchants—stand quite as high in Charleston as Roberts & Co. do in New York.   The bills will
be made payable to me, because by my endorsing them
to you there will be no trace of your having committed
high treason to his Majesty King Lincoln by, being a
subject of his, aiding, comforting, and assisting his
enemies.   This was a settler again, bringing Sing-Sing
once more into the foreground of the dreadful prospect.
Wall, says I, let's have done with it—endorse and hand
me over the bills.   'Taint likely, says he. Vanrynk
& Co., who are the intimate friends of most of Jefferson Davis's Cabinet, have told the officials here that
the *Cassius Marcellus Clay* that was is their property ;
but you don't suppose they are going to give their
draughts upon Roberts & Co. till you have signed the
necessary papers.   Don't be alarmed.   Your secret will

be safe with them for their own sakes.   I expect one
of the firm every minute to come here and finish the
business right off.   I offered to procure your signature,
to save you worry and trouble, of course; but they
declined concluding the transaction without a personal
interview with you.   They also, as you will see by
this note, think you ought to inquire as to the respectability of their firm before accepting their terms.   It
was a straightforward, business note, Captain Crosbie,
recommending that, as the transaction was rather a
considerable one, the owner of the *Cassius Marcellus
Clay* ought to apply personally to the gentlemen whose
names they gave.   One was the Mayor of Charleston.
This is quite satisfactory, Abram, said I.   There is
no need, I feel, of inquiry.   I hope the partner in the
firm will soon come on board.   Abram Dallard said
he expected him every minute.   He, Abram, did not
wonder at my impatience to be gone.   It was advisable
I should make tracks with the least possible delay.
Once across the Potomac, says he, you will be all right.
You must pass as a Unionist, suspected of disaffec-
tion by the Charleston people, and fleeing for safety
to the glorious Northern States, eh ?   Only, as you'll
be sure to be searched, in order they may be sure you
are not a spy, it will be necessary to have nothing that
can betray you on your person ; don't you think so ?'
Wall, Abram, says I, getting riled again at hearing I
was to tramp on foot to Washington,—wall, Abram,
says I, I don't know *what* to think.   But this I *do*

know, that if I could have imagined I should be led
this devil's dance, ten times thirty thousand dollars
would not have tempted me to join partners with you
in such an infernal maze.   Never !

"At last the senior partner of the firm of Vanrynk
& Co., Mr. Cornelius Vanrynk, made his appearance.
I never saw sober, straightforward respectability more
clearly stamped than it was upon his aspect, his general appearance.   I felt sure I was in good hands, and,
as far as he and his firm were concerned, was not mistaken.   His manner was very kindly.   He was glad to
meet in me one of the numerous friends of the South
dwelling in the Northern States.   The cargo I had
successfully run through the blockading squadron was
invaluable.   There were no articles of which their
gallant soldiers stood in such pressing need, and the
goods were truly of first-rate quality—all English
made.   Spence & Co. had made a great name for their
goods by such an admirable consignment; whilst their
astuteness in chartering the *Cassius Marcellus Clay*, a
Northern instead of a British ship, was beyond all
praise.   It would puzzle the cutest Yankee ever raised
to ditto that dodge—with a good deal more in the same
strain, whilst listening to which I could not take my
eyes off the stolid face of Abram Dallard, staring at
him in dumb amazement at his audacious lying, in
scowling admiration, as I may say, of a swindling
genius that could so successfully throw dust in the
eyes of the Southerners as to pass off condemned stores

as articles of first-rate marketable value. Well, Mr. Cornelius Vanrynk had brought the necessary paper, I signed and sealed, and Mister Vanrynk produced the drafts upon Roberts & Co., drawn in favour of Abram Dallard, who was about to endorse them, when Mr. Cornelius Vanrynk interposed. I and your relative, Mr. Sidebotham, says he, have talked matters over with especial reference to your own safety and the prevention of suspicion and legal annoyance when you reach Portland. You have full confidence, he adds, looking sharply at me from under his pent-house brows,—you have full confidence in your relative? What could I say or do? Wal, of course I nodded, and daresay said Yes. That, says he, makes it all safe and pleasant. Your relative, Abram Dallard, will transmit by safe conveyance—leave that to me—these bills to Portland, where they will arrive before you do yourself. Meantime, you go overland in the name of Septimus Brown. Our friend here has had a bill printed, offering five hundred dollars reward for the capture of Septimus Brown, who has been endeavouring to incite the slaves to revolt in this Confederate independent State. The likeness is coarsely drawn, added Cornelius Vanrynk, giving me the printed bill, but, for that very reason, it will, when found upon you, be an assurance that no *friend* of yours drew it. Wal, Crosbie, there was no doubt of that. It could not be called a flattering pictur'—not at all. At the same time you couldn't mistake whom it was meant for—certainly not. So, after a deal of backing and filling, and cross-questions and crooked answers, I signed articles, as one may say, and left Charleston as Septimus Brown, fleeing from the Southerners and Judge Lynch to the Free States, carrying my own advertisement in my pocket and one hundred dollars in cash—yes, one hundred dollars in cash, that's a fact, which, as I reckon, was about half a cent. in the pound. Wal, I made tracks north'ard, and in about five weeks reached here. Wife and boys and gals screaming glad to see me, of course—same myself. Wal, where was the *Cassius Marcellus Clay?* Sold. Glad to hear it. Got the money, no doubt. Wal, yes, the bank must have had it by that time. Ah, not before they wanted it, for they had paid bills of mine, for my honour, drawn at New York, for shoes, and saddlery, and things to over eighteen thousand dollars, including the drafts. Nonsense, Esther, says I. Eighteen thousand dollars! Why, you are dreaming, but myself at the same time feeling sick at stomach and fainty-like all over. It's a fact, Ezra, says she; eighteen thousand dollars, and a good deal over. Send at once and satisfy yourself. Ezra, says I to my eldest boy; Ezra, go to the bank and tell them to send me my pass-book. If it was eighteen thousand dollars, Esther, I have gained more nor double that by running the blockade, saying nothing of what I got for the brig. Running the blockade! says she, mighty skeared and savage. Why, what

devil's tantrums have you been up to? Tell you all
about it presently, old gal, but just now I'd like a
good gulp of peach-brandy. That did me good, that
did; and presently back comes Ezra from the bank.
'Haven't got the book made-up, father, but have
received this letter for you, care of them.' That skunk
Abram Dallard's handwriting, says Esther. Nothing
worth reading in that, *I'm* sure. I broke the seal
and read the letter—that is, the lines glared at me and
swam like before my eyes. Then down I slid on the
floor, was carried to bed, and it was nine weeks and
three days before I got up again. Here it is, Crosbie;
If you like, take a copy. I know the devilish thing a
thousand times by heart :—

" ' Charleston City, Confederate State of Virginia.

"EZRA SIDEBOTHAM—You are a bigger fool than your
brimstone wife, which is saying a good deal; to which
wife I am *not* related. I should be sorry. *My* name
is Seth Jones, but I was acquainted with Abram Dallard in the whaling trade. He was chawed up in the
Gulf by a shark, and I came into possession, being his
particular friend, of his papers, cash, and *the* watch.
Wall now, I have done well by them letters and watch
—about altogether close upon ninety thousand dollars.
I reckon you must be about cleaned out, Ezra. It is I,
not you, that have spoiled the Egyptians. The very
best British goods! Two of Stuart's regiments thoroughly equipped by Ezra Sidebotham of Portland,

State of Maine. Ain't that jolly, you old Northern nigger! My bosom swells almost to busting with patriotic pride, when I think of how we have run the blockade, and I have pocketed over eighty thousand dollars, allowing for discounts and deductions, which are always scandalous impositions. But we have all our crosses. Roberts and Co.'s bills were all right, which I remember you were doubtful about. Present my compliments to Mrs. Sidebotham ; kiss her dear girls, and kick your rascally boys for your very, *very dear* friend,

"SETH JONES,

"And formerly, when under a cloud, Abram Dallard.

"P.S.—I cannot conclude, friend Ezra, without mentioning how grievously my moral sense was offended by the assumption, though but for a period and purpose, of the baptismal name of your nigger President Abram. Disgusting! But self-sacrifice has always its reward. In my case, friend Ezra, it has counted up to a tall figure, eh ? Farewell, Sidebotham ; and if for ever, still for ever fare thee well. I think that's Longfellow."

"Now, Captain Crosbie, if that warn't enough to make a fellow hang himself in his own garters, I don't know a pumpkin from a potato. However, thanks to friends and Esther, and the gals and the boys, I've got over it ; am beginning the world again, quite chuff and cheerful. But I shall never forget running the blockade. Carry the marks of it with me to the grave, captain. Fact that is. I should only like just to have one chance of

leaving my mark upon Seth Jones, I should. 'Twould
be a comfort, that would. The worst was—well, not
the worst, but wonderful aggravatin'—was that the
first time I went to chapel, our new minister, the Reverend Ephraim Caiaphas Boreham, cousin to Wendell
Philipps, and a screaming Abolitionist, preached at me
point blank, from the text, "Be sure thy sins will find
thee out," proving from Scripture, though he mentioned no names, that that cussed Seth Jones was the
commission-agent of the Almighty to punish my national backsliding and craving after filthy lucre. And
Boreham hisself's movin' heaven and airth to get his
salary doubled, by reason that his wife always brings
twins !"

"You'll never have a shy at running the blockade
again, Mr. Sidebotham ?"

"Well, Captain Crosbie, I kinder think not—leastways, without I could plainly see a chance of being sure
to win, and had to do with honest God-fearing people."

"That scheme you were talking of—the Bermuda
scheme, you know—looks likely. Would you take a
share, say one-twentieth ?"

"Well, captain, my credit's good still, and there are
the gals to provide for ; and whoso neglecteth his own,
the Scriptures say, is worse than a heathen !"

"One-twentieth, then ?"

"Well, captain, Esther inclines that way, and s'pose
I say Done !"

"Done !"

"All right ; good-bye."

THE ALBATROSS.

NOT so very long ago five persons met in serious consultation at a well-known tavern in Liverpool. The
names I shall bestow on those five persons are Johnson,
Smithers, Reid, Selby, and Colborne. The three first
were first-class seamen. Captain Johnson, a Sunderland
man, had been apprenticed in early youth to the
master of a collier ; and since the expiry of his inden-
tures had looked death boldly in the face a hundred
times in the two Atlantics, the Pacific, and the Indian
oceans ; caught cod on the Newfoundland banks, and
whales in the South Seas. His age might be a little
over or under fifty—a hardy autumnal life, still glowing with spring-sap, and showing no sign of sere and
yellow leaf. His fortunes had, however, lately suffered wreck, and there were gloomy forebodings in the
previously blithe home, where, near Sunderland, dwelt
Mrs. Johnson and eight minor Johnsons. Captain
Johnson's version of the story was this :—He, by nearly
thirty years of fairly successful enterprise, had become
sole owner of the barque *Emily*—his wife's baptismal

name. The vessel, measuring five hundred tons, was built expressly for him, and he sailed her himself. The *Emily* was chartered by the British Government for the conveyance of military stores to Canada when it was anticipated there would be a shindy with the Yankees, arising out of the *Trent* business. The voyage was profitable both out and back, Johnson having obtained a full return cargo at a fair rate of freight. That cargo was consigned to Liverpool Soon after it was discharged, and the *Emily* again in sea-going trim, a Mr. Forsyth, we will say, and certainly an enterprising exporter, went on board and inquired if Captain Johnson was open to be chartered to convey a cargo to Bermuda. Johnson said he was. The rate of freight was settled, and the cargo, military stores, consigned to a British merchant resident in Bermuda, was shipped with despatch. No apprehension of being liable to capture by the Americans occurred to Johnson. He had carried military stores from Woolwich to New Brunswick for the Government, and who, in the devil's name—this was how he talked afterwards—who, in the devil's name, could have a right to stop him on the high seas, and steal his vessel and cargo, whatever that cargo might be, when again undeniably bound from one British port to another? Could a Yankee cruiser seize him if he was chartered to convey fowling-pieces, rifles, gunpowder from Liverpool to Glasgow? Where was the difference in principle? Captain Johnson saw none. The *Emily* sailed,

insured only against ordinary sea-risks ; was brought-
to by an American corvette when within a dozen
leagues or thereaway from her destination, carried to Key West, and condemned as lawful prize.
Johnson fiercely remonstrated ; the American Prize
Court laughed his remonstrance to scorn ; and Lord
John Russell, when memorialized by the ruined mariner, upon his return to England, said the American
authorities would seem to have somewhat stretched
their belligerent rights, but there was no ground for
the special interference of the British Government.
His lordship had, however, caused an intimation to be
made to the Federal Government, to the effect that
much exasperation was being excited in England by
the unusually stringent exercise of their right. Cold
comforting that, and I need hardly say that Johnson
was desperately savage. He had continued in a state
of chronic inflammation ever since, making his wrongs
and grievances the common talk on 'Change and in
City ; the seeming impossibility of having an early go-
in at the plundering Yankees eating his heart away
with passion. This humour of rage made me acquainted with him, and him with the very man he
needed—that very man being himself a Yankee, born,
raised in, and but lately a wealthy citizen of Boston,
Massachusetts. This gentleman was the Mr. Selby of
the assembled council. Smithers and Reid, the latter
Johnson's brother-in-law, were seamen, friends of
Johnson, whose skill and daring were well known to

him. Colborne was the agent of an eminent ship-builder. I, who made six in all, was a supernumerary; but having introduced Johnson to Selby, I was especially anxious to make sure that I had not unwittingly helped to bait a trap for the captain.

I was doubtful of Selby—very doubtful. He knew that I was; and as it was probable Captain Johnson would not admit him to a share in the proposed enterprise if I advised him not to do so, the Boston citizen had promised to remove all doubts as to his own good faith and unswerving earnestness. This was to be done as soon as we had dined, when, supposing the pledge of sincerity to be sufficient, business would be immediately gone into. A sinewy, wiry man was Enoeh Selby. He must have passed his sixtieth year, and much resembled Mr. Dallas, formerly American Minister to the British Court, both in person, manners, and speech, which would have been those of an educated English gentleman, had it not been for the fluent fierceness of his talk. I could not do away with the suspicion that he was a practised artist in bunkum, and clever enough to conceal his art, as a rule. To a close, mistrustful observer, like myself, the "actor" would now and then disclose himself—at least I fancied so. If he was playing a part, he certainly was no ordinary artist. The man, I repeat, *knew* I doubted him, and had, as before intimated, volunteered to effectually rebuke my want of faith in his professions and promises.

The circumstances were these : It was well known

7

in Liverpool that Captain Johnson, trusting to the promises of friends, had induced the eminent ship-builder to contract with him for an iron-sheathed corvette intended to have great speed, and carry an armament of eight rifled cannons. Difficulties arose during the progress of the vessel to completion. It was well understood that the *Albatross* was intended to run, and, if the necessity arose, *force* the Southern blockade. It appeared, however, if the Solicitor-General's opinion taken upon an A and B case was sound, that in order to render the nationality of a war-ship unquestionable, one-half of the crew at least should be subjects of the power under whose flag they sailed and fought. This position was disputed by another high legal authority, and the result of the imbroglio being that the *Albatross* could not be insured against war-risks by the underwriters, the eminent ship-builder announced that every farthing of the purchase-money must be paid before the corvette left the Mersey. The sum, a very large one, was difficult to raise, although Captain Johnson's plan of operations, when he should once be at sea, the main features of which he had somewhat rashly disclosed to friends, promised great results. The affair would, I dare say, have been finally arranged, but all obstacles were at once removed by a communication from Mr. Selby, offering himself to provide half the whole amount of capital required, not only for the completion of the purchase of the *Albatross*, but of her armament, which she could only receive when beyond

the jurisdiction—or at least the reach—of the British
Admiralty. No money was required for the purchase
of arms, ammunition, clothing, &c., with which to supply
the Southerners, Captain Johnson's plan being to lie
in wait for Federal vessels carrying munitions of war
from England to a Northern port, seize them, tranship
the cargoes to his own ship,—if that appeared to be the
most feasible plan under the circumstances—burn the
captured vessel if it was a Yankee, if English, release
it. This was, no question, an audacious scheme, and
if care were not taken to clearly ascertain that the military stores were Northern property, savoured of piracy
on the high seas. I intimated that opinion to Johnson : the argument did not disturb him. He would
take care to seize only Yankee property ; burn none
but Yankee ships. As to piracy, that was all moonshine. The villains who seized the *Emily*, and their
rascally abettors, the Prize Court, were pirates; no
one that had an ounce of brains could dispute that ;
and it should go hard with Richard Johnson but he'd
give the varmints a smart innings in *his* turn. "The
step-son of an American merchant," added Johnson,
with darkening rage, "and a half-Englishman on the
mother's side, of the name of Bence, I hear now owns
the *Emily*. She has been rechristened, and Bence is
to trade with her between the Federal States and
London. The father, I hear, is now one of the
Northern Secret Committee sitting in London, whose
special duty, you know, it is to watch our English ports,

and report to their Government and cruisers respecting suspicious ships. The step-father got the *Emily* for about a fourth of her value, but only let me have half a chance, and I'll get her again cheaper than that. I heard a bird—a blackbird—whistle only yesterday, and—— But I'm cracking on too fast as usual; I shall know more soon. Mind, lieutenant, you dine with us at the tavern to-morrow," he continued. "I quite share your doubts about Selby, and after hearing what he has to say, we can compare notes and queries."

The foregoing is the material portion of a conversation I had with Johnson at his lodgings on Copperas Hill, on the evening previous to the day upon which we were to dine at the "Lord Nelson" tavern. He walked with me to the door of the hotel at which I was stopping. "I shall steer by cautious soundings in this business, Mr. Warneford," said he at parting. "One thing don't lose sight of for a moment; whatever conclusions about Selby himself we may come to, I *must* have the ten thousand pounds he's so willing and anxious to embark in the scheme." There was a laughing expression in Johnson's eye as he uttered these words, the meaning of which I was too dull to even approximately interpret.

The dinner, an excellent one, had been done ample justice to; we had drunk half-a-dozen bumpers each to favourite toasts, and were in full swing with cigars, when Mr. Selby, with marked decision of tone, said—

"I think, gentlemen, we had now better turn our attention to business, to the enterprise we have on hand, and which, to be successful, requires, we all know, prompt and energetic action. I have offered to advance ten thousand pounds in furtherance of that enterprise, feeling confident as I do in the daring and genius of Captain Johnson to carry it to a successful, triumphant issue. But, gentlemen, the daring of a Nelson, the genius of a Dundonald, could not ensure the success of such undertakings, unless those engaged in them had perfect confidence in each other—confidence based upon well-founded, mutual respect. I am here to create, to vindicate that mutual respect and confidence. I cannot be deaf to the rumours afloat concerning me which have, I know, reached the ears and influenced the judgment of at least two gentlemen present—probably of every one. People say, and justly, 'How comes it to pass that Mr. Selby, well known in Liverpool as an almost fanatical Northern Unionist, whose speeches in Fanueil Hall surpassed in virulence, if inferior in other respects, the harangues of Sumner and Philipps, the printed rhapsodies of Garrison and Greeley, is become all at once a bitter enemy of the North, loudly predicts its ignominious failure in the attempt to subdue the South, and, it is reported, is disposed to, in every possible way, give aid to the rebels? Well, gentlemen, that is a very natural question—one which, if I cannot satisfactorily answer, my friend Johnson would be mad to admit me into part-

nership with him in the bold undertaking he meditates
—the parent, I will venture to predict, *if* it be successful, and it will be successful, of a hundred, a
thousand of like enterprises. This, then, is my reply
to that natural questioning, to those quite legitimate
suspicions. I fully admit that I was a furious, uncom-
promising Unionist; that the idea of our great Republic being broken into fragments almost maddened
me. From earliest manhood I have been accustomed
to ascend the Mount Pisgah of anticipative imagination and survey the vast, the almost illimitable terri-
tory of America, peopled by hundreds of millions of
republican freemen, the mere shadow of whose power
would awe into trembling submission the petty potentates of Europe. But this I will say, speaking as I
am to Englishmen, that never in the wildest moods of
that wild dream did I ever in thought pour contempt
upon the Ithaca from which the to be mightiest of
nations had originally sprung, or wish for a moment to
break the bow of Ulyssean greatness, which to-day at
least I know united America could not draw. What,
then, has changed the spirit of that dream?—wrenched
with rude grasp from my bosom, exalted aspirations,
alive with my life, and palpitating with the blood of
my own heart? Gentlemen, I will tell you in a few
words. The dreadful truth once spoken, let me beg
that it may never again be alluded to in my hearing.
Its memories are fiery arrows, piercing through heart
and brain!" Here the self-revealing impostor paused

in his fustian rigmarole of bounce and bunkum, to take
a cambric kerchief from his coat-pocket, and assume
the attitude, the shivering tones and spasmodic gasps
which pass on the stage for the expression of extremest,
irremediable anguish. He was but a vulgar common-
place charlatan and scamp after all—scarcely superior
to G. F. Train! I had egregiously overrated the fellow's mental calibre. Johnson's clear grey eyes, gleam-
ing through the tobacco-smoke, and fixed intently on me
with a sort of slight squint, showed that he, too, had
reckoned up as quickly as myself Mr. Selby's sum-total.
" I had been a widower twenty years," continued the
impudent harlequin. "My wife died in giving birth to
twins—girls, baptized respectively Rose and May, after
her mother and mine. They were the charm of my existence. Rose attracted the attention of a Mr. Martin,
a young, wealthy gentleman of Tennessee. They were
married, and at once departed for the husband's estate.
In six weeks afterwards May went on a visit to her
sister. Tennessee was and is a distracted, morally
divided State; at war with herself. Mr. Martin sided
with neither party, but was suspected of being a Non-
Unionist in his heart. I cannot say how that may
have been. The state was overrun by the rival armies.
Mr. Martin incurred General Pope's displeasure. His
house was occupied by the Federal soldiery, who believed themselves virtually warranted to commit any
outrage upon rebels. I can scarcely go on. Rose—
Mrs. Martin—the duplicate of her sister May, a

double cherry seeming parted—was very beautiful. My daughters had no protection but their husband and a few timid negroes. Need I say more. Poor Martin was shot through the brain whilst defending the honour of his wife. There was resistance on the part of the negroes; in the confusion Rose was mortally stabbed with a bayonet. An hour or less afterwards, May, by some means, obtained a loaded pistol, and slew herself, falling as she died upon the corpse of her sister. On the evening of that dreadful day I arrived at what had been my son-in-law's mansion! At once kneeling by the dead bodies of my children, I registered a vow in heaven of eternal hatred to the Northern cause — the Northern assassins. I will keep that oath!" Then back the mouthy humbug fell in his chair, with the cambric kerchief to his eyes, and his long shanks stretched out in helpless prostration. What a bat-eyed booby I had been! The fellow must surely have been a third-rate melodramatic actor at the New York Bowery or other Transatlantic play-house. But for a rapid warning gesture of Johnson's I should have burst into a guffaw.

"Now that is tragic," exclaimed the captain, with amazing power of face and tone. " I saw, many years agone, Vandenhoff play King Lear; but, Lord! the difference there is between real genuine nature and pretence! Wonderful! Mr. Selby," said he, rising and taking that afflicted individual's limp hand,— " Mr. Selby, any doubt respecting you, which I must have been a fool to entertain for a moment, has been blown away by that pathetic story. I understand you now as well as if your body and brain were a transparency and I could see the actual workings going on inside. Our bargain, as far as I am concerned, is sealed."

"Captain Johnson," said Mr. Selby, rallying his faculties by a supreme effort,—"Captain Johnson, your sympathy is reciprocated. We have both suffered at the hands of the accursed Northerners, though in very, very different degrees. You, I have no doubt, will pay your debt with compound interest. As to mine——"

"Don't, Mr. Selby; it's too harrowing. With respect to the ten thousand pounds?"

"I have Peabody and Co.'s cheque for the amount in my pocket-book. It shall be forthcoming directly we have come to a clear understanding from a business point of view."

"The clear understanding from a business point of view is, that you are to have one moiety of the clear profits. You also undertake to keep me well posted-up with respect to all vessels loading in British ports for the Northern states, the nature and probable value of the cargoes, and time of sailing."

"For doing which I have peculiar facilities, as you know. To make that knowledge available, I must of course hear from you by every opportunity, in order to know where letters will find the *Albatross*."

"Of course—of course."

" You have arranged as to the armament ?"

" All settled, Mr. Selby, except not being paid for. Your ten-thousand-pound cheque will not only liquidate the balance due for the ship, but clear the guns, powder, &c. We shall be able to take wing in about ten days, I believe, Mr. Colborne."

" No doubt of that, Captain Johnson."

" The *Albatross* clears for New York in ballast, the proclaimed intention being to sell her to the Federal Government; or, the offer declined, to open negotiations with the Mexican president. That's the story got up for—the marines. Very good. But about the armament; where do you ship it ?"

" Off Saint Mary's, Scilly Islands. It will take us out of our course; but I couldn't safely manage the business anywhere else. We can calculate to within an hour or two when the *Albatross* will be there, and two vessels, with the guns, shot, shell, powder, and so on, on board, will be waiting for her."

" Excellent. All then we have now to do is, with Mr. Colborne's help, to draw up the agreement in black and white—sign, and seal; which done, I hand over the cheque."

Little more was said. Mr. Colborne penned a brief but extremely cautious memorandum, of which nothing could be made, of the terms agreed upon: it was signed, witnessed, Messrs. Peabody and Co's. cheque was handed over to the ship-builder's agent, and the affair so far was finished. Two or three minutes afterwards, Mr. Selby's servant, a tall, fierce-featured negro, entered, to inform his master that Mr. Turnbull, a gentleman from London, was waiting for him at the hotel. Mr. Selby left at once; the black followed, and as he did so, contrived, unseen by that gentleman, to exchange a swift glance of mutual intelligence and triumph with Captain Johnson. Was this the black-bird which Johnson had heard whistle the day before?

The interest of the game was deepening!

Smithers and Reid had scarcely spoken a word during the conference, but they were eager, attentive listeners, and the result, it was plain, gave them intense gratification. They were to be second and third officers of the *Albatross*, and both enjoyed the entire confidence of Johnson. Reid, the Captain's brother-in-law, was a good-looking, smart seaman, of less than thirty years of age, Mrs. Johnson, his sister, being some fourteen years younger than her husband. Reid was unmarried; a circumstance destined to have then unguessed-of consequences. I did not remain long after Selby's departure. As I shook hands with Johnson, he said, with a peculiar look and smile (Colborne had previously left), "Come and breakfast with me the day after to-morrow; I shall have a tale to tell."

I had not the least doubt of that, and took care not to miss the appointment. Johnson was in glorious spirits, brimming over with glee. 'Such an out-and-out game, lieutenant!' he exclaimed, almost before I was

seated. "I wouldn't be out of it to be Prince of
Wales. But come, let's to breakfast, and eat with
both rows of teeth. I shall burst, if I'm obliged to
keep it in much longer."

"As to that, you and I can talk, listen, and eat too."

"To be sure. Well, then, I've found out all about
that land-lubber Selby. He was bankrupt about six
months ago at Boston; came over to this country, and
is now one of the Secret Yankee Committee sitting in
London, by whom the ten thousand pounds were supplied. Lord! aint it a game, though? Talk of Prince
of Wales; no, not to be Queen Victoria herself, I
wouldn't! Ho!—ho!"

This was somewhat incoherent, but perfectly understanding what he meant, I said, "Run the story right
off at once, captain; I am as eager to hear as you are
to tell it."

"This is it, then. But first, I must explain that my
informant is the negro Juba, Selby's servant. He was
a slave, the property of one Sickles, at New Orleans;
ran away with his son Pompey,—wonderful fond of
fine names are both black and white Americans!—
escaped to what people have the face to call the Free
States of America, and was benevolently taken in and
done for by Enoch Selby. I shall only waste so many
words upon this part of the story as to account for
Juba turning round, like a trodden serpent, and sting-
ing his master. Selby, though people didn't suspect it
then, became embarrassed in circumstances. Negroes

fetched a high figure ; Pompey was a strong, likely lad, about twenty years of age. So one day Selby, saying he was going to an old friend of his not many miles distant from Boston, took Pompey with him. He came back alone, having been three days gone. The Southern hunters had recognised and seized Pompey by authority of the Fugitive Slave Law, and the poor fellow was irrecoverably on his way back to New Orleans. The terrible news, whilst convulsing Juba with grief and rage, excited no doubt in his mind at first. Some circumstance, I don't exactly remember what, awakened suspicion in the father's mind : he caused inquiries to be made through some really sincere friends of the coloured race in Boston, and since his arrival in England has received positive information that Selby sold Pompey to a speculating slave-dealer, and that the young man is now the property of the principal blacksmith in Norfolk, of the name of Machin. Machin, who is said to be a decent fellow, will part with Pompey for two thousand dollars, though a very valuable hand. That sum I have agreed to furnish if, by. Juba's aid, I succeed in my designs."

"What especial service can the negro render you in the matter ?"

"Invaluable service ! The master, whom he hates with the deadly unappeasable ferocity of African animalism when once roused, has entire confidence in him ; and Juba is sufficiently a scholar to read and copy all letters he receives, or other private papers : I have

copies of all important ones. Now, you understand.
An objectionable proceeding—immoral, I dare say;
and pray wasn't the seizure of the *Emily* and her confiscation extremely objectionable—damnably immoral ?
I think so, at all events. So there's no use of your
preaching. I'd rob the robbers of my wife and children in a church, if I couldn't get at them elsewhere
—ay, at the very horns of the altar !"

" What, precisely, is Selby's game ?"

" A double one, old friend. In the first place, he is
desirous of keeping well in with the Federal Government and its London agents. He has therefore apprised
them that the *Albatross* will ship her armament off the
Scilly Islands, and given such other information as
would justify a Yankee cruiser in seizing her if caught in
the act of shipping that armament. The Committee do
not implicitly trust Selby. The Mr. Turnbull whom he
was called away to speak with is another of their spies :
he with Selby called upon me ; spouted a book against
the Northerners, and at last satisfied himself that he and
his cum-rogue had completely bamboozled me, and that
they both knew the chart I meant to sail by as well as
I did myself. Cute Yankees—very !"

" What is Selby's back-play, then, since the game is
a double one ?"

" You shall hear. But first let me tell you—though
I suppose it is hardly needful to do so—that that story
of Selby's about his daughters, was flam from end to
end. He never had a daughter—he *has* a step-son.

I will tell you about him presently. Good Lord, aint it a game?—and aint I the luckiest dog alive? Well —well, this is the double game. Selby isn't exactly a fool. There are a few grains of sense floating in that huge maelström of vanity, conceit, and bunkum. That modicum of common sense causes him to suspect that I'm not exactly to be depended upon, in his sense of the phrase. Therefore the Federal cruisers, failing to snap up the *Albatross,* in accordance with the settled programme—no blame attachable to him—he would like to go shares in my ample spoils of the Northerners. In order to have a reasonable chance of doing so, he has already supplied me with authentic information of the contemplated sailings, within a short period, of Yankee ships. I have tested his intelligence, and have no doubt that in that respect Selby is to be relied upon."

"A double traitor! Have you obtained a genuine commission from the Confederate president? Be quite sure on that point."

"I *am* quite sure. And now, friend Warneford, for the cream of the story. You will hardly believe your ears, I didn't mine, when Juba told me,—scarcely my eyes, when I read the letters of Selby's step-son— copies, of course."

"And what writes Selby's step-son?"

"That the *Columbia,* formerly the *Emily*—you may well sing out—is taking in at Great Yarmouth a cargo of rifles, powder, and the rest of it for New York, and that she is expected to sail on the 24th, just fourteen days from this. Aint it a game, Warneford, old boy? There never was such a one out before—never! There lieutenant, you'd have taken me for a downright madman, if you had seen me in this very room, after hearing that from Juba, and reading William Bence's letters. I danced a hornpipe to my own whistling—smashed that picture, 'The Prince of Wales in Washington,' with a poker—and altogether played old Harry and turn-up Jack, till the landlord brought me up with an intimation that his lodgers having mostly gone to bed, and two being ladies of consumptive habit, rest and quiet might be desirable for them if not for me. Well, of course, I shut off the steam, went to bed, and somehow managed to lie pretty still."

" You mean to capture the *Columbia?*"

" I mean to have my *Emily* again."

"I dare say you will succeed in doing so. Permit me, however, to observe, Captain Johnson, that your contemplated cruise, speaking of it generally, is a very hazardous and Quixotic one. You are, in fact, about to defy the whole American navy."

" I am going to *dodge* the whole American navy— that is, the Federal war-navy. No such difficult matter. The *Sumter* and *Nashville* have done it. A first-rate fellow is Nashville Preedy; I call him China' Preedy. You must remember the manly letter he wrote to the American newspapers concerning Admiral Hope's gallant failure in that country. 'Blood,'

wrote he, 'is stronger than water!' I say so too.
The Southerners are mainly of English descent,
whilst their enemies — with the exception of the
sailors, nine-tenths of whom are Englishmen, more
shame for them!—are a promiscuous rabble of all
nations, and——".

"Come, come. You mean, then, to *dodge* the Federal
war-navy. Judging by the past, I think with you
that that may not be so very difficult. Still they
ought to catch you; and they have iron-plated ships
in considerable numbers, remember."

"So we hear, such as they are. The *Albatross* will,
I have no doubt, be a fast ship, and will run away
even from a wooden man-of-war, unless she prove too
saucy. My business is to cripple American commerce,
help to send up the rates of insurance on their ships,
and thereby bring grist to our own mill. A score of
such vessels as the *Albatross* would well nigh give us
a monopoly of the carrying trade. In fact, I shall be
plundering, sinking, burning, destroying in the interest
of England, under the Palmetto flag. If driven to
bay," added Johnson, with flashing eyes, "depend
upon it the *Albatross* will prove a hard nut to
crack, even by half a dozen of the sounding brass and
tinkling cymbal Swede's *Monitors*. My crew are all
English, Scotch, and Welshmen—the very pick of this
port."

"I do not doubt that the corvette, manned and
commanded as she will be, would prove a *very* hard nut

to crack.   If compelled to fight, under what flag shall you go into action ?"

"Under the British flag, to be sure.   How can you ask such a question ?   I shall be faithful to the Confederate Government ; but the fight in which the *Al atross* will either win or go down, shall be recorded as of right in the naval annals of England."

I took final leave of Captain Johnson on the deck —a flush deck, by the way—of the *Albatross*, as she was about to drop down the Mersey. I never remember to have seen a ship in essentially finer fighting order ; not even the *Scorpion*, in which readers of "Tales of the CoastGuard" know I served as lieutenant, with the exception that there was not a gun, a musket, or a barrel of powder or board.   The crew, over one hundred and eighty men, were not only athletic, devil-may-care fellows, composed entirely of old salts who had served in men-of-war, and naval-reserve men, were, I could see at a glance, under the most perfect discipline.   Her armament once safely on board, the *Albatross* would undoubtedly prove an ugly customer for any single ship in the Federal navy to wait upon.   As I was about going over the side with Selby, the local commissioner of the Admiralty came on board for, I understood, the fourth or fifth time, and we remained to see the upshot.

"Captain Johnson," said the officer, "I do not feel at all satisfied with respect to the destination of this ship. The British Government is bound to prevent the fitting-out of armed ships in British ports to make war upon a friendly nation. It is true your papers are regular, and that you have no armament on board ; but you have a crew of over one hundred and eighty men, and the ship is iron-plated. Now really, captain, it is taxing one's credulity overmuch to have one believe you are simply going to find a market for the *corvette,* which could be sold here at a heavy price. It is simply *bosh !*"

" Simply *bosh,* is it ?" replied Johnson, his iron phiz as stolid as the figure-head of a man-of-war—" simple *bosh,* is it ? I cannot say whether it is or not, as I have never studied the 'Slang Dictionary.' However, as you are no doubt ordered to demand explanations, and your tone and manners are those of a gentleman, I will, though not bound to do so, give them. In the first place, then, you will not dispute my right to engage as numerous a crew as I please. The naval-reserve men shipped, have, I believe, complied with the regulations——"

" Yes, yes ; the thing has been skilfully managed."

" Much obliged, sir, for the compliment. Well, sir, it is highly probable that when the *Albatross* is put up to auction in New York, the competition between the Federal Government and the Mexican agents there—seeing that a great majority of the crew will, I expect, go with the ship—may fetch a tremendous price. Then, as to the iron-plating—besides that it

will vastly increase her value to both Jonathan and
Juarez, it *may* be that she will not reach the figure
the owners of the corvette set upon her. In which
case I am ordered to try back, run through the Gut,
and on to the Black Sea. There I should be sure to
find a liberal customer. Either Mohammed or Roma-
noff would purchase such a ship upon our own terms;
that is, Lieutenant ——, if the corvette upon examination proved to be sound. Now there is, we all know,
a worm in the Black Sea which speedily destroys
wooden vessels, whereas iron-armour——"

A burst of laughter, led by the officer himself, interrupted Johnson's impudent banter, in which the
captain himself joined. However, as the authorities
had no legal right to detain her, the Admiralty agent,
finding himself, as he had no doubt expected to be,
thoroughly baffled, took civil leave. A few minutes
afterwards I and Mr. Selby did the same. The bankrupt
Boston merchant appeared somewhat ill at ease.
Doubts and fears evidently beset him, that, although
he had two strings to his bow, they would scarcely
avail to bring down so wily a bird as Captain Johnson
I was decidedly of the same opinion.

As had been previously agreed, Captain Johnson
wrote, by every opportunity that presented itself, thus
furnishing me with a much more detailed log of the
Albatross than the regular one kept on board. The
guns, rifled upon the Whitworth principle, shell, shot

and powder, had been embarked in two coasters which awaited the corvette off Man, not Scilly. All was speedily got on board, and the main danger was at an end. The heaving in sight of an American cruiser an hour afterwards, in evident pursuit of the *Albatross*, would have occasioned not the slightest alarm, even if the speed of the corvette, which was remarkable, should not avail to shake off the pursuer.

The first thing was to lie in wait for the *Columbia*, *alias* the *Emily*, Captain Bence. This was an anxious time for Johnson, whose desire to recover his ship was intense, absorbing. Upon looking over what I have written, I find an omission of some particulars respecting Skipper Bence which I had better supply at once. The young man, though born in Washington, had not been in the States since his sixth year. Soon after the death of his American father, he had been sent to his mother's relations in Hull, Yorkshire, for the benefit of his health. The widow Bence became the wife of Mr. Selby, lived not very happily with him, according to the testimony of Juba, and died without issue by the second marriage. Young Bence had been well received by his mother's relations, who were in fair circumstances, his uncle Cornish being owner and master of a coasting schooner. To him William Bence owed what slight skill he possessed in seamanship. How the correspondence, which it appeared had been broken off between Selby and his step-son, was renewed, did not appear from the letters which Juba, inspired by implacable hate, had industriously copied for Johnson's guidance. William Bence had, however, it was clear, acted for some years as Selby's agent in London; and when the Boston merchant found his affairs irretrievably involved, he had dispatched the *Emily*, renamed *Columbia*, to Hull, with a valuable cargo—unpaid for, of course—consigned to Bence; a deed transferring the ship herself to the young man, in consideration of unliquidated claims for rendered services, being sent off at the same time. Selby himself, compelled to absquatulate sooner than he expected, arrived at Hull a few days only after the *Columbia*. Through Selby's influence with the Federal people in England, the *Columbia* registered at Boston, U.S., and sailing under the stars and stripes, was chartered to convey a very valuable cargo of military stores to New York, to be paid for on delivery there by Mr. Secretary Chase. Young Bence was placed in command of the vessel. His voyage out had a double object. His aunt Cornish—the uncle was dead—had a cousin, also a widow, living at Albany, the metropolis of New York State, and distant up the Hudson about one hundred and fifty miles from that city. The Harrison family had emigrated from Yorkshire eighteen years previously, and had prospered. The widow had one daughter living, British born, she having been only a few months old when the flitting took place. The widow and daughter having made up their minds to return and settle in the old country, communicated that intention to Mrs. Cornish; and that lady, who appeared to be very partial to her nephew Bence, at once conceived the project of procuring him Fanny Harrison for a wife, the dowry of the damsel having been settled by her father's will at five thousand pounds, with much more at her mother's death. Widow Cornish accordingly wrote, stating that the *Columbia* would sail for New York on such a day; passed a glowing eulogy upon the excellence of the ship, the skill, amiability, &c., of her young captain, and strongly advised her relatives to make the voyage home in said ship—a recommendation which would no doubt be complied with. I could not comprehend, when Johnson ran over those particulars, what interest *he* could take in them, or why he had persuaded Juba to copy the letters which set them forth. The logic of subsequent events enlightened me, proving that the lynx and the lion were yet more equally intermingled in Johnson's organization than I had supposed.

On the eighth day at sea, the eager watchfulness of Johnson and his mates was rewarded by the sight of a ship which the captain of the *Albatross*, as soon as she was within a couple of leagues' distance, had no doubt was the *Columbia*. Chase was immediately given. The *Columbia*, though fast for a canvas ship, was got up with in just no time; the Palmetto flag flew at the fore of the corvette, a heavy shotted gun was fired across the *Columbia's* bows, and Captain William Bence knew that his first outward-bound voyage had come to a disastrous end. Captain Johnson himself accompanied the prize crew, and so delighted was he at finding himself once more in possession of his vessel, that he kissed her masts, rigging, &c., over and over again, with as much eagerness as if, instead of being his ship *Emily*, she was his wife Emily, whom he had met after a long and cruel separation; which strange antics induced an impression in the minds of the captured crew that they had fallen into the hands of a maniac !

Captain William Bence was sent with his men—all of whom, except the mates, were British subjects, and over thirty in number—on board the *Albatross;* and the expectation was that, after removing such stores as were desirable to take, the *Columbia* would be burnt. Of course, nothing could be further from Johnson's intention. Smithers and Reid believed that the *Emily* would remain in company with the *Albatross*, and as soon as the corvette had herself secured a sufficient cargo, run the blockade under the convoy of the armed rover. Johnson had hit upon a very different scheme, which—if he found, by the ship's manifest and other collateral evidence, that, as the letters he had read correctly stated, the price of the munitions of war on board were to be paid to Captain William Bence upon their safe delivery at New York—would be carried out unhesitatingly. It *was* correct, he ascertained, that the cargo was to be so paid for—not in green-backs, but sterling coin. That capital fact ascertained, Johnson's mind was made up. A crew of the exact number taken from the *Columbia* was sent on board that vessel, placed under the command of his brother-in-law Reid, with whom he had a long consultation ; at the end of which Johnson returned on board the *Albatross*, and the *Columbia* made sail for New York. The account of the bantering seaman's first conversation with William Bence, a good-looking, good sort of chap enough, was somewhat amusing. The captive was of course dreadfully down in the mouth, and was evi-dently as much bewildered, mystified, as chagrined upon finding that his captor was Captain Johnson, the ship he had been forced on board of, the *Albatross*. Johnson asked if he would take dinner, the very mention of which seemed to increase the sickness at his stomach. He would, however, be glad of some brandy-and-water and a few cigars. Request willingly granted; and the two captains sat down facing each other in the state cabin, he of the *Columbia* staring silently in unutterable puzzlement at his captor till he had finished his fourth or fifth tumbler and as many cigars. Johnson, who could smoke five or six Ger-mans down, kept his countenance rigid and his tongue silent, eyeing his vis-à-vis as fixedly as he did him. Under the influence of his potations the colour slowly returned to Bence's calico cheeks, and he initiated the conversation, reported as follows by Johnson. If there be exaggeration in it, I am guiltless thereof.

"This is a dismal business, Captain Johnson, and what IS the meaning of it ?"

"Quite plain sailing, Mr. Bence, and far from dismal. The *Albatross*, Confederate ship, Captain Johnson, has captured the *Columbia*, so called, a ship hailing from Boston, with a very valuable cargo of warlike stores, Mr. William Bence, master. Very clear and simple, it appears to me."

"Clear and simple be——. I don't want to be rude or violent, captain, but how, in the name of the devil and all his angels, does it happen that a ship half owned by my father-in-law, Mr. Selby——"

"Step-father, my dear sir; Mr. Selby I understand to be Captain William Bence's step-father—a different relationship, quite."

"Pish! Well, then, Mr. Selby, my step-father, advanced, did he not, ten thousand pounds towards fitting-out this infernal steamer?"

"Correct—hoping to recoup himself off the Scilly Isles. But you know, Mr. Bence, that the best-laid schemes of mice and men break down sometimes."

"The devil take both mice and men. What I want to understand is, why the *Albatross*, half-owned by my step-father, captured *my* vessel on the high seas? *That's* what I want to understand."

"A very reasonable request, Mr. Bence. First, however, as to your estimable step-father having advanced ten thousand pounds, you are somewhat in error. The Federal Committee in London found that money."

"Which is, of course, irrecoverably lost. Lord, Lord, what a precious sell!"

"A fine haul, Mr. Bence, a decidedly fine haul. Flotsam and jetsam, Mr. Bence, which means valuables that float of themselves like, into one's lap."

"Well, it's of no use crying over spilt milk. Of course you will give me my private papers and set us all at liberty at the earliest opportunity. Some part of British America *I* should prefer, for particular reasons."

"Amongst your private papers, Mr. Bence, were, I remember, two sealed letters, addressed, one to Mrs. Harrison, the other to Miss Harrison, Albany, New York State. *They* cannot be given to you, having been forwarded to their address by a sure hand. As to your men, every one has volunteered to serve under the Confederate flag, except the mates, whom I wouldn't have, if they were willing, at any price. It pains me to add that the exigencies of the particular service in which I am engaged will not permit me to send either them or your worthy self on shore for a long time, perhaps for many months to come, and——"

"Particular service be——. Don't aggravate the case, captain. My blood's boiling already. *Why* can't you put us ashore, and who has those letters—tell me that."

"I was about to do so—but pray replenish your tumbler."

"Curse the tumbler! Tell me *why* you can't put me ashore, and who is the sure hand that has undertaken, confound his impudence, to deliver the letters?"

" Willingly, Mr. Bence. The case is this :—Finding there is a very large sum to be paid for freight and cargo, on delivery of the same, for which I am very happy to find the English manufacturers have been paid ; that Captain William Bence is not personally known in the States ; the *Columbia*, formerly the *Emily*, has proceeded to her destination, New York, where her present commander, personating Captain William Bence, will receive the cash——"

" Why, what an infernal, scoundrelly do ! It's scandalous. It makes one's very flesh creep and one's hair stand on end——"

" 'Like quills upon the fretful porcupine'—exactly. Captain William Bence will next deliver the letters, as in person, at Albany. The widow Harrison's daughter, Frances Harrison, is, I am told, a very handsome girl. Reid, my brother-in-law, who is a bachelor, and fine-spirited young fellow, hopes to make himself agreeable to the young lady, particularly as she has a fortune of five thousand pounds, and much more in expectation."

" I'll be hanged if you must not be Beelzebub himself !" shouted Bence, springing to his feet and glaring with flaming eyes at his tormentor. " Do you think a man is made of wood or iron ? It's infamous ; it's tearing out one's very vitals—that's what it is !" and the exasperated young man continued to pour forth volley after volley of indignant vituperation, greatly to the amusement of Johnson, till strength and breath failed him, and he fell prostrate on the cabin locker in an agony of suffocating rage and mortification. It certainly could not be denied that, up to th attime, Johnson, singularly favoured by circumstances, had played his audacious game with wonderful good fortune. To finish, however, with the particular adventure entrusted to Reid, I have to state that the *Columbia* reached New York in safety; that the only real danger to be apprehended—treachery on the part of one or more of the crew, who had, however, been carefully selected by Johnson—did not occur, and that, after somewhat tedious formalities had been gone through, the pretended Captain William Bence received the amount due from the Washington Government. Reid, grown daring by success, endeavoured to get the *Columbia* chartered with military stores for New Orleans by the Federal naval authorities, and sent in a low tender in furtherance of his design to that department. He was disappointed. Secretary Willes decided upon forwarding the stores by a steamer, and the *Columbia* left, ostensibly for London, in ballast. Reid had had a very narrow, touch-and-go escape. Twenty-four hours after the *Columbia* sailed from New York, the *Persia* ran in; on board of which splendid vessel was Mr. Turnbull, who *knew* the real William Bence. Of course, he suspected nothing, and wrote by the next mail a congratulatory letter to his friend, Mr. Selby, upon his step-son's success; assuring him that the young sailor had made a most favourable impression upon the Federal officials with whom he had been placed in communication.

During his compelled stay at New York, Reid, who could not, I should say, have slept very soundly at nights, determined—upon the principle, I suppose, that a man may as well be hanged for a sheep as a lamb— to proceed in one of the fast river-steamers up the Hudson, and deliver the letters to Mrs. and Miss Harrison. He was received with great cordiality by those ladies, both of whom he found were zealous partisans of the South. Upon that hint, he spoke to Miss Fanny, a very amiable and lively young lady, confessing the imposture he was carrying out, and informing her where the real Simon Pure was at that moment held in captivity. The gay damsel was delighted with the story, so was her mother ; and it was tacitly understood, perhaps openly avowed by Miss Fanny, that they should be glad to see him in Yorkshire when they returned to England, which they did in the *Persia* at her next departure after leaving Mr. Turnbull. That person had brought a letter for them from Mr. Selby, and to him they expressed a highly favourable opinion of Captain William Bence.

All this news reached Captain Johnson, when off Halifax, to which place he sent a boat for newspapers and letters. Having read them himself, he handed the papers and Reid's letter to his captive, Bence, with the expression that he hoped they would interest that despondent gentleman. They must have done so, as he at once took to his bed—sleeping-berth, I mean—and did not reappear on deck for a fortnight.

I now return to the log proper of the *Albatross.* Two days after parting company with the *Columbia,* Captain Johnson fell in with the United States ship *Neptune,* nine days out from London, and laden with military stores. The crew and stores were taken out —an operation which, as there was a heavy sea on, occupied nearly three days. It was not too soon accomplished, as the *Albatross'* men were still on board the prize, when two heavy steam frigates, carrying the Federal flag, hove in sight, and, perceiving what was going on, got up full heads of steam, and came swiftly up to the rescue. Johnson at once gave orders to fire the *Neptune,* and returned with his men to his own ship, bringing two of the *Neptune's* boats. Anxious to disembarrass himself of prisoners as quickly as possible, he placed the captured crew in those boats, and steamed away; slowly enough, however, to make himself certain that the boats were seen, and would be picked up by the approaching frigates, the names of which, when I last heard from him, had not been ascertained. Satisfied on that point, he put on full steam, and very quickly found that the American ships had no chance of overhauling the *Albatross.* Had they been swifter than the corvette, Johnson believed they would have been no match for his armour-plated corvette. The *Neptune* had been so effectually fired, that two minutes after the *Albatross'* men left, she

was a mass of flame. During the next three weeks
seven other vessels, four outward bound with military
stores, were captured ; six, after having been despoiled
of everything valuable to the captors, were burnt.
On board the seventh, the *Diamond* brig, all the seven
crews were placed, and the brig proceeded with them
to her destination, Bristol. The corvette was now
full, and Johnson at once hastened to meet the
Columbia at the appointed sea-rendezvous, about twenty
leagues northward of the Bermudas. He readily found
her, and was informed by Reid that the port was
closely watched by a sloop of war and a gunboat.
The *Columbia* had herself been brought-to by the
Montgomery gunboat ; but there being no suspicion
that she was not what she pretended to be, had been
immediately released. A council of war was immediately held, at which it was debated whether or not
the *Albatross* should escort the *Columbia* into Bermuda,
where a contraband cargo for her could be easily obtained, and, if necessary, fight the sloop and gunboat.
The proposal was negatived, inasmuch as the *Rinaldo*
British frigate and the sloop *Desperate* were there,
who would certainly refuse to allow a ship that had
engaged in British waters the United States vessels, to
enter that harbour. The next question was, should
the *Columbia*, rechanging her name, go on to England.
That too, upon consideration, was negatived. The
Federal London Committee would be sure to scent out
the secret, and as neither of the belligerents were per-

mitted to bring prizes into British ports, the hapless *Emily* would be ordered to leave forthwith, and become an easy prey to the Federal cruisers in wait for her. The conviction was forced upon Johnson that he should be obliged, if lucky enough to convey her safely into a Southern port, to sell her there,—to him a bitter mortification. There happened to be half a gale of wind blowing at the time from the north-east, a great advantage to the barque, enabling her whilst it continued to hold her own with the steam corvette. This was decisive, and it was at once resolved to run for Chesapeake Bay, and evade or force the blockade at the first favourable opportunity.

The two ships gave the still vexed *Bermoothes* as wide a berth as possible, but notwithstanding that precaution they were seen by the *Montgomery* gun-boat, which, unaware of the force of the *Albatross*, gave instant chase. The gun-boat was remarkably swift, and seeing it would be impossible to drop her, the corvette slackened her speed to allow the *Montgomery* to come within cannon range, then to unmask the Confederate cruiser's battery, and settle the gun-boat for good and all. The *ruse* failed. The Federal captain must have suspected a trap, for he also slackened his speed, and kept beyond range of the corvette's guns; he, however, kept on constantly firing, of course to attract the attention of Federal cruisers.

The port ultimately fixed upon for the grand effort was Norfolk, arrived within some twenty leagues of which the gale died away to a faint summer breeze, and the *Columbia*, but for her powerful friend, would have been quickly overhauled by the gun-boat, which her assumed character would not again deceive. The *Montgomery* continued to play a safe game, keeping her distance, firing at intervals, and keeping signals constantly flying. The situation was a trying one for Johnson. He would almost as soon have parted with one of his limbs as with the *Emily*, and yet he knew, as did every man on board of her and the *Albatross*, that if the barque was to be prevented from falling into the hands of the enemy, and the corvette was to have a fair chance of successfully running the blockade, with her, to the Southerners, priceless cargo, the *Emily* should be scuttled or fired without delay. The appearance of three United States cruisers, all heavy ships, one or more possibly iron-plated, in quick succession, attracted by the firing, put an end to Johnson's hesitation. Reid was signalled to hasten with his crew on board the corvette, having first scuttled the *Emily*. The order was promptly obeyed, and long before the *Montgomery* could come up with her, the *Columbia*, alias the *Emily*, had disappeared in her sea-sepulchre.

All disguise and mystification was then thrown off. The British ensign was run up at the main, the palmetto at the fore; full steam was got up, and the corvette's formidable battery unmasked and made ready. The leading American frigate—plainly a wooden ship—was then about half a league distant, and had commenced firing. Johnson, determined to stop her barking, as an example for the others, instead of holding his course so as to pass her, put the helm up, and steered directly for her. The frigate continued firing, but her balls, when they struck the *corvette*, were of no more effect than cherry-stones flung at a stone wall. The *Albatross* kept steadily on without returning a shot till within pistol distance, then gave the Yankee her broadside at one dose. She did not require another, and the corvette, sweeping up to windward, again resumed her course. But though the *Albatross* was not injured by the American frigate's fire, Johnson's left arm was smashed by about her last shot. The force of the blow knocked him off his legs. He was up again—this I know from the brother-in-law—in a moment, called for a tourniquet to stop the effusion of blood, and continued to give his orders as coolly, calmly, as if nothing had happened. The two remaining American ships, and the gun-boat, made aware that they had to do with a plated ship, carrying a very heavy armament, declined to close with the awkward customer they had fallen in with. The *Albatross* stood gallantly on, the blockade was forced, and the immense contraband cargo taken from Federal ships safely landed at Norfolk. Johnson's arm was amputated. Anticipating that the Washington authorities would, as soon as they heard of his exploit, detach ships to *blockade* the *Albatross* herself, through

9—2

which it would be impossible to force his way, and though he himself must have been suffering intensely from his wound, the corvette left Norfolk on the third day after her arrival there, and again successfully braved the blockade, this time to break her way out of, not into, a southern port. Since then I have not heard much of the *Albatross*. I believe Johnson has changed the scene of his enterprise to the Pacific, up towards California. Captain William Bence and the two American mates were, I suppose, left at Norfolk. Reid has, I know, returned to England in general, and Yorkshire in particular, and is, I dare say, a jolly, thriving wooer. Nothing more likely, but I know nothing positive upon the subject. Nor do I know if Mr. Selby is still in the flesh, and a trusted member of the Federal committee. I should guess not. I had almost forgotten to mention that Johnson fulfilled his promise of redeeming Juba's son from slavery, and that Pompey is now living with his father in this country.

THE IRISH WIFE.

AT the Earl of Bute Hotel, Cardiff, I met with a gentleman who favoured me, in substance, with the following narrative :—

The port of Cardiff, Wales, is well known to be a rapidly rising one, and no question has a highly prosperous future before it. Amongst the numerous persons whose fortunes have grown with the growth of the port, are two mariners, Owen Jones and Owen Pryce. These men had sailed from and returned to Cardiff many years before the splendid quays, warehouses, and other vast maritime appliances had been projected by the Bute family. They were first cousins, born in the same house, baptized by the same name, were apprenticed to the same coasting skipper, and remained fast friends through life, and this notwithstanding both formed an attachment to the same young woman, Mary Williams, whom Owen Pryce married. One boy was born of this marriage, whom, as it seems, Jones felt as much parental pride in, and affection for, as did the young man's father himself. At the time

this narrative opens (1861), Pryce and Jones—who,
I have omitted to say, were born the same year—had
attained the respectable age of sixty-four.   They were
still hale, vigorous men. Seafaring men, if they escape
being drowned in spirits or the sea, generally steer
clear of disease and death for a much longer spell of
life than landfolk.   These men, in the aforenamed
year were in affluent circumstances for their class in
society.   Their joint savings had enabled them to
build a brig of large tonnage, copper-fastened, and well
found in every respect. She was named the *Earl of
Bute,* and when at sea was commanded each day alter-
nately by Jones and Pryce.   When either was not
captain, he was first-mate ; the son, David Pryce, an
athletic, skilful young seaman, was second-mate. Mrs.
Pryce, my informant says, was a notable, industrious,
worthy woman, and out-and-out Methodist after the
straitest pattern.

"Early in 1861, the *Earl of Bute* was chartered to
convey a cargo to Cork Island, and bring back a return
freight made up of butter, bacon, and other agricultural
products.   The brig was detained in the Cove of Cork
for various reasons much longer than had been expected, a delay patiently borne by the brother mariners, inasmuch as the demurrage to which they were
consequently entitled would amount to a goodly sum,
and nothing to do for it.   At length the return cargo
was securely shipped, but the departure of the brig
was still delayed.   David Pryce could not be found,

though anxious search was made for him in the city of
Cork and the neighbourhood. The Blue Peter had been
angrily flying at the brig's main for more than two
nights and days, and the distracted mariners began to
entertain the frightful dread that David had been
waylaid by Ribbonmen, Peep-o'-day-boys, or some
similar gang of ruffians, when the lost sheep made his
appearance, looking extremely sheepish ; and no wonder, for he brought off with him, in a shore boat, Mrs.
David Pryce, a handsome, merry-mannered Irish
damsel, whom he had married the day before ! The
joint-owners of the brig must, my friend imagines, have
simultaneously fallen into a fit, perhaps a trance, of
some duration, as the *Earl of Bute* had cleared the
Cove, and was stretching out into Saint George's
Channel, when those astounded mariners distinctly
realized in its entirety what had happened.   The
young wife, directly she found her father-in-law was
in a condition to appreciate her attentions, first half-
throttled him with her daughterly embrace, then knelt
down and asked his blessing.

"Not a 'Roman,'" gasped poor Pryce, over whose
mind a dreadful suspicion flashed. "Not a 'Roman.'
Dont say *that !*"

"Certainly I am a Roman Catholic," replied the
young woman, springing up, and her eyes flashing fire.
"Do you suppose, old gentleman, I would give up the
true Christian faith for the finest husband that ever
trod in shoe-leather ? If you do think so, I make

bold to say you are mightily mistaken in your daughter-in-law, Mrs. David Pryce."

The "old gentleman" must have gone off in a swoon again, since it was not till next day that the two friends were sufficiently composed in mind to take tolerably calm council with each other. They, as placable a pair as ever lived, would there and then have forgiven David, and drank the young couple's health in bumpers, but for the spectre immovably painted on the retina of each with about equal distinctness,—Mrs. Pryce, senior. How was the awful business to be broken to that sternly-spiritual woman and deadly abominator of the Scarlet Lady? Pryce declared that sooner than walk into his house at Cardiff with such a daughter-in-law, he would prefer dropping down, like Daniel, into a lion's den. That couldn't last very long; but this dreadful business—oh dear! Irish *and* Roman! Good Lord! Fire from heaven—lakes of brimstone! Finally, after a large consumption of tobacco and scheidam, the two friends unanimously voted an adjournment of the difficulty. Mrs. David Pryce, who, though not worth a copper, was in possession of high certificates to character, was the daughter of a not long since deceased skipper of Cork, with whom at first, for the benefit of her health, she had made frequent trips to the Levant. She was accordingly accustomed to live in a ship. Why not, then, arrange that she should remain aboard the *Earl of Bute?* Richards and Company of Bristol had settled to charter the brig for Marseilles, France. The return cargo.

was to be delivered at Bristol. Very well. An immediate discovery was impossible, and who knew what time would bring forth, and so on. The affair was so decided.

The Phocian city was safely reached by the *Earl of Bute*, the cargo discharged. Pryce and Jones, who, spite of themselves, had become attached to their comely, interesting relative, were fishing for a return cargo, for London they had hoped ; but this was found difficult, if not impossible, when a liberal offer was made to them by a Southern agent at Marseilles. Mr. Jefferson Davis' emissary had accumulated a vast quantity of French, English, and Belgian rifles, and was exceedingly anxious to ship them forthwith for the Confederate States. He was willing to pay handsomely, but French skippers, the most *un*adventurous class in Europe—in a commercial sense—turned a deaf ear to his proposals. So he sounded Jones and Pryce. They, too, were at first indisposed to having anything to do with running the American blockade. But just upon the God-speed of it, and when it seemed that they could not for many days longer delay returning in ballast to Cardiff, a parcel arrived, containing a long letter from Mrs. Pryce, whose mind, it seemed thereby, was much alarmed and inflamed by the thought that they were sojourning in a popish city. As a shield to guard against such peril to their immortal souls, she had sent them a large number of the latest evangelical pamphlets, &c. &c.

No doubt this message, intensifying the conviction

always simmering in their minds, that to take Mrs.
David Pryce to Cardiff was equivalent to breaking up
their home—of poisoning all the remaining years of life,
determined the friends again to put off the evil day.
Mr. Mostyn's offer was accepted.   By some means,
analogous to those contemplated by O'Connell when
he boasted of being able to drive a coach and six through
an Act of Parliament, the *Earl of Bute* was enabled
to clear with her cargo of rifles from Marseilles.   The
charter-contract was not very wisely arranged on the
part of the Welsh mariners.   The freight was settled
at a very high figure, but the condition of liability for
two-thirds thereof was that the blockade should be *successfully* run.   Considering that it was next to impossible
to insure the *Earl of Bute* against the risk of capture,
the bargain was a very one-sided one.   Pryce and
Jones were essentially coasting mariners, and almost
completely ignorant of ocean navigation.   Their son
was better instructed, but his theoretical knowledge not
having been tested and confirmed by experience, did
not inspire even himself with much confidence.   It was
resolved, therefore, to insert an advertisement in the
Nouvelliste of Marseilles, that the services of a petty
officer who had passed a French examination, and
obtained what is called a "longue cour" certificate,
might have a berth, with liberal remuneration, in the
Earl of Bute.   One peremptory condition was knowledge of the English language and English sea terms.
One Jacques Le Breton, who had sailed several times

as *second* in ships bound for long voyages, presented himself. His certificate was complimentary, his moral character vouched to be unquestionable, and M. Le Breton was engaged. This man had no doubt the qualifications required ; his moral character in the main *was* unexceptionable. There was but one fatal flaw ; he was afflicted with intense Anglophobia ; as hundreds of thousands of honest Frenchmen are. His father had fallen in a frigate action with the English, his two much older brothers at Waterloo. His hatred of the English was consequently venomous ; and being an aged though hale widower, with no children, no ties strongly attaching to earth and life, he, I have no doubt, from the moment his eye rested on the notice in the *Nouvelliste,* determined to strike one blow before he died at *les maudits Anglais.* That is not my friendly informant's opinion. He believes that Le Breton, intending honestly at first, was surprised by, and yielded to a great temptation. My opinion is reinforced by the shrewdness of the young Irish wife, Mrs. David Pryce, *born* Mary Mahony. The *Earl of Bute* had not been three hours at sea when Mrs. David Pryce told her husband, told her father-in-law, and Owen Jones, that they had a traitor on board ; that Le Breton was a rascal. She could give no reason for her opinion, except that of Dogberry anent Borachio, "She didn't like his looks." A shrewd woman, though not much past her teens. The value of the *Earl of Bute's* cargo was estimated at over forty

thousand pounds—cost price—three times that value
at the very least if successfully run ; the brig herself,
being over six hundred tons, and A. 1 ½—not launched
a twelvemonth, could not be worth less than from nine
to ten thousand pounds.   The extent of the venture
to which our two Welshmen had committed themselves
was rather considerable.

The *Earl of Bute*, bound ostensibly for New Zealand,
was compelled by stress of weather to put in at St.
John's, Newfoundland.   The brig remained there but
a few days only.   Quite sufficient time for a man of
LeBreton's readiness and resources to arrange his plan
of definitive action.   The *Wave of the Sea*, a United
States cruiser of small force, carrying only two guns,
with a crew of some forty men, had also been
obliged to put into St. John's by stress of weather.
She had carried away some part of her top-hamper, to
replace which would necessitate her stay at St.
John's for some considerable time.   The *Earl of Bute*
would be able to proceed on her voyage directly the
furious gale had sufficiently abated to enable her to do
so with prudence.   Mrs. David Pryce went on shore
with her husband, partly for a change, partly to en-
quire if a relative of hers, one Patrick Lynch, a seaman, who had been long engaged in the Newfoundland
fishery, might perchance be there.   Patrick Lynch was
there, as it chanced, out of a berth, and pretty nearly
hard-aground.   He was a practised navigator and

fair seaman, but addicted over much to whisky. Mrs.
David Price got him a berth on board the *Earl of
Bute*, and was the more anxious that he should be
engaged forasmuch that she, her husband, and Patrick
Lynch had seen Le Breton in earnest eager consultation with Captain Wallace, of the *Wave of the Sea*.
Wallis, it was subsequently ascertained, had several
conferences with the skipper of a Yankee schooner
named the *Pensacola*, which forthwith hurried the
preparations for departure, and in effect *did* leave St.
John's, at some risk from the violence of the weather,
twenty-four hours or thereaway before the *Earl of
Bute*. The workmen employed upon the *Wave of the
Sea* were, moreover, worked day and night to hasten
the departure of that vessel. The aspect of affairs was,
to draw it mildly, menacing—Things, as Francis Moore,
Physician, would say, began to look black in the South ;
the two master-mariners had strong misgivings that
the presence on board of a votary of the Scarlet Lady
was shedding disastrous influence over their too hastily
undertaken voyage. They could, however, keep a
sharp look-out for squalls ; and since Lynch was fully
acquainted with all the bearings of the American
coast, they might pull through and reach port in safety,
after all.

Lynch and Le Breton had a serious difference of
opinion when the *Earl of Bute* had been about two
days out ; the Irishman insisting that it was advisable
to take a more south-easterly course than they were

steering. Le Breton, on the contrary, argued that the boldness of more nearly hugging the northern coast would preclude suspicion of their intention to run the Southern blockade. This was plausible, and Lynch yielded the point. Le Breton, who knew the man's weakness, quietly managed to supply him with means of drinking himself dead-drunk,—an opportunity which Lynch, could not resist, and to the infinite, annoyance and disgust of his relative, Mrs. David Pryce, he swilled himself into a state of utter helplessness, and the navigation of the brig was perforce wholly intrusted to Le Breton.

The owners of the *Earl of Bute* had not long to wait for the result. Lynch, partially recovered from his drunken bout, staggered upon deck about noon one day, aroused with great difficulty by the angry insistence of David Pryce's wife. Two cruisers were in sight, bearing the Federal flag, and it seemed doubtful that the Southern port said by Le Breton to be Charleston, distant, according to him, about one hundred and fifty miles, could be reached, if no other cruiser hove in sight ahead. There was a stiff breeze blowing, and Le Breton certainly evinced great zeal in getting as many knots out of the brig as was consistent with the safety of her spars. Neither the *Brandywine* frigate, nor the *Wave of the Sea*, by which the *Earl of Bute* was pursued, appeared, however, after a while, to gain very much upon them; and hope revived in the troubled bosoms of the Welsh skippers. The chase had lasted from early dawn, and if Le Breton was

not strangely out in his reckoning, Charleston would
be gained before either of the Yankee cruisers could
bring a gun to bear with effect upon the brig. That
pleasing hope was rudely dispelled. Lynch looked
long and steadily as he could through the glass for
some time, doubting the evidence of his muddled senses,
but thoroughly convinced at length that he was labour-
ing under no drunken illusion, exclaimed, with a fierce
oath—"Sandy-Hook by —— ; steering straight for
New York." The Frenchman attempted a bold denial,
iterating his assertion that they were fast nearing
Charleston. The state of the weather since the day
after St. John's was left had precluded the possibility
of making an observation, but Lynch was not to be
bounced. It would, he argued, have been quite impossible to have made Chesapeake Bay since the *Earl
of Bute* left Newfoundland ; and as for saying yon was
not Sandy-Hook, they might as well tell him his name
wasn't Pat Lynch. He was believed ; the direction of the brig's course was confided to him ; and in
a few minutes the *Earl of Bute* was careering over the
waves really in the direction of Chesapeake Bay. That
Lynch was right, an additional proof was quickly
afforded. The Federal cruisers, guessing what had
happened, put on full heads of steam and sail, and unless the brig could keep beyond cannon-fire till night-
fall, which promised to be dark and dirty enough, the
chase was virtually at an end. To try that last chance,
a yet greater press of sail was got upon the *Earl of
Bute,* the early result of which was, that the main-top-

mast snapped, and top-gallant and topsail fell over the side. Further struggle was useless, and in about half an hour the brig and cargo were the lawful prize of the Federal frigate. All over with the *Earl of Bute ;* the legality of the capture could not be disputed, and the savings of the two honest Welsh skippers, through nearly half a century, were swallowed up for ever. It must have been an inexpressibly bitter moment for them both, and rendered more agonising, from knowing that the primary cause of the irreparable misfortune was the marriage of David Pryce, their tenderly beloved son, with an Irish Papist. A heavy, but no doubt just, judgment upon him and them.

The officers and crew of the American frigate were naturally much pleased to find they had not been deceived as to the large value of the intercepted prize ; and though this occurred before the recapture of the *Emilie St. Pierre,* yet as more than one attempt had been made—unsuccessfully, it was true—by captains left on board captured vessels to get their own again, by overpowering the prize-crew, the commander of the *Brandywine,* in view of the vast stake at issue, determined to leave nothing to chance. Twenty able seamen were accordingly told off and placed on board the *Earl of Bute,* under the command of a lieutenant. Of the officers and crew of the captured brig, all were carried off in the frigate except nine persons, three of whom were Mrs. David Pryce, her husband, who had slipped down the forecastle hatchway, so spraining his ankle that *he* as a fighting man was nobody ; and

Patrick Lynch, found dead drunk in his berth ; Owen Jones and Owen Pryce were left in the brig as a matter of right, it being a recognised principle in such cases that owners of captured ships have a right to appear in person before the court whose duty it would be to adjudicate upon the legality of the capture. The remaining four permitted to remain, or more properly ordered to remain, on board the brig, were Thomas Williams, cook and steward, Hugh and John Evans, father and son,—stout able-bodied seamen, who seem to have been selected to assist in working the ship on account of their vehement entreaties *not* to be left in her, the loss of time consequent upon being examined by a prize-court being ruinous to poor fellows whose families at home depended for their daily bread upon the father and husband. The ninth was one Wilkins, cook's mate, and apothecary at a pinch. Welsh, all of them, with the exception of the wife and her rela- tive, Patrick Lynch. All could consequently hold dis- course in unknown tongues, seven in Welsh, two in Irish, Mrs. Davis Pryce, moreover, having with natural aptitude already sufficiently mastered her husband's native language to be able to keep him well *au courant* of all that was going on. I presume that the first resolu- tion come to by the Welsh owners and their people, as soon as it had been clearly ascertained that there was neither a native Irishman nor Welshman amongst the prize crew, was to talk openly, loudly with each other, in those, to the world at large, incomprehensible, untaught out of Ireland and Wales, dialects. This after a short time might excite no suspicion, whereas whispered talk amongst the captives, certainly would. Another circumstance much favouring any chance that might present itself to Pryce and Jones of getting their ship again —and any chance, however slight, desperate as it might be, they were thoroughly resolved to seize,—was that the *Earl of Bute* was ordered to Key West, although there were Northern ports so much nearer. The weather, too, proved unusually calm, so that five days after being ordered to fill and make for Key West, the brig had not progressed more than about fifty marine leagues. I having omitted to state that Le Breton was placed on board the prize, in addition to the twenty Americans.

The Irish wife, who was the soul of the plot for retaking the *Earl of Bute*, was not only a very handsome, personally attractive young person, but a sweet singer of the songs of Ireland. She laid herself skilfully out to please and bamboozle the lieutenant in command of the prize crew, who would listen enraptured to her Kathleen Mavourneen, and such like ditties, of a still evening upon deck for hours together. In brief, he became outrageously spoony about her, doubting not to win her to his wishes, and before long too. What could she really care for that disabled cripple of a husband, who, according to the report of Wilkins, would never recover the use of his foot? or for the drunken relative Lynch, who, continuing to drink like a fish, though where he got the liquor was a mystery ! had not been one minute able to leave his berth (he would have been handsomely flogged to his duty, but that he *was* her relative). Her father-in-law, too, was a beggar. It was Wall Street to a pumpkin-pie in his favour. He would have been enlightened upon that point had he heard and understood the mocking merriment of the disabled cripple's wife when amusing her husband with details of the infatuated dupe's folly.

At length the officer's heart-strings having been wound up to the highest bearable pitch, decisive action was resolved upon. The morrow, 20th of June, was his charmer's birth-day, and she was desirous that her American friends should celebrate it in a quietly convivial way. When the *Earl of Bute* was at Marseilles, she confidentially informed the lieutenant, a considerable parcel of excellent wine and spirits had been taken on board. It had been successfully concealed when the brig had been made prize of; but *she* knew where it was hidden, and would show him secretly, for she would not for the world her husband and other relatives should know that she had betrayed their confidence even in so trifling a matter. It might be accidentally discovered, and a pleasant banquet improvised, enlivened with singing, &c. The lieutenant was delighted, especially as the liquids on board, mainly tainted water, were detestable. One of the seamen was admitted into his and the lady's confidence—the

precious wines and spirits were *discovered*—the place
of deposit made known confidentially to every one of
the American prize crew before many hours had
passed, and that on the morrow evening a modicum of
the same would be served out to each of the sailors.
Now this was a damper to every American on board.
The delay was objectionable; in the next place, a
modicum meant, most likely, a wineglass-full to drink
the lady's health!   Then the place of concealment was
easily accessible; the lieutenant himself did not mean
to wait till the morrow, for William, the acting-
steward, had been seen to carry a number of bottles to
the cabin.   Why should they wait more than he? The
quantity in secret store—especially of the spirits—was
not known, but on the morrow the bottles would certainly be numbered; the champagne brandy gauged!
As men and Americans they were entitled to liquor
whenever it was possible to do so.   As soon, therefore,
as the lieutenant, and the middy, a relative of his,
the lady always insisting that he should be present when she honoured his superior officer with her
company), were safely booked for the evening, they, the
common fellows, it was tacitly resolved, would have a
good innings whilst the ball was at their feet.

The plot, it is well known, succeeded to admiration,
though the navy department (Lieutenant —— having
influential friends in high quarters) hushed it up.
Both wine and brandy had been craftily qualified by
Wilkin, a clever fellow in that line.   A dead calm,

moreover, prevailed, so that comparatively no deck-duty was required to be done. The men had consequently leisure to fully enjoy themselves. Everything fell out as hoped for. The lieutenant and middy, whilst basking in the lady's smiles, found themselves insensibly rocked off to sleep upon the silver waves of her sweet singing, and awoke from uneasy slumbers to find themselves handcuffed prisoners, and bowling along—*not* to Key West—under the pressure of a nine-knot breeze, over quite other sort of waves. The crew had fallen just as easy victims, been effectually secured by the two skippers, David Pryce, whose sham sprain had suddenly left him, Lynch, whose continuous drunkenness was sham also; the two Evanses, Williams and Wilkins. Only one on board was capable of showing fight—the Frenchman, Le Breton. He had always suspected that some plot was hatching, that Mrs. David Pryce was fooling the infatuated lieutenant, and was therefore constantly on the watch. His attempt at resistance of course availed nothing; and as soon as more urgent matters had been attended to, he was seized up, and received three dozen well-earned lashes. My friend added, upon the authority of Patrick Lynch, that when the American lieutenant began to stir restlessly in his sleep, and drowsily open his astonished eyes upon the state of things in general, the siren who beguiled him assisted his awakening perceptions by warbling in her sweetest strains some such vile parody on his favourite song as the following :—

" O, doodle doo, Yankee, the grey dawn is breaking,
    The cuffs of thy country bind fast thy own wrists,
    This may be for weeks, and it may be for months, dear ;
    Then, why dost thou slumber, my own doodle doo ?"

Atrocious, if true, which I can hardly believe it to be.
After many narrowly-escaped perils of recapture, the
Earl of Bute successfully ran the blockade at Mobile.
She attempted three or four times to run *out*, failed to
do so ; the sworn-brother Welsh skippers sold her, and
themselves and friends ultimately got safely away from
another Southern port in a French vessel. So effectually was the affair " hushed up," that for several
months after its occurrence the captain and officers of
the *Brandywine* frigate, whose disappointment at not
finding their rich prize at Key West may be imagined,
believed the *Earl of Bute* had gone down at sea. The
elder Mrs. Pryce died suddenly of bronchitis during her
husband and son's absence ; and the Irish wife now
reigns in her stead. I may add, that a second *Earl of
Bute* is now on the stocks, to be commanded by David
Pryce—Owen Pryce and Owen Jones having wisely
resolved to lay up in ordinary for the remainder of
their lives.

CAPTAIN ARNOLD.

ONE of the most zealous officers engaged in the hazardous business of supplying the Southerners with contraband of war, is a naturalized citizen of the United States, and was till lately a commissioned officer of their navy. Captain Arnold, as I shall call him, was born at Truro, Cornwall, in the year 1804, and is consequently now in his fifty-eighth year, but looking ten years younger at least. The story of his life, as I have heard it related, is a somewhat remarkable one. His father, a man of daring courage, but irascible, violent temper, was serving as boatswain on board the *Lapwing*, sloop of war, in 1807, when he received a wanton blow from one of the midshipmen. It was promptly returned with tremendous interest ; in fact, he half killed the astounded stripling—and he, the son of an Admiralty lord, too—before effectual interposition could be made. The mutinous boatswain was immediately put in irons, and notwithstanding the provocation he had received, would, no question, have been sentenced by a naval court-martial to condign punishment; he, however, managed to escape. He was a great favourite with both captain and crew, and the former he always believed must have connived with the men who actually managed the business. John Arnold got safely off to America, settled in Nantucket, engaged in the whaling-trade, and was soon in a condition to send to Truro for his wife and two children—a boy and girl. They sailed in 1808 in an American vessel, which experienced a long, stormy passage, during which the girl died. The mother and son arrived safely out. John Arnold was prospering more rapidly than his wife had ventured to anticipate. He had immediately upon landing taken the necessary steps to become naturalized, and was remarked for displaying, in season and out of season, extravagant contempt and hatred of the British Government. The breaking out of the war in 1812 between England and the American Union found John Arnold quite ready to take eager part in it. He had built, fitted out, and armed a fast brigantine, which he named the *Hawk*, and that vessel was one of the first privateers which left the American ports to prey upon British commerce. The *Hawk*, under John Arnold's energetic command, was a great success, and the ex-boatswain's name became a familiar word in the Atlantic seaports. He obtained pudding as well as praise, having realized by the close of the war over sixty thousand dollars. There was one drawback to his good fortune—a serious one. In a disastrous fight with a British 10-gun brig,

;he character of which he had mistaken, John Arnold had both his legs carried away by a chain-shot, and it ras with difficulty the *Hawk* escaped capture. This was Arnold's last cruise; the war being soon afterwards brought to a close by the mediation of Russia. The *Hawk* was sold, and Arnold, with wife and son, settled in Maryland, near Baltimore, where Arnold had purchased a handsome and improving property. There the ex-boatswain of the *Lapwing* closed his eyes in peace in 1830, his son, who had been naturalized at the earliest possible opportunity, being then in his twenty-sixth year, and an officer in the United States navy.

The widow followed soon afterwards, and Lieutenant Arnold found himself sole master of a property the value of which had trebled since his father made the purchase. The young officer then retired from the service — retaining his rank, reduced pay, and liability of being at any time recalled to active service. Captain Arnold was, it will be found, "a good hater," like his father; as unforgiving, inflexible as he. The son did not, however, inherit John Arnold's bitter hatred of the English. The reverse rather, which he owed to the example of his mother, who lived and died a true Cornishwoman, and but that her husband's grave was in Maryland, would have caused her own bones to be transported across the Atlantic, and deposited with those of her parents in the old churchyard at Truro.

Captain Arnold was a first-rate seaman, but he made a miserable mess of it as a planter. Still, the property was so large that it was not all gone till just before the outbreak of the civil war now raging in America. Lieutenant Arnold's downcome was of course accelerated by a wife and nine children; the wife a Southern lady. Altogether an impulsive man, unsobered by time or experience, Captain Arnold seems to be, but of his blunt truthfulness I have not the slightest doubt. He, I believe——though the subject was avoided by him, seemed distasteful—was connected more or less intimately with Walker's filibustering exploits. He had been arrested and held to bail by a marshal of the United States. This circumstance he more than once incidentally mentioned. No further step was taken in the affair, which was probably therefore a preventive measure only. Necessity makes us acquainted with strange bedfellows, and Arnold is essentially a man of action.

Such was the disastrous condition of things in Arnold's household when the cannon of Fort Sumter roused the angry passions of the North, initiating the suicidal struggle still in direful progress. Lieutenant Arnold determined immediately to set off for Washington and solicit active employment. He hoped to obtain the command of a sloop of war, a confident intimation to that effect having been conveyed to him by a superior official in the Navy department. He set out for the Columbian capital in high spirits. Mrs. Arnold and family had still a home at the old place; gaunt and grim poverty's black feet were on the threshold, but not yet thrust among the children's on the hearth.

There was quite as much official red-tapeism amongst the office-holders at Washington at the commencement of the contest—a great deal more, according to Arnold—than the British government could be charged with during the Crimean war. The President and Cabinet could not or would not look the gigantic task before them boldly in the face; and, as we all know, Mr. Lincoln called for seventy-five thousand men to subdue and keep in subjection a country as large in extent as Europe. The Navy department was almost equally sluggish, and Arnold was kept dilly-dallying about for months, promise-crammed plentifully enough, but an actual appointment as far off as ever, when his hotel bill (he was well known in Washington, and generally believed there to be still a man of substance), had reached an enormous sum. Under such circumstances, a man of Arnold's temperament would eat his heart away with rage, imagine affronts where none were intended, and be eager to follow up the slightest quarrel to deadliest issue. The Bull Run race came off whilst he was still dancing attendance on the Naval authorities; Arnold remarked upon the celerity of movement displayed by the Grand Army of the Potomac with sarcastic bitterness at the bar of the hotel in presence of several officers of that army. One of those gentlemen, during the heated discussion which followed, corrected a statement of fact made by Arnold, which, in his angry bitter mood, he chose to consider an insult, giving him the lie, in fact, and only to be atoned for by immediate personal satisfaction. This was demurred to by the party challenged, who commenced an explanatory apology, peremptorily brought to an end by a blow from the challenger. Of course, the only question then left to decide was whether rifle, pistol, or bowie-knife should be the final arbiter, without appeal, in the dispute. The choice fell upon pistols, which decided against the challenged officer. Arnold shot him dead at the first fire.

These "difficulties" in transatlantic cities, where life is so eager, feverish, brief, excite but a passing attention, and the death of Captain —— in fair duello would have had no sinister influence upon the future of the gentleman by whom he had been honourably killed, but that the slain officer was the relative of a highly influential member of the government that had been recently installed at the White House.

A few days after the duel, Lieutenant Arnold received an official note informing him that his application to be restored to active service could not be entertained. He was between fifty and sixty years of age, and nothing had been found in the archives of the Navy department to warrant a departure in his case from the rules of the service.

Not many days had passed when Lieutenant Arnold was at Richmond, cooling his heels in the ante-rooms of President Davis's official residence. Routine and redtape everywhere, even amongst enthusiastic revolutionists! Arnold passionately urged that the first, all-important duty of the Southern Government was to fit out light, fast, armed cruisers—anything that could sail or steam, and carry a gun to prey upon the rich sea commerce of the Northern States ; and that this should be done before the immensely preponderant maritime force of Lincoln's Government could effectually blockade the Southern ports. The theoretic reasonableness of the proposition was admitted, but the exigencies of the land service so taxed all the resources of the Confederate States, that the construction of a corsair fleet was adjourned till a more convenient season. In thus deciding, Jefferson Davis, as all the world now perceives, committed a great, almost irreparable error ; perhaps the only signal military error of his administration. He has at last bestirred himself in the right direction, but a dozen *Alabamas* at sea, as they might have been had Arnold's advice been taken eighteen months ago, would have quickly sickened commercial America of the insane attempt to subjugate the South.

The sagacity of private individuals is almost always superior in its appreciation of proposed expedients than the collective wisdom of governments. Mr. Durley, of Charleston, an ardent patriot and most estimable gentleman, who saw, and frequently conversed with, Arnold at Richmond, warmly urged the soundness of his views upon such members of the government as

he had access to ; and it is very possible that the tardy
fitting out of those comparatively inefficient vessels,
the *Sumter* and the *Nashville*, was in part due to his
energetic backing of Arnold's representations.   Be
that as it may, Mr. Durley proved the sincerity of
his convictions by purchasing a schooner, the *Wave*,
fitting her out as a miniature war-ship, carrying four
old twelve-pounder guns—two completely honey-
combed, and dangerous only to those who should venture to fire them, the command of which formidable
ship he offered to Arnold, by whom it was eagerly
accepted.   The *Wave* measured about one hundred and
thirty tons, her scantling was of the slightest, and she
carried a crew of thirty men.   Nevertheless, had she
been propelled by steam instead of canvas, she would
have fluttered the Northern mercantile marine, as the
youngest hawk would a dovecote.   As it was, the
Wave did some rather striking things.   When two
days at sea, she captured the United States brig
Oriana, from Jamaica to Boston in ballast.   The condition upon which he consented to release her, throws
a striking light upon the mingled yarn of Arnold's
character.   It was that the captain of the *Oriana* gave
a bond, supplemented by his word of honour, that he
would pay one Lieutenant Arnold's hotel bill in
Washington.   Arnold had assumed in the Confederate
service the name of Brown, and for an excellent reason.   His pay in the Federal navy as a retired lieutenant was a principal support of his family, to whom he

had directed the same to be handed over. The excuse he made to the captain of the *Oriana* was that he had incurred a large gambling debt—a debt of honour, with the individual who had eloped from Washington, leaving his bill unpaid, and that he, Captain Brown, had given his word to liquidate the debt as soon as possible in part payment of the debt of honour. A lame story —a tale for the marines. The captain of the *Oriana*, however, swallowed it ; or at all events, which was the essential point, he paid the bill, rejoiced, no doubt, to have got off so easily, the *Oriana* being a fine new brig of large tonnage.

The *Wave* had been sixteen days at sea when she came to grief. During that time, she had brought to and captured no less than seven vessels of various values belonging to citizens of the Northern States, and burned them all, it being impossible to spare one prize crew out of the *Wave's* thirty-two men. The crews of these vessels, far exceeding in number the *Wave's* complement of men, were all in irons on board the schooner, when the *Georgia*, Federal steam-cruiser, hove in sight, and gave chase to the *Wave*, which she had heard of a few hours previously by the captain of a vessel which the schooner had perseveringly chased, and as ineffectually fired at. There was a stiff breeze blowing, and the *Wave* at once spread all her wings for flight. Escape was, however, soon found to be hopeless. The *Georgia* was a remarkably fast paddle steamer. The cruiser was well known to Arnold, and the worst of it was, her officers and crew well knew *him*. That was a circumstance to flurry Arnold's pulse if anything could. He, an officer of the Federal navy, actually drawing pay from the Federal Government, caught *flagrante delicto* capturing and burning merchant ships sailing under the stars and stripes, was unquestionably liable to be hanged, and if the captain of the *Wave* would avoid making his final exit by that pleasant passage to the bourne from whence no traveller returns, it behoved him to play all he knew, or the game of life was assuredly lost. Arnold remarked that he had never realized the peculiar peril of his position till he recognised the *Georgia*, and found that escape was impossible. From the first moment of sighting the cruiser he had stood in for the land— the nearest being Salt Island, as it is usually termed, one of the Bahamas; but the *Georgia* herself, to say nothing of her cannon-balls, would be up with the schooner long before she had reached to within a marine league of the British island shore, even if the captain of the *Georgia* would in such a case respect the maxim of international law, which forbids pursuit of an enemy within that distance from a neutral shore. The sun was near its setting, and darkness, duskness more correctly, was falling over the waters, but there was no hope, not the slightest, that night would be early enough or black enough to conceal the *Wave* from her pursuer, who was coming up hand over hand. In that terrible emergency Arnold proved himself to

be a man of singular coolness, audacity, and resource.
After a brief consultation with his chief officer, who,
alone of all on board, knew Captain Brown to be
Lieutenant Arnold, the smallest of the *Wave's* boats
as lowered over the side, a bag of biscuit, cask of
ater, keg of spirits, and two light sculls placed in
her, the schooner at the same time luffing, heaving-
to, and offering readiness for fight to the Federal
steamer, by rapidly firing her two serviceable
guns. The object was to conceal by the bulk of the
schooner, assisted by the shrouding smoke of the guns,
the boat in which were seated Arnold and an equally
powerful oarsman, pulling with a will away from the
schooner. The *Georgia* was still considerably more
than two leagues distant, and her people must have
thought the captain of the *Wave* had gone suddenly
mad. Of course she did not return the puny schooner's
fire, but kept steadily on, quite secure of her prize.

Arnold was an immense favourite with all on board,
and faithfully they served him in that most perilous
hour of his life. The "reason why" of their Captain's
departure soon flew through the vessel, "and it was
wonderful to hear and see," remarked Arnold, "the
rapidity with which such comparatively untrained
gunners fired the two 12-pounders, and the clouds of
smoke they raised, which floating slowly aft to leeward,
materially lessened the chance that the look-out on
the steamer's top would observe the departure of the
boat.

11

Half an hour thus passed, the schooner's firing kept up the while with unabated spirit, when the acting-commander of the *Wave,* finding that he himself, knowing in what direction to point the glass, could only discern a speck on the waters, which might or might not be a boat, ceased firing, filled, and went off at her best speed, determining not to throw away half a chance in assuring Arnold's escape. A man must be made of sterling stuff to win the unhesitating devotion of his officers and crew in so short a space of time.

When the schooner filled, the *Georgia* was within about one mile of her. At the relative speed of the two vessels the steamer would range up abeam of her prey in about half an hour. She did so. The *Wave* hauled down the Palmetto flag in token of surrender, and was taken possession of, the lieutenant who boarded her asking James, the acting captain, if he and his fellows were all madmen broke loose from some lunatic asylum? James laughed, and said, "they liked to have some fun for their money, or money's worth," adding, that "he and the gunners, being new to the work, were not very good judges of distances!" And so the affair passed off. It was then as dark as it would be during the night; but James knew he had successfully done his duty—he is still Arnold's chief officer and trusted friend—and by no help, even of tropical stars, could the *Georgia* follow in the track of the *Wave's* boat. One of the liberated prisoners who had been taken out of Arnold's last capture, remarked that James was not the Captain Brown who commanded when he was brought on board. The man's words appearing to have no significance were unheeded. The crew of the *Wave* were made to exchange conditions with their captors, and the schooner, under charge of a lieutenant, was sent to the nearest Northern port. The reader will understand that though the crew of the *Wave* knew that Captain Brown was an officer in the Federal navy, only James knew his name, and that he kept strictly to himself.

A fortnight afterwards, Lieutenant Arnold walked into his old hotel, Washington, ascertained that his bill had been discharged by the Captain of the *Oriana*, and forthwith resumed his siege of the Navy department, not with any thought of obtaining a command, but to give him an excuse for finally retiring from the service in a huff. The opportunity was afforded, and promptly taken advantage of. " If Lieutenant Arnold would call on the morrow, the formal document necessary to prove that he was no longer an officer of the United States Navy would be handed to him." This was done, and Arnold was—not exactly "Richard" but a Cornishman again. For the naturalization humbug he didn't care one cent : he knew Great Britain has always maintained that her Majesty's born-subjects cannot, without her special permission under the Great Seal, throw off their allegiance, nor she her duty of protecting them—the relations, rights, and duties being reciprocal. True, General Jackson set that doctrine at defiance by hanging Anstruther; but that was in the disastrous dawn of the peace-at-any-price policy, especially peace that should ensure a supply of cotton, when England was the best-bullied nation in the world. But not now our Cornish countryman knew —not now. Oh, no! a thousand times—No.

Yes; but though Lieutenant Arnold had slipped his neck—not without an unpleasant sensation about that region of the human frame—out of a hempen necklace, if, indeed, he was quite sure of *that*, how about the family in Maryland, the young ravens there, and the parent-bird? Ah, well! he had found on board one of his prizes about five hundred dollars in sterling specie. He had not forgotten those dollars when ordering bread, water, spirits, compass, and sculls to be placed in the boat; the only difference was that he took them into the skiff himself. Half that sum would temporarily suffice the young ravens; and with the other half?—well, that was in the hazy future— and he himself, the chief ass and foals in the Navy department had pronounced to be an aged (meaning worn-out) man. For all that, Arnold believed he had vigour enough left to hew out for Mary, Clara, John, &c., a path to a pleasant, permanent home near that Truro of which his mother murmured in her dying dreams, and he thought he discerned the entrance to that path.

No question that he did discern it, and marched towards it with the steady tread of a man who knew that he did. That business of burning ships and cargoes at sea, though the true game of the Confederate Government, is not, as a private speculation, very profitable. The want of ports into which prizes can be taken and turned into cash—a want which, if the United States Navy be worth its salt, will be more and more severely felt—was a dreadful drawback. And shoes in Richmond were worth from four to five dollars a pair, blankets just anything you may ask; and rifles, gunpowder, cannon! I could hardly open my mouth wide enough to say what a well-appointed Armstrong field battery of 12-pounders would fetch—the genuine article, with the Government broad arrow upon it, not to be had—of course not; but the mercantile duplicate does not much differ. The margin for risk was tremendous. He should venture, if he could find, beg, or borrow the sinews of war.

It was somewhat after the foregoing fashion that Arnold argued the commercial chances of attempting to run the blockade, having always in his mind's eye the figure of old Silas Hartley, who had in the outset assisted his father in equipping and provisioning the famous *Hawk*. Hartley, though perhaps fourscore years of age, was as greedy of money as ever, and one of the old man's most favourite reminiscences was the prodigious per-centage he made upon his venture in the *Hawk*. He was enormously rich, though he lived meanly in New York. Would he advance the funds necessary to carry out the speculation? That Arnold would ascertain without delay.

Captain Arnold explained that when he said Silas Hartley lived meanly, he only meant that he did not maintain an establishment at all commensurate with his wealth; very comfortable, luxurious even, and the resort of influential personages, but which would not have been thought extravagant in a man not one-tenth part so rich as Hartley. A hard-headed man, according to Arnold, was this Hartley, not to be easily tree'd by all the bears and bulls of Wall-street and the London Stock Exchange combined. He had always manifested friendliness towards the son of his old friend the captain of the *Hawk ;* but when, under the pressure of an extreme necessity, that son ventured to ask the old hunks to loan him a thousand dollars for a few days or weeks, the request was met by a point blank refusal. "Not a cent, sir, not a cent : the thousand dollars would but go into the bottomless pit which has swallowed up all your father's earnings. No—no—not one cent—not one cent !" And it was to this man that Captain Arnold resolved to apply, and with good hope of success, for an enormous loan ; which shows that, although the lieutenant or captain was an unlucky cultivator of tobacco, he was not unskilled in moral agriculture, having once studied the peculiar attributes of the human soil which he proposed to plough, harrow, and sow.

There must have been a good deal of preliminary fencing between the needy applicant and the cautious grantor. However, when Arnold had clearly developed his scheme, to which Hartley listened with eager interest, Arnold felt almost sure that the rich man—in the hope of adding another heap of gold to the heaps which, except in the sense of *power* they afforded, were of no real value to the possessor—would enter into the scheme. He judged rightly as to the result, but not accurately as to the motives by which Hartley would be actuated in entertaining such a proposition. Greediness of gain had, no doubt, much to do with his accession to the conspiracy against the Federal Government, but there were other promptings. Silas Hartley would sleep upon the matter, though the subject was not unfamiliar to him.

Certainly not unfamiliar : that was quite plain to ex-lieutenant Arnold the next morning. After clearly satisfying himself that the son of his old successful friend had broken all bonds with the Washington Government—stood, in fact, within its danger—Silas Hartley opened his mind. He, Silas Hartley, was a Southerner to the back bone, to his finger and toe nails, not only on account of his reverence for State rights—meaning the right of each sovereign State to legislate for itself, and cast itself adrift from the loose Federal bond, whenever such sovereign State should deem it expedient to do so, but that—a minor consideration, in a moral sense, still not without its influence—he had, about twelvemonths before the outbreak, purchased a location in Georgia, on the border of the Savannah, of General Briggs. He had paid down two hundred thousand dollars for the property, the main element of which was the numerous niggers employed in its cultivation. He had placed in possession, as his *locum tenens*, his only grandson, as smart a fellow as ever lived. The property had fallen in value since that rail-splitter Abe Lincoln had come into office, at least fifty per cent. In fact, it would not realize at all, and Silas Hartley considered himself a grossly injured man. That was a dreadful business ; but he had been otherwise persecuted by the Federals. Naturally anxious to assist the Confederates in holding their own and his own,—in accordance with the Apostle's injunction, that "whoso doth not is worse than an infidel "—he, Silas Hartley, commissioned, under the rose, an agent of his at Liverpool, County of Lancashire, England, to charter a ship to convey military stores to New Orleans. The commission was duly executed, the barque *Connecticut*—a judicious name —measuring twelve hundred tons, and A 1. register, embarked a cargo, for which bills had been drawn apon him to the tune of between forty and fifty thousand dollars. Well, that patriotic enterprise (in an Independent State sense) had been frustrated ; the *Connecticut* at that moment anchored off Staten Island, had been snapped up by a Federal cruiser, brought in and of course condemned by the Prize Court. The ship and cargo had been appraised for the captors, and the grand army of the Potomac being sadly in want of the stores—the Washington Government had purchased ship and cargo. The transaction—atrocious

swindle, Silas Hartley, though usually a man of
chastened speech, called it—had only been concluded
the day before, and it had, he, Mr. Hartley, had been
that morning informed—it had been determined,
instead of breaking bulk, and sending the stores on
piecemeal to Washington, which would cause delay
and enormous expense, to send the *Connecticut* accompanied, and if necessary towed, by a steamer to the
Potomac, where she would discharge her costly cargo.
"All this" said Arnold, "was addressed to me with, if I
may so say, a savage significance, the meaning of which
I could not at the moment fathom. I could see, however, that old Silas was in deadly earnest, whatever
his meaning might be. 'The *Connecticut* sails this very
afternoon' added Hartley—'the *Connecticut* sails, I say
this very afternoon, and I lose—for I am responsible
for the ship herself under the charter-party—well nigh
on to one hundred thousand dollars, if she casts anchor
at the mouth of the Potomac, instead of before New
Orleans. The profits,' added Hartley with as much
fiery zest as if he could possibly live to enjoy the fruits
purchaseable by that profit,—' would in the latter con-
tingency be at least three hundred per cent. ! Three
hundred per cent. Lieutenant Arnold, upon fifty
thousand dollars outlay—to say nothing of the barque
—think of that—think of that, my bold sailor, you who,
going on for sixty, have not saved a cent for the winter
of your own life, or your wife's—nothing for the spring
and summer of your children, who, if they are not to

become weeds, castaways, will require so much helpful culture, protection—protection which only money gives.' " Arnold, much surprised, interested, said he felt there was a portentous meaning in the words so vividly emphasized by Mr. Hartley's burning eyes and palpitating voice, but that meaning he could not even guess at. It was a dreadful loss certainly, but after all, calculating the loss, say the total loss of the Georgia estate, Mr. Hartley would be sufficiently well off— besides ——

"Have done with that drivel," interrupted the old man, feverish, trembling with passion,—"have done with that drivel. When your name was sent into me yesterday," he went on, "I was about, knowing you to be a poor hampered devil, to bid the help order you away. Then it struck me I could make use of you, and Lieutenant Arnold was admitted."

[The reader will understand that I am paraphrasing, avoiding Americanisms, the narrative of the seaman I name Arnold, in order to bring out the facts more vividly.]

"Very plain, but not so polite," remarked Arnold.

"I hardly need say," resumed Hartley with a fire which one could hardly believe burned beneath the frosts of fourscore years—"I hardly need say that no one in New York, in America, imagines that Silas Hartley has any concern in the *Connecticut*. Well, Arnold," he added, with a burst, "I will give you the *Connecticut* and ten thousand dollars in cash, if you will take the *Connecticut* to New Orleans. Your father's son ought to be able to do that !"

More and more mystified, Arnold nevertheless protested energetically that if the *Connecticut* barque of twelve hundred tons burthen and ten thousand dollars were to be won by man—he would have a shy, though failure involved immediate kingdom come.

" I feel sure of that. Now then to business. Captain Hosken appointed to the command of the *Connecticut*, who has been staying at Astons, owes me somewhere about ten thousand dollars, for which I have long since obtained judgment. He has been arrested at my suit at an early hour this morning. No—no— not at my suit nominally, that would not do, but really so."

" Well, Mr. Hartley, and then ?"

" I have powerful influence amongst the New York agents of the naval department ; and can, I doubt not, obtain the command of the *Connecticut* for Lieutenant Arnold, ex-lieutenant if you please, but whose loyalty to the rail-splitter is not questioned. Do you see a little further now into the foggy future ?"

" I do. You wish me, having obtained command of the *Connecticut*, to take her to New Orleans. There is nothing objectionable in that. But how to accomplish it is the question. I shall be one man amongst a crew, I suppose, of fifty at least ; and a steamer—an armed steamer, no doubt—you said will escort, and, if necessary assist the *Connecticut*. Really, sir, it seems to be about the same thing as attempting to gratify the whim of a child who cries for the moon."

"You have put your finger upon the two obstacles to success—not, however, insurmountable obstacles. When I told you yesterday evening that I would sleep upon your proposal, I really meant that I would work during the hours of sleep with the means at my disposal, to make success, with your aid, possible. I believe I have succeeded. I expect every moment an official letter, appointing you to the command *pro tem.* of the *Connecticut,* and unless trusty agents have for once failed me, one half at least of the *Connecticut's* crew, on temporary leave ashore, will be in no condition to go on board when that leave expires. And then? your look asks. Why, this; the new captain—Captain Arnold—will have to engage men to supply the runagates' places. He will not have far to seek for those men. They are already selected —and are of the right sort, depend upon it—Englishmen, every man Jack. *My* countrymen are just as good, perhaps better seamen—don't sneer Mister— but they wouldn't back you up against Americans as those fellows will."

"The fog is clearing, Mr. Hartley; the *Connecticut* and the ten thousand dollars looming through, are more distinct — tangible. But how about the steamer?"

"The steamer is a screw; and if ex-lieutenant

Arnold does not know how to foul the screw of a steamer just ahead, abeam, or astern of him, he may as well go home to his mother for any use he will be to me. Besides, the *Connecticut* carries a sixty-pounder swivel gun."

"That is a stouter stay to hold by than the chance of fouling the steamer's screw ; which, however, under favourable conditions, might, of course, be accomplished."

The foregoing is, I think, a fair rendering of the conference between Silas Hartley and Captain Arnold, as given by the latter. It was interrupted by the arrival of an official messenger, informing him that Lieutenant Arnold had, through his recommendation, been appointed to the command *pro tem.* of the *Connecticut ;* and that it was necessary that officer should, without delay, present himself at the office (I myself know nothing of New York, and what office Arnold meant I did not inquire—I suppose a local Admiralty office), should without delay present himself at the office to receive full verbal, as well as written instructions. I remember Arnold remarking that that which surprised him most was the virile passion for gain, for money, —the rage at the losses he had met with manifested by a man fourscore years of age, for whom the world, with all its wealth, vanities, and ambitions, would so soon be shut out by the darkness of the grave. He had to learn that the palsied palm of age closes upon gold with a far more clutching tenacity than does the liberal hand of careless youth.   But Silas Hartley was inspired, in part at least, by higher motives.

The well-spun reel ran smoothly out.   The sailors engaged to fill the places of the hocussed men on leave were first-rate fellows, who appeared to comprehend, without certainly having been told so in words, that they would be expected to take part in a serious, out-and-out rumpus — a great attraction that to your true old salt, your genuine English sea-dog.

To Captain Arnold's great surprise—it will be well now to drop the "Lieutenant"—to Captain Arnold's great surprise, Mr. Silas Hartley came on board a few minutes only before the anchor was brought home. He was pale, excited, breathed heavily, but merely said—"I shall find a comfortable berth, no doubt.   I have business at Washington, and the doctors recommend a sea trip."   With that he hurried below, and the large quantity of luggage he had brought was hoisted upon deck.   Not very many minutes afterwards the *Connecticut*, towed by the *Monteray*, Captain Pons, was on her way through the Narrows to the Potomac or the Mississippi, as fate might determine.

Arnold was in a difficult position.   Mons distrusted him—was possessed of a vague feeling that something was wrong somewhere.   I had better, perhaps, allow Captain Arnold to tell this part of the story in the first person, and, as nearly as I can recollect in his own words :—

"I don't know exactly how to account for it, but

Mons and I had not exchanged a hundred words before
each felt that he was in the presence of a resolved, un-
scrupulous enemy. That was my feeling, at any rate.
Mons was a stout, square-built fellow, with iron jaws
which snapped together when he was in a rage, like an
iron rat-trap. That, however, was only animal energy.
I knew my man. Before we lifted anchor, I noticed
him, shortly before Hartley came on board, confabulating
in under tones with three or four of the old crew. I
soon made up my mind how to deal with such a
bounceable fellow as Amos Mons, if ever he came
across my hawse. Off Sandy Hook, he signalled me
to lie to. I did so, and he came on board, black as
thunder and as noisy. 'Lieutenant Arnold,' he began,
without a civil word of introduction,—'Lieutenant
Arnold, I can tell you plainly, I have my doubts
about you.' 'Have you,' said I, 'then that's more
than I can say, for I have no doubt whatever
about *you*. I can reckon up M. O. N. S. quite correctly, without the help of a ciphering-book.' 'You
are impertinent, sir.' 'Same to you and all your
family,' said I. 'You are a Britisher born, I am told.'—
'Whoever told you that, Captain Mons, is a gentleman
and a friend of mine.' 'But you have been naturalized a citizen of the Great Republic for now going
on forty years.' 'I don't see why, my noble Captain
Mons, you should without any provocation fling that
in my teeth. I have never, I believe, insulted you,
and a man's misfortunes, undeserved misfortunes,

should ——.' 'I am not here to bandy insults with a rascally traitor, as I believe ——.' 'Most noble Captain,' said I, rising (we were seated opposite each other at the state cabin table), 'most noble Captain, I had a difficulty once with a gentleman at an hotel in Washington, which you may have heard of. Ah! I see you have ; the lily displacing the rose on that handsome phiz of yours is sufficient proof. That we will call Difficulty No. 1 ; now, are you disposed to solve Difficulty No. 2 after the same fashion?' 'You shall not fasten a personal quarrel upon me, Mr. Arnold ; but remember, I shall have an eye upon you for the future.' 'I have *two* upon you, Mister Mons, at this moment ; but as I live and breathe they have once or twice in my lifetime rested upon more attractive objects. Fact, I assure you, though you may not believe it.' I think I had the best of the chaff, but I well knew all the while that though it would have been utter folly to have humbled to the squinting bully ; we were at his mercy, the *Monteray* mounting six Dahlgrens, while the *Connecticut's* 60-pounder swivel-gun was of no more use to us than a child's popgun. The bore of the gun was eight inches in diameter, and the balls on board were *ten* inches in diameter. That was a sweet mistake. However, Mons did not know that— yet I am not sure—very possibly he did. He had gone on deck, but presently returned accompanied by a lieutenant of marines. 'I have requested,' said he, 'this gentleman to witness that I now formally warn you, that if the *Connecticut* is not sailed and steered as I from time to time shall direct, I will sink her.' 'Think twice before you do that,' said I, 'most valorous Captain; or the Grand Army of the Potomac will be dreadfully inconvenienced. There are many thousands of pairs of shoes on board, and they say that in the rapid running at Bull Run, the soles of the Grand Army's shoes, from the tremendous friction, caught fire and ——' Mons and the Lieutenant stayed to hear no more. I confess to you, Mr. Warneford, that the banter I indulged in was not in very good taste, but you would excuse it if you knew what a pretentious pump and Hail Columbia humbug Mons was and is. I had a long and anxious conference with Hartley afterwards; when he confessed to me that all he had in the world was embarked in the *Connecticut*, with of course the exception of what the estate in Georgia might be worth. He had sold off all his scrip, stock in New York, and if we foundered in our enterprise he and his, myself also, would be in the deep bosom of the ocean buried. The position was not a pleasant one—decidedly not; especially when an order came from Captain Mons directing me to hoist a red light at the fore as soon as it fell dark. Furthermore, the steamer would, every night when it was possible to do so, take the *Connecticut* in tow by a chain cable. 'It's all over,' groaned poor Hartley, when I showed him the order. 'Poor Rebecca, Child of Calamity— Child of Calamity! Your grandfather is a broken

12

reed in whom you have vainly trusted.' I had never, Mr. Warneford, heard of Rebecca, Child of Calamity, before, but I saw by the tears which ran down the old man's withered cheeks, that his grief was genuine, and so, as my motto is Never say die, I said it was rubbish about its being all over with us. We were not to be picked up in that sort of way, and should see—what we should see. You know, Mr. Warneford, the trick I played Mons?"

"I saw a somewhat confused account of it in a Liverpool newspaper."

"Well, this was it. The *Monteray*, the weather being exasperatingly calm, took us in tow every evening, casting us off at dawn. The nights were dark as only nights in those latitudes are when they are dark. That was my basis of confidence, only it behoved us to be very quick. The *Connecticut's* crew I had divided into two watches—one composed of the old lot, the other of *my* men, as I called them ; and upon whom I knew thorough dependence could be placed. Well, we were in tow of the *Monteray ;* the night, early night, dark as the inside of a tar-barrel—darker, blacker. It was my fellows' watch ; the others had turned in, but did not turn out again in a hurry. They were all quietly secured ; no noise, no botheration ; that was the first move. Poor Hartley ! I pitied him. I had told him that on that night I meant to win the horse or lose the saddle ; and there the poor old man lay in his berth—he who was so fierce and valiant of tongue, perspiring with fear ; and yet I have seen that same man, in defence of one of his great grandchildren, confront a grizzly bear. To be sure, he would have been, as the Yankees say, chawed up in no time, had not more effective aid been at hand. But he placed himself, not being compelled to do so, betwixt the child and the brute—a great, brave act, I say ; and yet that man was being almost distilled to jelly in his berth, when his fine sense of hearing—he was wonderfully acute in that way—apprised him that the hour of fate, of death or life, of happiness or misery, had struck. I have no respect, neither have you, Mr. Warneford, for those lingering, hesitating, indecisive men !

" We had plenty of spare spars, and in about a couple of hours a raft was constructed, and an upright pole raised thereon. Our light was doused, but at the same moment the red light at the top of the pole gleamed forth, also the bight of the chain cable was transferred and secured to the raft. On went the steamer ; on went the raft, the strain upon the chain-cable being I suppose rather more than if the *Monteray* was towing the *Connecticut*, and our glorious barque was loosed. Hartley had crawled, stumbled up the companion stairs, and seeing the success that had hitherto attended what I had done, immediately rose into the seventh heaven of assured triumph. We should be at New Orleans in just no time ; he with his Rebecca, no longer a child of calamity (it is thus that the facile impulses of feeble natures run the gamut from despair to delight), but a thousand times over rewarding with her dear caresses, the careful love of her doting grandfather. Pleasant, but wrong. God bless you, my dear Mr. Hartley, I am not going, said I, to New Orleans just yet. I should be very sorry. That ass, Mons, as soon as he finds by day-dawn to-morrow what he has got tied to his tail, will look for us in that direction. Not likely to find us thereaway ; eh, Mr. Warneford ?"

" Not unless you were as great an ass as you make him out to be ; you sailed south-east of course. But allow me to interrupt your narrative for a moment, by this remark. You appear to have a contemptuous opinion of American sea officers which facts do not justify. I have made the acquaintance of a considerable number of those gentlemen, and they really appeared to be a fair average of the class to which, in the family of maritime nations, they belong. Your Cornwall birth and mother's whisperings have given in this respect a twist to your judgment."

" I don't think so. That the bouncing and bullying of the Americans about their 'Decaturs' and the rest have, though I am a naturalized son of America, often got my dander up, is true. But what in essential respects is maritime America to maritime England ? Scarcely upon a par with France—but for the British seamen in its service, far below France. If that be not so, how is it that the Cunard has destroyed the

Collins line of packets, that all the great sea highways are practically monopolized by England? Rule, Britannia, depend upon it, is but the hyperbolic expression of a plain, prosaic truth. Still, you are quite right. Yankee bunkum and braggadocio should rather amuse than anger us. But where was I with the story?"

"Where the *Monteray* was steaming ahead in triumph with the raft, upright pole, and red lantern."

"True. Well, there was a ruffling breeze blowing, and as soon as it was prudent to do so—for the sheen of white canvas gleams in the darkest night a long distance off—I made sail for the African coast. Having thus destroyed all trail, as it were, of our track, the *Connecticut's* bows again looked westward, and after some nine or ten days' pleasant sailing we sighted the deeply-indented coast of Louisiana. Soon sighted much less agreeable objects. Off the mouths of the Mississippi, but considerably asunder, were two Federal cruisers, both, fortunately, sailing vessels. The *Connecticut* carried the British flag; but as a ship can hoist any kind of bunting she pleases, that did not avail to ward off suspicion for an instant. Both cruisers made sail immediately we were seen, to interpose between the *Connecticut* and the mouths of the Mississippi. The wind during the previous half hour had increased to half a gale, and blew dead from the eastward. It was quite useless to hesitate, and running up the Palmetto flag at the fore, we, with studding-sails outspread, spite of the risk, for it was neck or nothing, ran boldly on. If no spar gave way, the chances were in our favour. No spar did give way; nor did the cannon-shot of the cruisers, when they found us slipping through their fingers, damage us. We ran the gauntlet bravely, and I had the honour of landing at New Orleans the most extensive cargo of military stores that has, I believe, arrived at any Southern port during the war.

"Silas Hartley was generously grateful. He not only made over to me the *Connecticut*, and stumped up the ten thousand dollars, but threw in a handsome bonus over. 'Rebecca,' I found, was a dearly-loved grand-daughter, whose facile-tempered husband had in some way ruined himself and family, and would have been sold out but for grandpapa's arrival with no end of rhino, causing that child of calamity to dry her tears, and look so bright and smiling, like flowers kissed by the sun after an April scud, that had neither of us been married, I had not been hard on for sixty, and she considerably less than half that, I really think that she, being so grateful——but that's neither here nor there. I sold the *Connecticut* at a fair price, feeling convinced that only steamers, and fast ones, have a fair chance of successfully running the blockade. You know I have tested the truth of that. The *Palmetto*—checky, eh?—built here, my present craft, has done the trick once, cleverly, and two or three days hence we start for a second shy, and Master Jonathan will need get up early, and then he'll be too soon to put salt on her tail, depend upon it."

"You are a lucky man, Captain Arnold. Mrs. Arnold and family have safely arrived, I was told yesterday."

"Oh, yes, a month agone, and are safely housed near Truro. Only this one last trip accomplished, and I settle down with them for the scant remnant of my days."

JOHN SHIPLEY, OF NORTH SHIELDS.

THE Shipleys, humble, honest folk, had dwelt in North Shields, from, practically, immemorial time; the men and lads were seafarers, the women and lasses industrious housewives and notable girls, who all married seamen when they did marry. A Shipley was Anson's favourite coxswain, and sailed with that admiral round the world. In 1840, the long sea-line of the Shipleys was suddenly broken to the great disgust and mortification of the family. Margaret Shipley married a cotton-spinner, or weaver, in a small way of business at Preston, where she had gone on a visit to distant relatives. The husband's name was Orfey, and he appears to have been a decent man in his general relations, and a kind husband and father. One reason for the young woman taking for better for worse a spinner instead of seaman, was that her father, whose housekeeper she had been, married a second time, and with a woman of such a fiery temperament as soon to render the house too hot to hold stepmother and step-daughter. Margaret, however, stood it as long as she

could, chiefly for the sake of a man-child (in the complete sense of the phrase), an only issue of her father's
second marriage, as she herself was of the first.
John Shipley was nine years of age when Margaret
married, and parting with him was the sorest trial she
had to encounter in leaving, as she knew for ever, the
old house at home. The father, Robert Shipley, a
fierce, determined man, never forgave his daughter for
casting off the maritime line of the Shipleys, never
after the marriage mentioned her name, and sternly
forbade his wife and son to do so, either in or out of his
hearing. John Shipley, nevertheless, retained and
cherished a tender remembrance of his sister, visited
her by stealth as soon as he was sufficiently his own
master to command sufficient leisure and funds, and
became much attached to his nephews and nieces, of
which there sprung up a goodly crop. Margaret's
marriage was an unfortunate one, in a money sense.
Orfey, never more than one of the pettiest of the
cotton-spinning hierarchy, was by a succession of rapid
falls reduced to the lowest ranks, and he, his wife, his
children, as soon as they reached the legal age, toiled
to sustain hard life in a mill. In 1857 Orfey died.
John Shipley, then in his twenty-seventh year, and
first-mate of the *Hyacinth*, a Liverpool ship, generally
chartered for the United States, after vainly endeavouring to awaken compassion in the father's heart
for his sore-struggling daughter, at once set aside half
his earnings for the support of Margaret and her

children. This he could not do in a direct way through the owners of the *Hyacinth*, his father, who had scraped together a goodly amount of gear, having an eighth share in that ship. The transaction would consequently have become known to the inexorable old man, and John Shipley, as regarded his father, have been himself a castaway. He could, therefore, only transmit the moiety of his wages to Margaret when he himself was in England and received the money. I need not say that such a man had often aided his sister before her husband's death, not perhaps at any very great inconvenience to himself, he being a young single man, of very temperate habits, and in constant employment. It was very different now. John Shipley had been courting for some time a North Shields lass—a cousin, and a Shipley—to whom, when he returned from his next voyage, he was to have been married. Now, as he could not keep a wife and family upon a mate's half wage, his union with Jane Shipley must be indefinitely deferred. The necessity of this was recognised, and bravely acquiesced in by the young woman herself, who faithfully kept John Shipley's secret. A girl that, worthy of John Shipley. All these particulars, and many more, I have heard from Margaret Orfey's own lips.

An unforeseen difficulty arose when the *Hyacinth* next returned with a cargo of cotton from New Orleans. Robert Shipley, who generally sailed the ship himself, had been laid up with the lumbago when the ship left Liverpool, and the command, with consent of all the owners, had been entrusted to the first mate, his son. Now what the stubborn old seaman could not comprehend was why John's marriage with a cousin, a Shipley, and a North Shields lass—a match after his own heart—should not come off at the time agreed upon ; and hearing there was a hitch somehow or somewhere in the business, he sternly demanded of his son *why* he was not going to be spliced to Jane Shipley, according to articles agreed upon. John Shipley, who had anticipated such a query, replied that he could not afford to marry for a long time to come. He had lost a good deal by the several ventures he had made on his own account (this was a fib ; he had neither won nor lost), and had not ten pounds in the world. After long deliberation, for Robert Shipley held his hard-won gear with a tenacious grip, the veteran decided that want of needful cash should not postpone a wedding upon which he had set his heart ; so he announced that he should furnish a place for the young couple, and make them a present of fifty pounds to start with. It was impossible to make further objection, had John Shipley wished to do so. The marriage took place ; and by the time the American war broke out John Shipley had given hostages to fortune in a wife and three children of his own, besides a sister with her family of seven whose support in a great degree depended upon his earnings. Had that not been the case, I doubt that John Shipley, who had always been a sincere foe to negro slavery, and believed, though a really fairly educated young man, "Uncle Tom's Cabin" to be the next best book after the Bible, would have suffered himself to be persuaded into attempting to break the American blockade. The ties of blood and kindred hold firmly under a strain that would break asunder the strongest bonds of speculative philanthropy. This is the explanation of my motive for prefacing the narrative proper of John Shipley's exploits in running the blockade, by an account of his previous domestic history.

The blockade of the Southern ports had been proclaimed by the Federal Government, the *Hyacinth* had brought to Liverpool her last cargo of cotton,—agents of the Confederate States were already busy in chartering ships for furnishing the Southern armies with the indispensable supplies of which they stood in such grievous need. Amongst others, the owners of the *Hyacinth*, a stout roomy barque, though by no means a fast ship, were applied to. A profitable bargain was immediately struck, one of the most ready to conclude it being Robert Shipley, who did not in the least participate his son's negro-sympathies. The cargo was to consist chiefly of shoes, blankets, cloth, and such like stores. The shipment of these commenced forthwith under the active superintendence of Captain Shipley, who, quite free from lumbago, determined to take the command on the first voyage himself — the nominal command, strictly speaking.

His son would be the real skipper.   The Shields-sea-
man fire still glowed hotly in the old man's bosom,
fanned to fiercer flame by the danger of the enterprise.
He had besides, a particular crow to pluck with the
Yankees.   Fifty years before (1812), he then a mere
lad, whilst serving in a fruit and wine vessel from
Malaga to London, had fallen into the clutches of an
American privateer, and been kept prisoner till the
peace.   I don't suppose he made any very searching
inquiry as to whether the privateer hailed from a
southern or northern port.   He knew she sailed under
the stars and stripes, whilst the *Hyacinth* was chartered
by a Government whose flag was the Palmetto flag.
That was quite sufficient for Robert Shipley.   Of
course the *Hyacinth* cleared for a British port, Halifax; and though everybody knew her real destination, there was not the shadow of a pretence for
detaining her.   Shoes, blankets, &c., are not contraband of war, though without them winter-battles
could hardly be fought with success by the bravest
soldiers.

John Shipley was all this time at North Shields
with his wife and family, having the while visited his
sister at Preston.   The *Hyacinth* being just ready for
sea, Robert Shipley took rail for his native town, to
bid the auld wife farewell, and return with his son
John was of course informed of the true intent of
the charter-party entered into by the owners of the
Hyacinth; upon which he at once blurted out an

indignant refusal to iu any way assist slave-owners in perpetuating slavery.   The irascible old man, who in his secret soul believed a negro to be only a slightly superior chimpanzee, was savagely angry, hot words ensued, and finally Shipley senior left the house with a grim intimation that if John, persisting in his nigger-nonsense, refused to help his father in running the blockade with the *Hyacinth*, he would no longer be that father's son.

Here was a charming fix for that son. Old Shipley had been fairly generous since his marriage, but his expenses were onerous at that nick of time. His sister Margaret, considerably in debt and with two children down in typhus fever, expected a promised remittance of twenty pounds; there had been long-continued sickness in his own family; his wife was still ailing; required the best medical attendance, and the most nutritive diet, wines, &c., that money would purchase; and his purse was almost void. Of course there could be but one termination to the conjugal debate which ensued immediately upon the old seaman's departure. What on earth to John Shipley were a parcel of black fellows whom he had never seen, in comparison with his own wife and children, of his sister and *her* children? The wife could no more understand that sort of stuff than the father did, who had promised to let her husband have, unknown to the old woman, another fifty pounds.   Well, John Shipley put on his hat, sought his father, declared his willingness to sail in the

Hyacinth, and do his best in running the blockade, concluding with a hint, that the wife was in some need of those fifty sovereigns. The postscript, as it were, to his son's else gratifying announcement, caused the old seaman to wince considerably : he grumbled out something about Jane Shipley, having *for* a Shipley, turned out not the genuine thing, the domestic expenses, allowing for doctor's stuff and all that, being frightful to think of. However, she must have the fifty pounds, if less would not do. These words were told slowly, reluctantly out, Shipley senior taking occasion to inform his son that he had given instructions to a lawyer in Liverpool to make his will, which he should execute before embarking upon a trip from which he might never return. By that instrument his eighth share in the *Hyacinth*, and his unquestioned right, transmittable to his son, to the skippership—was worth between two and three thousand pounds, would be bequeathed to him, John Shipley ; and all other property the testator was possessed of to the old woman. 'Now you understand,' added Shipley senior, 'that you have a serious risk in this go-in against the Yankees, which warms the cockles of my heart but to think of. D—— them, don't I remember their iron handcuffs—their swamp prison ? I think I do. The *Hyacinth* being cleared for Halifax, cannot of course be insured for her real destination, you understand, John. She *must* run the blockade, and you are the lad to do that if any one can : I will say that of you. The risk is tremendous—

to be sure it is; the profit also. I shall be able to lay
up comfortably with the old woman here, and you can
have my share in the *Hyacinth* at once, whilst I live.'
I left my brave, honest, prejudiced father," said John
Shipley in relating the story to me—" I left my brave
honest, prejudiced father with a heavy foreboding
heart, scarcely lightened by the chinking gold in my
pocket. I saw that he had incurred a most serious,
unwise risk;—but I also knew you might as well say
to the waves, 'Be still,' as endeavour to turn Robert
Shipley from any enterprise upon which his mind was
set. Clearly, it was my imperative duty to land, if
possible, that cargo of shoes, stockings, and blankets at
Charleston; for after all, had not the Southerners as
much right to govern themselves as the thirteen States
had which threw off their allegiance to England? Pro-
found, philanthropic reasoners were Clarkson, Wilber-
force, Brougham. I was familiar with their writings,
—agreed in theory with all that was printed in those
weighty volumes; but placed in the scale against my
wife and children, Margaret and her children, those
volumes were not a feather in countervailing force.
Selfish, I dare say, but it is written that 'whoso pro-
videth not for his own is worse than an infidel!'
Yes, and I had long secretly participated the smothered,
contemptuous rage excited throughout the sea-service,
military and mercantile, by the eternal Yankee boast-
ings of their *fudge* naval triumphs in 1812–13. Certainly I should do my best to successfully run the

blockade, Jane,' said I to my wife, as I threw the fifty sovereigns into her lap. ' My conscience is at rest.' ' Of course it is,' said she, 'and I'll send the bank-order to Margaret by this night's post. Rot the nasty niggers, what are they to us, I wonder ! Children of Cain every one of them.' "My wife," added John Shipley with a smile, " sat under a clergyman who had peculiar negro-notions in an ethnological Moses-sense. I have never interfered with her religious crotchets, believing, as I do, that sort of thing will only be valued according to pure purposes at the final reckoning.

" We made fair weather of it for some fourteen days," continued John Shipley ;—" but the *Hyacinth*, as I mentioned before, was by no means a fast craft. One grave omission had been made in the equipment of the ship for her voyage. In the owner's anxiety to avoid an excuse for the barque's detention, at the instance of the American Consular representatives, by the British Government, it had been determined not to ship a swivel-gun, though one of large calibre had been ordered and paid for. Every ship has an undoubted right to carry a reasonable defensive armament ; and the *Hyacinth* was absolutely defenceless. We had half a dozen flint muskets on board, and a few charges of powder and ball—nothing more. This was a fatal error, but for which the voyage would, I have little doubt, have had a different termination. The course agreed upon by John Shipley was the frequent one of hugging closely as safety permitted the African coast, and when

sufficiently south bear up westward, and reach Charleston, a hoped-for port, by help of the Gulf Stream.
This at the commencement of attempts to run the
blockade was often successful.   The Americans, who
are far from being the 'cute critters' they have bounced
so many thousand of people into believing them to be,
seldom suspected a ship sailing north, and had passed
the Gulf, of any intention to run the blockade.   That,
however, is not the ease now, and has not been for a
long time.   The *Hyacinth* had passed the Florida
peninsula, and, helped by a stiff southerly breeze as
well as the force of the stream, was nearing the
entrance of the river, not then partially blocked by
the sinking of the stone ships, and in twenty-four
hours at furthest, if no mishap occurred, the *Hyacinth*
would safely bring up in Charleston harbour.

"Not half that number of hours was vouchsafed to
us.   The United States' steamer *Flambeau* sighted,
suspected us, and immediately gave chase.   My father
being in nominal command, I went below to consult
him as to what should be done.   The veteran had
been sadly down upon his luck during the entire
voyage.   His old boisterous cheer of mind had left him,
and, to quote his own often-muttered expression, he
had a presentiment that he should not leave his bones
where he found them.   He came on deck at my request,
took the glass, pointed it at the steamer, but the sinking of the vital flame, as I concluded, having dimmed
his eyes, he did not recognise the flag carried by the

Yankee cruiser : the star-spangled banner he took to be Saint George's ensign.   I felt it was useless to any longer consult him as to the command of the ship, though I of course forbore to say so.   There could be so little doubt that the stranger was a Federal cruiser, that I had already changed the course of the *Hyacinth*, and was stretching away with all our wings spread towards the Bahamas, under a stiff breeze abeam—the *Hyacinth's* best point of sailing, a rare thing for a square-rigged vessel, even a barque, whose mizen-sails of course help greatly in such a case.   We were getting about five knots out of the strong, stout tortoise, and if, as the lady says in the play, some opportune Phaeton would have whipped the chariot of the sun to the west and brought in cloudy night some two hours before, by the world's clock, it should sink beneath the horizon, the *Hyacinth* might have a chance of giving her pursuer the go-by.   That not being so, capture was certain.   My father himself admitted it after a while, and proposed that ourselves and the crew should take to the boats, having first fired or scuttled the barque.   I was anxiously pondering that proposition when I perceived that the speed of the *Flambeau* (of course I did not then know the steamer's name)— that the speed of the *Flambeau* had much abated.   We much more than held our own with her, and hope of escape brightened in our brains.   I afterwards read in the American newspapers, that some part of the steamer's machinery had broken down : one account said she fouled her screw, but that could hardly have been the case, which it took an hour to repair—a precious hour to us, but not enough for salvation. On again came the steamer, though not quite at her old pace, and as night was fast coming on, commenced firing with her heavy bow-gun shotted, upon finding we paid no attention to her blank gun, directly she was within range. Now, if we had shipped the swivel-gun purchased in Liverpool, it is plain that the *Hya-cinth* would have had as good a chance of crippling the *Flambeau* as the *Flambeau* had of capturing or sinking the *Hyacinth;* but we had not that chance; and all we could do was to stagger on unresistingly under every stitch of canvas we could set. Twice during the next half hour we were hulled, not dangerously; ten minutes or so afterwards a shot struck us below the water-line, causing a frightful leak, and it was neces-sary to at once rig the pumps. The sun was, however, near his set, and you know how suddenly night falls in these latitudes. There would be no moon, no stars—for a few hours at least, thick darkness—darkness that might be felt. The firing continued without more hurtful effect than now and then hulling us, and snapping a few ropes. The *Flambeau*, though she gained upon us, was manifestly much crippled in speed; she was becoming dim in the distance, when an unlucky shot struck and splintered the main-top gallant yard. One of the falling fragments struck my father on the head. He fell, mortally stricken, on the deck. His

presentiment was realized, and by the very last shot
fired by the infernal Yankee. He had been, taken
altogether, a good generous father to me, and at the
sight of his white hairs, his withered face streaming
with blood, a devouring rage took possession of me
which will never be slaked. I carried him below.
Precisely how long he survived, I could not say.
His last words I well remember: 'Take care of
Margaret, John; poor Margaret! I have been a
hard father to her. The Lord forgive me!' Then
after a long pause, incoherently, but in substance he
murmured—'This ship's gone — all's gone, John!
But you are young and bold. Trust in God. Better
if your father had done so more than he has. Tak
to the boats, John. Sink or burn the ship; never le
the Yankees have her.' After that, though his lips
moved, I could not distinctly catch what he said,
except the sacred names of Lord—Christ—over and
over again repeated. My poor father was praying.
He died praying, not again recognising his son.

"I rushed on deck with a hell of fury seething at
my heart. What I purposed to do could not have
been known to myself, except that the accursed Yankee
should not have the ship, if it should be my own, th
crew's sepulchre, as well as my father's. The night
was dark as the inside of a tar-barrel. The barque
had been hove-to by the second mate, he having mistaken something I said, when about to carry my father
below, for an order to that effect. It was the best

thing that could be done. The *Flambeau* had already
passed us ; her light was seen at half a league distance
floating like a star through the night. Thoughts of
home, of wife, sister, children, came thronging back
upon me. I had much to live for, in addition to the
duty of avenging the white-haired old man stiffening
in death below. An unchristian sentiment, say you ?
The Federal captain had only done his duty ! True,
that is how calm men reason ; not as, when boiling
over with grief and rage, they feel !

"The greatest danger now was the leak ; one of the
pumps had become choked ; the other was utterly in-
sufficient to sensibly affect the deluge of water pouring
into the doomed ship. I was fully alive to the exigency,
and immediately ordered the boats to be lowered, and
furnished with every necessary in the way of provisions, water, spirits, compass, glasses, that could be
required. There would be plenty of time to do all
that leisurely, carefully ; time also for another solemn
ceremony—the committal to the deep of the brave old
veteran killed by the Americans. That was reverently
done.

"The boats, amply provided, cast off from the sinking ship ; soon enough, but not too soon. At the distance of four or five hundred yards we could not see
her, so black was the night ; but we could hear in the
deep silence, as we lay upon our oars, anxious to witness by ear, if not sight, the end of the stout ship, the
rushing gurgle of the waters eager to engulf their

prey, and the plunging, heeling, righting of the struggling ship, till in despair of avoiding she accepted her
destiny, and went down into the depths, whether bow
or stern foremost, we could not say ; but that she had
gone down was unmistakably proved, not only by the
mighty sob—sough, if you like it better—with which
the *Hyacinth* took the final plunge, but the down-
draught, which it required, distant as we were, smart
pulling to avoid being drawn into.

" A dismal night, but not of long duration. Morn
rose in beauty—the lustrous beauty of a tropical
clime—and calm, blue, as a Mediterranean summer
sea. At noon we ascertained that we were distant
about ninety miles only from Nassau. This was
nothing in such weather, and two days and nights'
alternate and combined sailing and pulling took us to
that hospitable port—all well."

All well! except that John Shipley, whose modest
narrative but incidentally reveals the sterling heroism
of his character, had lost all of worldly goods that he
possessed *in posse* or *esse*. Not one farthing would be
recoverable from underwriters for the loss of the
Hyacinth, and he had to begin the world anew, trudge
forth again on the world's thorny, stony path, with
two women and ten children buckled to his back!
Well, we must set a stout heart to a stiff brae, and
John Shipley's was unquestionably a stout heart. The
frame, however, sometimes fails the spirit, and John
Shipley was seized with fever a few days after landing

in Nassau, from which his recovery was slow and tedious.

He did recover; and, about seven months after he sailed from Liverpool in the *Hyacinth*, landed at that port from one of the Cunard steamers. He found his domestic affairs in a terribly embarrassed state. Mrs. John Shipley and children, but for credit readily accorded, must have starved or gone to the Union, that harridan Mrs. Shipley senior having denied all assistance. This was so keenly resented by John Shipley that, though his own mother, he would never see her afterwards. Truly, he inherited from his father a full share of the old Adam. Matters at home put a little straight, John Shipley, with but a scant purse, proceeded to Preston. His sister—his ever-beloved sister Margaret —and her children, one of whom had just died, were paupers—literally paupers, subsisting upon parish relief. The mill at which they worked had been one of the first that stopped, and they were perishing of the cotton famine. "The remorseless Northerners!" screamed in spirit, John Shipley. "Ah! if England will not interfere to arrest this desolation, or punish the desolators, individual Englishmen will—John Shipley for one." He has fulfilled that wordless vow, is still, as I write these lines, fulfilling it. Does the Government of England imagine that our seamen, who know the remedy for the dreadful distress in the North, and by whom the order to open the Southern ports would be hailed with yet wilder enthusiasm than Nelson's Trafalgar signal, are stocks and stones?

John Shipley—need I repeat that this is not the real name of the daring blockade-breaker?—John Shipley, during convalescence in Nassau, and during his voyage home, had steadfastly meditated the problem of supplying stores to the Southerners at the least risk and greatest profit to himself and owners. His African sympathies — never, I suspect, having very deep root in Caucasian soil — had completely vanished. His father's death had thoroughly cleansed his bosom of that sham sentiment stuff; and he had to recoup himself for the loss of his eighth share in the *Hyacinth* destroyed by the Yankee cannon balls; to re-illume the darkened homestead in North Shields, and provide means of healthy livelihood for his sister and her children. John Shipley nothing doubted that he could do so; though his whole stock-in-trade—his capital, as one may say—was his reputation as an honest man, and a bold, skilful, intelligent seaman,— a large capital in maritime England—he knew that.

John Shipley first waited upon the joint-owners with his father, of the *Hyacinth;* asked them to charter a vessel of about the same tonnage as the unfortunate barque, for the express purpose of running the blockade. Burnt children dread fire, and those gentlemen, though hesitatingly, declined the venture. Shipley next applied to the chief agent of the Confederates in Liverpool. A true man himself, that gentleman readily recognised a true man. An understanding was soon come to; a commission in the Confederate naval service, signed by the President

the seceded States, was filled up with the name of
John Shipley, and in a very few days the *Arabia*
schooner, a wall-sided, cranky, slight thing, not over
a hundred and fifty tons, dropped down the Mersey.
There was no gun on board. That purchased for the
Hyacinth was offered by the owners of the barque
to John Shipley, and would have been shipped, but
it transpired that if that were done, the Customs
would refuse the *Arabia* a clearance—that the schooner
would not, in fact, be permitted to leave the Liverpool
docks. Necessity has no law, and the *Arabia* left without the gun—an unarmed vessel, technically speaking.
But she carried John Shipley, himself worth many
guns, and a crew of seventy men, fellows who could
face the flash, roar, and shot of a frigate's battery
without winking ; pistols and tomahawks sufficient
to arm every man were concealed on board, and
there was sufficient powder for John Shipley's probable
needs. Only about half the crew were on board when
the *Arabia*—which by the bye had been purchased for
a mere song, being quite unseaworthy—left the dock ;
the other half were waiting at the Mersey's mouth
in two first-rate new boats ; one of which boats, strange
to say, happened to contain the identical swivel-gun
which it had been found inconvenient to put on board
the *Arabia*. A timid mariner, John Shipley ! He
feared, and with reason, to cross the wild Atlantic in
such a wretched craft as the *Arabia ;* a vessel so
crank that, if struck by the slightest squall, she

would be pretty sure to turn turtle. Still John Shipley might surely make up his mind to go or not to go; either to venture across the herring-pond or return to Liverpool. He did neither, kept standing off and on, at never more than ten or a dozen miles distance from the estuary of the Mersey, and often within half that distance. A peaceful-looking vessel. The swivel gun had been mounted, but keenest eyes through Dollond's best glass could not have discovered it through the heap of canvas, turpaulin, cordage, flung in careless confusion thereupon. And never more than half-a-dozen men were to be seen at once upon the deck of the *Arabia*. One of those men was constantly sweeping the mouth of the *Mersey* with a day and night glass. When he took absolutely essential rest, that duty was discharged by his first officer, Jeddes Brown. This lasted over eight days and nights. The crew did not quite understand it, but an old salt on board, a North Shields man, who knew the Shipleys, after making the oracular remark that there were wheels within wheels, said the main thing to attend to was keeping their pistols clean, their tomahawks sharp, and ready at hand; that done, they would be ready to do their duty in the station to which it might please John Shipley to call them—which was all they need trouble themselves about.

The facts, well known to hundreds of persons in Liverpool, were these. A splendid steamer, built at Boston—the *Sagamore*, we will say, and measuring over eight hundred tons—was taking in a cargo of war-stores for the Federal Government, at the time John Shipley had his interview with the principal Confederate agent in Liverpool. The *Sagamore* was a fine specimen of American naval architecture, and, though Yankee shipbuilders are scarcely a patch upon those of the Thames or the Clyde, was a very tempting prize, apart from her cargo, to such a man as John Shipley, with John Shipley's purposes. She was very stoutly built; her scantling was that, or nearly so, of a corvette, and she carried, one aft, one forward, two swivel one hundred-pounder guns. Her crew numbered fifty odd men, but of these twenty were Mexicans; many of the others were steamboat American *river*-sailors; not more consequently than about twenty genuine sea-dogs. Her commander—we shall call him Captain Rouse—was a gallant, courteous gentleman, with whom I have passed many pleasant hours, and hope to pass many more. This was the ship which John Shipley was waiting for with such eager impatience, in that crank, crazy schooner, the *Arabia*. Were it the morning of his marriage, he could not have been more impatient to embrace his bride than to closely hug the *Sagamore*.

"Here she comes at last," exclaimed John Shipley, closing his glass with a snap, at about 2 bells p.m., on the ninth day after the *Arabia's* departure from Liverpool,—"here she comes at last, and the wind

favourable as if we had bespoke it. All right.
Jeddes Brown, fill and make all sail the crank old tub
will bear. I shall go talk with our fellows below."

The *Arabia* slipped through the water away from,
but in the track which the *Sagamore* would certainly
take, at a fairish rate. It would be five or six hours
and dark, before the vessels could possibly close with
each other. Shipley's scheme was so to steer that the
schooner would apparently be in danger of being run
down by the *Sagamore*. How easily that could be
managed under favourable circumstances, the *Arabia*
being well to windward, a seaman will easily understand.

It was pitch dark, the *Sagamore* not more than a
quarter of a mile astern and to leeward, when the
Arabia hove to and began firing minute-guns in token
of distress ; at the same time jets, spirts of flame, shot
up from the schooner's hold. There could be little
fear that so good and brave a man as the American
captain would pass a ship apparently on fire without
an effort to save the crew. That was a safe calculation ; but should it fail, the heavy swivel-gun, pointed
by a practised gunner, would in all likelihood so
damage the *Sagamore's* machinery as to enable the
schooner to close with and board her. Sails were
also in readiness to be flung overboard, which, drawn
in by the suction of the *Sagamore's* screw, would foul it.
This, all practical men know, is the great danger to screw-
propelled vessels, and no certainly effective preventive

has yet been devised. John Shipley had thus more than one string to his bow. For all that, I should, as I have told him, have bet, knowing all the conditions, five to one that he would fail.

The screw of the *Sagamore* ceased to work as that splendid ship ranged up abeam of the schooner, and not more than two hundred yards off. "What ship is that?" demanded Captain Rouse through a trumpet: "and what's the matter?" "Her Britannic Majesty's Revenue schooner *Zephyr*. We are on fire." "Have you boats enough?" "Yes." "Send the crew then on board this ship." "As fast as possible—many thanks."

Everything being ready to the minutest detail, the four capacious boats of the *Arabia* were quickly filled. Each man had in his right trowsers' pocket a loaded six-shooter, and concealed under his jacket a sharp short-handled tomahawk. Two boats pulled direct away for the *Sagamore*, ostentatiously as one may say:—the other two worked round, concealed by the thick night, and propelled with muffled oars. Not a soul was left on board the schooner, the wheel of which was so secured as to render the rudder of no effect.

The crews of the two leading boats were soon upon the deck of the *Sagamore*;—a peculiar "call" assured John Shipley that the others were immediately at hand, and scarcely interupting Captain Rouse's somewhat anxious questioning, he, at the same time waving his hand to the armed seamen, in-

formed the commander of the United States Ship
Sagamore that that vessel was a prize to the Confederate schooner *Arabia.*

The surprise was complete. Captain Rouse was no
doubt as brave a man as ever lived ; but what chance
would such a crew as his have with the forty grim devils
already on deck, and pretty nearly the same number who,
as Shipley spoke, came clambering up the *Sagamore's*
side? None whatever — not the slightest. Captain
Rouse recognised and at once accepted that fact. "I
surrender the ship," he said, "under protest; as I
believe all these fellows to be Englishmen. I know
you, Mr. Shipley,—and of course the schooner, instead
of being Her Britannic Majesty's *Zephyr*, is the piratical
schooner "*Arabia,*" which left the Mersey seven or
eight days ago, and I supposed was in the latitude of
Newfoundland or thereabout, by this time. However,
there is no help for it. Of course, the schooner is not
on fire ?"

"No, Captain Rouse : a rather clever make-believe
that—pyrotechnics—fireworks, you know. A dodge
not to be sneezed at, permit me to say. The *Arabia*
is all right; plenty of stores on board ;—but you may
take out of the ship any quantity you please in addition, for your own and crew's personal needs."

"We are then to go on board the *Arabia* ?"

"Just that, Captain Rouse. An exchange of ships,
nothing more. Only your people must bear a hand."

Thus was achieved a daring exploit, which, like

almost all other humiliations sustained by the Federal
Government, has been carefully ignored; and I need
hardly say that John Shipley, having clearly brought
himself within the meshes of the Foreign Enlistment
Act, was not anxious to proclaim his liability to
ruinous penalties. He is a certificated captain, and an
enrolled member of the Naval Reserve. The Federal
Navy he was quite willing to defy, but there were
nests at home to be lined with down, not strewed with
thorns.

A valuable prize was the *Sagamore*. In addition to
her more especially war-stores, John Shipley read in
the ship's manifest that she was carrying out a large
quantity of quinine—a specific for ague and fever of
which the Southerners were in pressing need. Twice in
the latitude of the Bay of Fundy was the *Sagamore*
challenged by American cruisers. The correct number was of course displayed, and on went the gallant
ship without further molestation, the usurped stars and
stripes floating out grandly from her main. She ran
the blockade successfully to Mobile, but had a terribly
narrow escape. Captain Rouse reached Liverpool with
his crew in the *Arabia* only about an hour before the
Persia, the fastest ocean steamer yet launched, left
Liverpool. That vessel consequently took out intelligence of the delightful trick that had been played
him, from Captain Rouse. The *Persia* touches at Halifax, and thence electric messages reach the Washington
Government in a few hours. The result was, that three

war-steamers, one from New York, two from Boston, were immediately dispatched to recapture the *Sagamore*.   They failed to do so : had they succeeded, we should have heard enough and to spare about the *Sagamore* and her captor's capture, in the columns of the New York press.

The *Sagamore's* cargo was purchased by the Confederate Government at a figure which, after repaying their agent at Liverpool for the advance he had made in furnishing funds for the purchase of the *Arabia*, paying the crew the high wage which in such a service seamen command, and all incidental expenses, left John Shipley a great profit, exclusive of the *Sagamore* herself, which he might or might not get clear away with.   One thousand pounds he placed, humanly speaking, beyond the reach of fate, by transmitting it through well-known channels to England, *viâ* Boston and Halifax, insuring the safe delivery thereof at a heavy premium.   One-half went to the wife at North Shields, the other half to sister Margaret Preston.   Two dear English homes would be made bright and cheerful, whatever became of himself and the *Sagamore*,—which, by-the-bye, he renamed *Mary Jane*, the names of his two girls and wife.

John Shipley proposed to purchase a heavy cargo of tobacco, contrary to the advice of his Confederate friends, and especially of Jeddes Brown.   The shrewd seaman argued that if the *Sagamore*, or rather the

14

Mary Jane, in ballast, were captured in the endeavour
to run the blockade outward—and it was known a
sharp look-out was kept for her—John Shipley would
only lose the ship. But a cargo of tobacco—good
Lord! In addition to his own all invested therein,
there would be a loss of thousands to friends who,
at enormous prices, had agreed to fill up the ship
with the, in a money sense, precious material. John
Shipley could not be dissuaded; he could rely upon
his crew. Two had fallen ill, and must be left in
Mobile; but the rest were stanch and true. He
knew sailors. By loading with tobacco, he would be
able to offer them splendid *prize-money,* should the
Mary Jane, a peaceful British trader, of course, get
safely anchored in the King's Road, Bristol. They
would fight all creation with that reward in view;
and as to getting away without fighting, such a notion
was nonsense!

John Shipley was not more daring and positive
than he was shrewd—practical. Much meditating
the venture, and not unforgetful of Jeddes Brown's
warning words, he concluded to purchase, on credit,
nine-tenths of the tobacco cargo. The price would, of
course, be a speculative one, so to speak; there were
plenty of men in Mobile anxious to run the risk. It
was a toss-up, no doubt; but if he so acted, it would
really be "heads," I win; "tails," I don't lose—much!
This was prudent conduct, and was so gradually improved upon, that when the *Mary Jane* brought her

anchor home, and, amidst the thundering cheers of thousands of spectators, steamed away from Mobile, all, except the steamer, which John Shipley possessed, consisted of gold coin and unexceptionable bills upon London, carefully locked up in his private cabin. A prudent, practical man, no question, is my friend John Shipley—knows how many beans make five as well as any man in existence. Nevertheless, he will fight to the death for that tobacco, though it does not belong to himself.

There was no chance of eluding the blockading ships; this was soon evident. It was just possible the *Mary Jane* might fight her way out—barely possible. The *Albany* gun boat was her first assailant; she came on in the assurance of easy victory, and was only undeceived when the two 100-pounders plumped their tremendous shot into her almost simultaneously. So much for the *Albany*. It would take her many hours to repair damages, and the *Mary Jane* sped unmolested on, her small band striking up derisively the tune of " Yankee-Doodle."

" Yankee-Doodle" was an ugly customer after all, to be got rid of. By no means by two lucky shots, even from 100-pounders. A heavy and fast steam-frigate, the *Rappanhook,* according to Captain Shipley, but a mistake in name, I think, gave chase, and spite of every exertion to shake her off, she, after a long run, gradually closed with the *Mary Jane.* It was far into the night, when it became obvious that there was no

14—2

escaping the Yankee frigate, and fighting her was equally out of the question. Shipley called his crew together, and spoke frankly to them : he had lost his ship, the merchants who freighted her their tobacco; but they themselves had nothing to apprehend beyond a temporary detention, and the loss of the moneys they would have been entitled to had they succeeded in reaching Bristol. Against even that loss he would personally guarantee every mother's son of them who, as soon as possible, within a month it must be, joined him at the Havannah, Cuba, from which they were then distant about eighty miles. He himself, and a few men whom he had spoken with, were about to embark in the ship's yawl. Jeddes Brown would remain in command, and as soon as the Yankee frigate came within cannon-range would haul down the Palmetto flag, and give up the ship. There must be no fighting ; it would be folly. But he promised plenty of that sort of fun to those who joined him in Cuba— plenty of prize-money too. It is nothing like dark enough to give us a chance of losing the infernal frigate ; but a boat getting away will not be observed. He then asked if they were agreed ? An assentive shout was the reply ; and after advising them to stick by Jeddes Brown, and shaking each individually by the hand, John Shipley, and eight chosen men, went over the side into the amply-furnished yawl—the bills on London, and gold, had not, you may be sure, been forgotten—and lay still upon the water, the *Mary Jane* passing on, with fullest head of steam.

The *Mary Jane* was overtaken and captured soon after dawn on the following day, sent to Key West, and of course pronounced a lawful prize. It was deeply regretted John Shipley had in some unaccountable way escaped.

The yawl arrived at the Havannah, all well. The fascinations of the Cuban capital appear to have for a time taken John Shipley off his feet; and I suspect that when talking over his adventures with Mrs. John Shipley, he draws particularly mild—in very faint water-colour, if not omitting altogether—his experiences in the Havannah during his first three or four weeks' sojourn there. The arrival of his crew restored him to healthful life. By connivance, as I believe, with the Captain-General of Cuba, John Shipley purchased a powerful gun-boat—*El Reyna*, renamed by him the *Mary Jane*. This vessel—she was a steamboat and very swift—mounted one gun only, a rifled forty-pounder. At the Havannah, several Yankee vessels were taking in cargoes chiefly of cigars, tobacco, &c., for the Northern States and Europe. Shipley fixed his mind upon the *Delaware*, a brig of large tonnage, bound for London with a valuable cargo. Well, the *Delaware* was captured by the Confederate gunboat *Mary Jane*, when going through the Bahama Channel; sent on with a choice crew of discreet men under the command of Jeddes Brown, and satisfactorily disposed of, ship and cargo, at the Havre-de-Grâce, at which port she had been compelled by stress of weather to put in.   Several other valuable prizes have been seized by the *Mary Jane*, alias *El Reyna*, two of which, laden with stores useful to the Southerners, have successfully run the blockade ; one is under the personal command of John Shipley ; the other in attempting to run the blockade was captured.   John Shipley himself— who has indulged in a trip to the old country, just to see his wife, sister, bairns, nieces, and nephews, has gone back to Cuba, and the *Mary Jane* is, I doubt not, again in full and formidable play.   Had John Shipley anything approaching to an equality of force, I should greatly rejoice to hear of his encounter with Commodore Wilkes.   I should have a painting of that battle, by the best artist I could afford to engage, handsomely framed, hung up in my parlour by the side of an engraving of Turner's matchless War-Ship going to be broken up.

EX-LIEUTENANT MAITLAND.

I RELATE the following story upon the authority of Colonel Zauas, by whom it was told to my good friend Captain Weekes, a first-rate officer in the service of the Oriental Steam Navigation Company.

We all remember the filibustering raid upon Cuba by Colonel Lopez and his associate ruffians a few years ago, its ignominious failure, and the reckless execution of the captured pirate invaders. It is right to say, that those ruffians were, with scarcely an exception, Southerners. The Southern States of America, improving upon the Monroe doctrine, that no European Power should be permitted to extend its *de facto* dominions on the American continent, favoured the expedition to Cuba, being resolved that the Queen of the Antilles should not be "Africanized"—that is to say, Cuba, made a State in the Union, should be compelled to rescind her comparatively mild laws affecting the coloured race, and become, in the Southern meaning of the phrase, a Slave State. This is an unquestionable fact; and although, as previous papers abundantly prove, my sympathies are with the South in their present struggle, the truth is the truth, and should be told.

One of the filibusters was a young man, a mariner, whose father was a native of Saint Jago de Cuba. Whether he was connected, as supposed, by ties of natural affinity with General Lopez is a matter of doubt, and is of no importance. José or Jeseph Lopez fell in the first encounter of the filibusters with the Spanish troops. He was shot though the lungs, through the right lung, and was left for dead upon the scene of the encounter.

Not far from the scene of that encounter resided Señor Velaseo, a wealthy planter : he, a benevolent gentleman, intently perused' the field of death with several negroes after the conquerors and conquered had departed. Coming to the apparent corpse of José Lopez, who lay upon his back, his striking features illumined by a full Cuban moon, he fancied he saw a resemblance in those features to an old friend of his whose son had some five or six years before run off to sea. This, though a mistake, quickened his compassion, so to speak, for the seemingly slain young man : he felt for the pulse, at the wrist, over the region of the heart, believed he detected the throbbing, the faint throbbing of yet undefeated life ; called his negroes, who made a litter upon which José Lopez was gently, tenderly borne to Velasco's residence. The wounded sailor ultimately recovered, thanks to skilful medical treatment and assiduous nursing. Velasco was an influential personage, and no inquiries were made by the authorities respecting the young American. He turned out villanously. There was a Doña Inez Velasco, sole daughter of the house and hearts of her parent—an amiable maiden, but very susceptible. Climate has much to do with that. Inez was not more than sixteen, but that is ripe womanhood in the tropics. It became necessary that young Lopez should marry Dona Inez; the ceremony took place, and three or four months afterwards the wife was a mother. The union was not a happy one. The discordance in religious faith was one element of unhappiness. The Velascos were rigid Catholics, the young Lopez a free-thinker, as bigots of unbelief are usually called. Señor and Señora Velasco did not live long after the birth of the grandson, and within a few weeks of each other. The estate and personals were devised to Madame Lopez, which was the same thing as bequeathing the property to her husband, so entirely was she under his influence, his control. Joseph Lopez, after the death of his wife's parents, gave loose rein to his evil propensities. He drank, gamed to excess, frequented the haunts of loose women, became, in short, a reckless, shameless scamp. His unfamiliarity with the Spanish tongue and his professional proclivities caused him to affect the society of American and English seamen, who abound in the Cuban capital. Amongst these was a young officer of the name of Maitland, who, once third lieutenant in the *Nimrod* British sloop of war, one of the African slave squadron, had been dismissed the service for unofficerlike and ungentlemanlike conduct—drunkenness, namely, and abusive language, when in that state, addressed to a superior officer. Charles Maitland's vices were, however, upon the surface : he was a true man at heart, and despised himself for those vices more than it was possible for any other person to despise him ; vowed amendment a thousand times, and as often broke his vow. He became extremely intimate with Lopez, who found in him, as he believed, a reprobate after his own heart. Maitland was introduced to Madame Lopez, who from the first moment interested him greatly. Her moonlight comeliness, the patient sorrow which vibrated in every tone of her soft low voice, touched him profoundly. He heard that Lopez had dissipated all the property, or nearly so she had inherited ; that in a few months she, her husband, their son, would become outcasts, beggars. Reckless Ruffian as Lopez might be, he was not quite impervious to the fiery arrows of remorse, and in a paroxysm of self-accusing rage, he told Maitland all ; confessed that his ruin was complete, and asked counsel of his friend. Maitland, who must have had an undefined inchoate idea floating in the mists of his mind for some time said he would take a few hours to consider ; but first, how much ready money could Lopez raise immediately if there was a fair chance it could be so employed as to retrieve his position. As the shameless waste and extravagance he had indulged in was not matter of general notoriety, except amongst the swindlers who profited thereby, and very few knew that Madame Lopez had been mad enough to guarantee his chief liabilities, Lopez said his wife could, upon her bond, obtain a very large sum. But being a scrupulous, religious person, had only a day or two previously refused to do so, forasmuch as she felt convinced that if everything she possessed was sold there would be scarcely enough to satisfy their creditors. For the first time the wife had firmly refused her husband's request, passively defied his imperious command. But she would waive her scruples if by a bold venture there was a reasonable chance of repairing the ruin which gaming and other pleasant pastimes had wrought. Lopez had no doubt that she would, and Maitland promised to see her in presence of Lopez in four hours from that time.

This was in 1861. Charles Maitland's first care was to obtain a commission in the Confederate naval service : there was no difficulty about that ; his next to ascertain if one Señor Martinez would take Madame Lopez's bond in payment of sufficient goods—cigars, sugar, oil, &c.—to freight a ship of from six to seven hundred tons. Señor Martinez would willingly do so. That important point settled, Master Maitland proceeded to the firm of Serrano and Company, shipping agents, ascertained that the fine American ship *Powhattan*, at the Havannah, was waiting for a freight, and that her captain would be glad of conveying such a cargo as Maitland named to Halifax, British North America.

There was not likelihood of much profit accruing from such a venture;—much more probably a loss would be incurred. The shipment of a costly cargo to Halifax, and its sale there, was, however, but the prologue to the pleasant project contemplated by the ex-lieutenant of the British navy. That project fully explained to Madame Lopez obtained her approval; the bond was given, charter-party signed, and the good ship *Powhattan*, Captain Deedes, cleared and sailed for Halifax, having on board as joint supercargoes Joseph Lopez and Charles Maitland.

There was a loss, not a very large one, upon the cargo sold at Halifax, and Maitland prospered, with the reluctant assent, pretendedly so of course, to clear for Bermuda, and purchase a cargo there of such army requirements as might meet with profitable sale at New York, Boston, or other Northern port that might be finally determined upon. Captain Deedes, an enthusiastic Unionist, cordially agreed, remarking at the same time that a large portion of the goods required might be profitably purchased in Halifax. His counsel was deferred to; about a thousand pounds' worth of the required articles were bought and shipped; the *Powhattan* sailed for Bermuda, could not there make up more than half a cargo, and, after much grave consultation, it was decided to run as far south as the Bahamas, where at Nassau military stores might be had in abundance by any one who could pay for them. I cannot doubt that they might have been obtained in any quantity at Bermuda, but that would not so well have answered Maitland's purpose; and poor Captain Deedes, whose reliance upon that sprightly gentleman's sympathies with the Northern people, and inherent detestation of slavery and slaveholders, was not tinged by a shade of doubt, appears to have been hoodwinked and bamboozled throughout—as easily led by the nose as asses are.

A Federal cruiser off Nassau brought to and boarded the *Powhattan*, but her papers and purpose being quite satisfactory and patriotic, Captain Deedes himself well known by reputation, if not personally, to the Federal commander, she was not unnecessarily detained a moment. Commander Featherstone wished his compatriot Deedes success, and advised that when the stores were shipped, the *Powhattan* should sail direct for Boston.

There was no difficulty in obtaining and shipping stores at Nassau, and the next move upon the board had to be played. The British authorities would not have permitted Captain Deedes and his crew to be dispossessed of his vessel by force; and how to manage the business, when the time for action arrived, did not appear so easy of accomplishment as when looked at from a distance.

Maitland was advised to ask the counsel and help of squinting Joe Masters, a fellow half crimp, half contrabandist, whole rogue, who Maitland, when serving in the slave squadron, had in some way become acquainted with. Squinting Joe Masters was a local celebrity who had a numerous following amongst the raffish, loafing foreign sailors who hang about Nassau ; a bold fellow, of resource too, and not particular to many shades if a job could be made worth his while. He was said to be a native of, or, at all events, had been many years a sojourner in, the Southern States, which he had quitted precipitately. Lopez would not hear of seeking assistance of Joe Masters ; would not, he said, call in the help of, or be seen in the same street with, such a discreditable scamp. This surprised Maitland, he having chanced not many hours before to see Lopez entering a drinking place with Masters. He, however, made no allusion to that, but determined to see Masters himself, and engage him on his own hook. He did so ; found his man quite willing to undertake the duty required of him, and fertile in suggestions for its accomplishment. Maitland having given him earnest-money, Masters laughingly remarked that that was the second retainer he had received for agreeing to perform the same service. "I shall stand word with both you and Lopez," said he, "and I shall hold both to your bargains."

"Lopez has engaged you ?' exclaimed Maitland.

"Just that, Lieutenant Maitland; and mind you are on board an hour at least before the time he will tell you is agreed upon. That devil's chick has no notion of going shares with you in a venture which he says will have been carried through with his own money."

"His own money be ——!" retorted Maitland; "his robbed, swindled wife's money, or, more accurately, the money of his wife's creditors."

"As to that, my noble lieutenant, you must excuse me," said Masters. "I know his wife well, a flaunty jad at Saint Louis, who keeps a grocery store, and has a sore struggle to make both ends meet. She believes her husband was rubbed out with General Lopez and the other filibusters. Why, how skeared you look, lieutenant! I'm only telling you a plain fact. Lopez, when this little business is finished, means to rejoin his wife and young uns: he has two or three alive; and he is a precious sight older than he looks, I can tell you, in more ways than one. Sell the grocery store, the *Powhattan*, buy niggers, and set up as planter."

"You have almost rubbed me out," said Maitland, greatly agitated. "Lopez has a wife and son in Cuba, a charming woman whose property he has squandered."

Squinting Joe Masters gave a prolonged whistle, curiously eyeing Maitland as he did so.

"The sly varmint!" said he presently. "That's a smart dodge, that; and if I were Lieutenant Maitland,

I'd get what I could out of the critter at once, and not trust my life at sea with Lopez when he's in command of the ship."

"Lopez will *not* have the command of the ship, Mr. Masters. *I* am a commissioned officer of the Confederate Government — *not* he. You carry out our plan, procure reliable fellows, and I'll take care of myself and Lopez too, never fear. What you have told me respecting his having a wife at Saint Louis but hardens my determination neither to lose sight of him or the *Powhattan*."

Maitland added, in his anxiety to win over Masters to his side, that if he himself would sail with them, he should have one-fourth of the sum which the ship fetched if the blockade was successfully run, and he would sign a bond to that effect. Masters caught eagerly at the offer; the mode of action was anxiously discussed, and at the close of the conference little doubt of the perfect success was felt by either.

Captain Deedes and his first and second officers received an invitation to dine with the Lieutenant-governor, whose house was about five miles distant from the town. It is deemed a duty to accept such invitations, and the *Powhattan* being quite ready for sea, and awaiting only the formal clearance for the Customs, which could be obtained on demand, the three American officers set off for the Lieutenant-governor's residence at about three o'clock in the afternoon, intending to return about ten. The third mate, who had been gained over by Masters, was instructed to obtain the clearance papers, and, should the wind continue favourable, Captain Deedes intended to sail at early dawn the following day. Masters was baffled upon one (to him) important point; he was anxious to leave Lopez behind as well as Captain Deedes and his officers, and tried one or two ingenious dodges to effect that object, but Lopez was not to be had. Whether suspecting treachery, or determined to run no possible risk, Lopez turned in to his sleeping-berth under a pretence of feeling unwell, and did not leave it till the *Powhattan* was at sea.

Meanwhile the third mate, having cleared the Customs, sent two-thirds of the crew on shore, in gangs of five and six, to bring off stores of different kinds to be fetched from considerable distances from the harbour. The *Powhattan* then cast off from the pier, the boats in which the sailors went on shore had been pulled to the upper inner harbour, followed after, filled with the men engaged by Masters and that worthy individual himself. No one noticed that the sailors were not those which had shortly before left the ship; the nine or ten men of the American crew who remained in the *Powhattan* were sternly overawed, the sails were let fall, and before Captain Deedes and his officers could have reached the Lieutenant-governor's residence, the *Powhattan* was clear of the harbour, and standing to the north-west under a spanking breeze. She carried the stars and stripes at

15

the main, was recognised by the Yankee cruiser by whom she had been overhauled when going into Nassau and allowed to proceed unchallenged.

It was Maitland's intention to run the blockade by the Savannah, distance being a weighty consideration ; but the appearance of the Federal gunboats near the entrance to that river compelled him to hold on north-ward and well away from the coast line. The weather was thick, squally, and on the second day after leaving Nassau it blew a gale of wind. The *Powhattan* was a fine sea-boat, and made fair enough weather of it, careering through the water at a high rate of speed ; and as the gale, after some chopping, finally blew steadily from the south-south-east, there was every chance of making the James River successfully. That hope was rudely shaken. A powerful war-steamer loomed through the cold grey dawn whilst the *Powhattan* was still considerably distant from the James or any other river-refuge, and immediately gave chase, but finding she did not gain so fast on the *Powhattan* as was desirable, ran up the Palmetto flag, and commenced cannonading the fleeing ship. Maitland, all aboard in fact, believed the Palmetto flag to be a ruse to induce the *Powhattan* to heave to and speak a friend, her stars and stripes not deceiving her. At all events, the steamer was determined to ascertain if the *Powhattan* had a right to fly the Federal bunting ; and the fire of her bow-gun was sustained, much too close and accu-rate to be agreeable to the captain and crew of that ship. Still a stern case is a long chace, even by a fast steamer pursuing a sailing ship when the sailing ship happens to be a clipper, and she is running before a gale of wind. The fear was that some important spar would be shot away. That misfortune had not, however, occurred, when the look-out at the masthead hailed the deck to announce another large steamer right ahead, and making direct for the *Powhattan*. She appeared to be about the same force as the pursuer, and carried the Federal flag. Escape appeared hopeless, when, to the surprise of Maitland and his mates, the first-seen steamer luffed, and stood away to the south-east. The fast approaching frigate almost at the same moment altered course to follow directly in the other's wake. It seemed evident, therefore, that the Palmetto flag was rightfully carried by the steamer which had done its best to cripple and capture the *Powhattan*.

"What ship is that?" shouted the captain of the United States frigate, as she passed within speaking distance.

"The *Powhattan*, Captain Deedes," was the prompt response, "from Cuba to Boston."

On swept the war-steamer in eager chase of the Confederate ship. In a short time both were lost to view, and before sundown the *Powhattan* had gained the James River. The blockade by a lucky accident had been successfully run; Maitland had made a great hit, fully compensating, in a pecuniary point of view, his dismissal from her Majesty's service.

15—2

The stores realized extravagant prices at Charleston; the *Powhattan* was also disposed of at a heavy figure. Then thunder fell upon Joseph Lopez. The reader is aware the *Powhattan* was freighted by Madame Lopez, as she believed herself to be. Lopez did not suspect, it seems, that his old acquaintance Masters, to whom he had promised a large reward, had betrayed the awkward fact that he had a wife and children living at Saint Louis, and he was just becoming angrily impatient for a settlement upon the terms agreed upon at the Havannah between herself and Maitland, who had dexterously managed—helped by Masters, who, it would appear, had some bitter grudge against his quondam acquaintance—to get the entire proceeds of the sale both of cargo and ship into his own hands.

The discovery that the fatal secret had been disclosed, and that Maitland had thoroughly made up his mind not to hand him over one cent of the money, rightfully belonging to the lady he had so foully wronged, first stunned and then nearly drove him mad with rage. He flew like a tiger at squinting Joe Masters, who retaliated his blows by a few inches of bowie-knife. He did not die of the wound, and as soon as he was able to travel absquatulated from Charleston.

Charles Maitland got back to the Havannah, honourably accounted with Signor Velasco's daughter, to whom he was shortly afterwards married. They removed to Georgia; and Maitland now holds the rank of Commander in the Confederate service. Before, however, he led Donna Inez to the bridal altar, he had a difficulty with Captain Deedes. That gentleman, furious at having been so outrageously swindled, as he considered it, out of his ship, proceeded to the Havannah for the purpose of instituting legal proceedings against Maitland for the recovery of the vessel's value. As, however, the charter-party was entered into by him with Joseph Lopez only, and Maitland, when he obtained possession of the *Powhattan*, held a commission authorizing him to sink, burn, capture, destroy, Federal ships, legal redress was out of the question. He sought such satisfaction as a duel might afford him, and got nothing by that except a slight flesh-wound by his adversary's pistol-bullet. I think, however, that Mr. Maitland was amenable to the Spanish and British Governments for having violated the neutrality of the harbours of the Havannah and Nassau.

WILLIAM STUBBS, OF FALMOUTH.

In jotting down these " Blockade" narratives, one disadvantage, always present to my mind, clogs my pen:
that being shut out from the exhaustless field of fiction,
and confined to one topic, the stories must necessarily
resemble each other.   To be thus cabined, cribbed, confined, through 320 pages is very unpleasant to a writer,
and the inevitable sameness, in however carefully varied
colours the sketches may be painted, will possibly prevent this little volume from catching the breeze of
popularity which has now for some years kept in floating motion the trifles which I have ventured to launch
upon the dangerous ocean of modern fugitive literature.
It is, however, idle to complain of the necessary conditions of a task voluntarily undertaken, and I am
glad to believe that the incidents which make up the
following story, save it, at all events, from the almost
inevitable sameness I speak of.

It will be remembered, that Captain Tobias Crosbie,
who is substantially the narrator of the *Cassius Marcellus Clay* story, initiated, in fact, in a loose way con-

cluded, an arrangement with Ezra Sidebotham with respect to a certain 'Bermudan' scheme for running the blockade, the shamefully victimized deacon consenting, as Esther was favourably inclined, and the "gals" had to be provided for, to take a twentieth share in the contemplated venture. Before Crosbie left Portland, Ezra had advanced his bid, first to a tenth, and lastly to a fifth share therein, always with the indispensable proviso that he should only have to do with honest God-fearing folk. The meditated project did not, however, come off, for various reasons. Crosbie sailed for England, visited his native place, Falmouth, where he remained several weeks,—before taking command of the *Robert Peel* and sailing for New Zealand.

Falmouth was the birth, and would in all probability, be the burial-place of William Stubbs, master mariner, —*Bill* Stubbs of late years in the vernacular Cinque-Port Vulgate. There is quite a stone fleet of Stubbses, rated from one to one hundred years, in Falmouth churchyard.   William Stubbs, born Anno Domini 1800, deceased 18——, the two last figures not ascertainable he hoped for a very long time to come, would, in the natural course of things add another unit to the Stubbses awaiting in consecrated-ground a glorious resurrection, it being a remarkable fact, that the Stubbses had been mariners for three or four centuries, and (in this resembling the Shields Shipley family)—not one had been drowned. They had in sooth, Crosbie told me, an antipathy, a lodged hate for water taken internally, and it seemed that water reciprocated the dislike. But for the confidence generated by so long a course of seemingly miraculous impunity, I should not have to record William Stubbs's exploits in his attempt to run the blockade. He might be hanged, that was within the range of possibilities, but a Stubbs could never be drowned. Crosbie seriously assured me that this was a superstition not confined to the Stubbs' family, but acquiesced in generally by the Falmouth sea-folk.

William Stubbs at all events illustrated his faith in the non-drowning destiny of his family by practice. He had been a fairly fortunate master-mariner up to the year 1859. Then a series of calamities, which we all know come, when they do come, in battalions, befel him. His only son died of typhus fever; his uninsured homesteading and all which it contained was consumed by fire ; and, to crown all, his brig, the *Sailor Boy*, employed in the coasting-trade, and sailed by himself for a quarter of a century, was wrecked in sight of port—the port of Falmouth. He himself and the crew, five men and two boys, escaped with life in a boat, but the crazy old craft was driven on shore, and when Crosbie arrived at Falmouth previous to embarking for New Zealand, was lying a painted simulation of a sea-going ship upon the Falmouth sand-beach.

Poor Stubbs had refused to accept the annihilation

of the ancient *Sailor Boy* as an accomplished fact—had, with such help as his wasted purse permitted, furbished up the crazy old craft by a lavish expenditure in putty and paint, so that to an unskilled eye the *Sailor Boy* looked, if anything, younger than she first sprang from the stocks to embrace the fond wave.   The man really believed, Crosbie said, she was ' all his fancy painted her,' and seriously contemplated recommencing the coasting-trade, with his rejuvenated brig.   The design was baulked by a seemingly insurmountable obstacle. Shippers, as a rule, will not consign cargoes which they cannot insure, and Lloyd's agent resolutely declining to have anything to do with the *Sailor Boy* at any premium, William Stubbs was becoming desperate. Lloyd's agents have a pestilent habit of using augers against which paint, if laid on with a trowel, is powerless ; the rottenness within is inexorably brought to light, and insurance is impossible.   I need hardly say, that if the ship itself cannot be insured, no cargo shipped in the condemned craft could be insured. This was a poser. It was quite in vain that Skipper Stubbs argued, he should sail the *Sailor Boy* himself, and the notion that a Stubbs could be drowned was absurd, as all Falmouth knew.   It would not do. Reversing the recent saying imputed to Pius IX., that though the Lark of St. Peter was guaranteed against wreck, her crew was not, shippers protested, that though Stubbses were not susceptible of drowning, the *Sailor Boy* might founder, and kindly, but firmly, declined to freight the very good-looking deceptive brig. William Stubbs was in despair. He even in his extremity tried to sell the *Sailor Boy* by auction, but the highest bid amounting only to her value in firewood, no sale was effected.

Such was the state of affairs when Crosbie shook hands with his old friend, William Stubbs, on the Falmouth Sands, after having parted with him something like nine years previously. Crosbie had been in some way, I don't know in what way, effectively helped once upon a time by William Stubbs, and Crosbie's nature is grateful and generous. He and Stubbs were consequently often together, and divers plans were canvassed, by which it might be hoped the still hale old seaman's position in life might be bettered. In the course of those conversations, Ezra Sidebotham's blockade-breaking venture was related; that the swindled Deacon, moreover, would not be averse to have another go-in, provided that his associates were God-fearing people. The moral, so to speak, of those debatings, urged by Captain Crosbie, was that William Stubbs should emigrate to America with as much cash as he could command,—the *Sailor Boy*, even at the price of firewood and old marine-stores, would fetch something,—he, Captain Crosbie, would give him a letter of introduction to Ezra Sidebotham,—he would get ample credit at Portland, and might there, untainted by commercial failure, obtain a good coasting connexion. Captain Crosbie did not confine his good offices to mere advice. William Stubbs was much respected in Falmouth, and Crosbie heading the list with his own fifty, raised, by zealous exertion, between two and three hundred pounds, which he had the pleasure of placing in the hands of his early friend, together with a letter to Ezra Sidebotham, to whom he had also written by post. The next day Captain Crosbie left Falmouth, and will probably first hear the sequel initiated by his active efforts on behalf of William Stubbs, in these pages.

William Stubbs, though he lost his son, had his son's wife and an infant child to support. He was greatly attached to the young woman, in some degree perhaps a reflected love,—and he doted upon the child as only grandfathers and grandmothers do. The daughter-in-law had a brother, a lawyer's clerk, and a chap who had all his buttons on. After Crosbie's departure from Falmouth, Stubbs and Bob Richards had frequent conferences, the subject-matter being the contemplated emigration, the disposal of the *Sailor Boy*, and other cognate matters. Of course, Ezra Sidebotham's misadventure was often talked and laughed over.

Now Bob Richards was unusually well posted-up in international maritime law : it was a pet topic of his, upon which, *à propos* of the *Trent* business, he had given a lecture at the Falmouth Mechanics' Institute. Much reflecting upon the position and prospects of his sister's father-in-law, and the possibility of himself crossing the Atlantic to the great betterment of his own prospects, he mentally drew up a case, which he submitted *in extenso* to William Stubbs.   The kernel of the nut which he counselled the dubious mariner to crack was this :   That a Stubbs not being, or not fancying himself to be, in danger of drowning, would not hesitate to cross the Atlantic in the *Sailor Boy;* and there would be little difficulty in finding a sufficient number of hands to navigate her,—by taking the vessel round to Plymouth or some nearer port where her exact condition would not be known or curiously inquired into.   Now, a certain factor in Birmingham well known to his governor, and to whom an introduction could be given, had always large quantities of military implements on hand, such as rifled muskets, pistols, &c., which not being up to the Regulation mark,—defective weapons,—not perhaps so murderous as might be wished,—but not dangerous to use; could be had at a very low price.   This germ, as it were, of Richard's idea was, he admitted, suggested by Seth Jones's dodge, but the main feature of the proposition was emphatically his own. Mr. Chuck, the factor he was speaking of, was a *bond fide* exporter of arms to South America. For the three or four hundred pounds William Stubbs had on hand, paid down, and a lien on the bill of lading, Chuck would unquestionably furnish a full cargo for the *Sailor Boy,* of which ship it was presumable he had never heard.   If he had, Bob Richards was sure he would run the risk.   Well—and this was the *gist* of the scheme,—the said cargo must be a genuine consignment to some well-known merchant, say at Rio Janeiro; and proof that it was a genuine consignment to that place must be ready to be produced when it was expedient to do so. Good. But before sailing, the Yankee spies at Plymouth, if it was determined to sail from that port,—or Yankee spies at any other port,—must be made to believe, by means of anonymous letters through the post, that the *Sailor Boy*, Captain Stubbs, meant to run the blockade. Thus, Captain Stubbs taking no particular care to avoid such a misfortune would ensure the *Sailor Boy's* capture; the brig would be carried to Key West or other Federal port, and proceedings would be instituted before the Prize Court of such place, to get her condemned as lawful prize. Good again. Now the Yankee's Government being desirous, for a time at least, not to quarrel with Great Britain, would never condemn a vessel which it could be proved clear as day was *bonâ fide* bound to Rio Janeiro. When the vessel was seized, Captain Stubbs, confined to his berth by a dreadful complication of maladies—gout, gravel, and what not—was incapable of giving that perfect information, and producing documents which might possibly have prevented the *Sailor Boy's* preliminary seizure, and so on. The brig would of course be pronounced to have been captured by mistake, and, as in the case mentioned in the President's last Message to Congress,—that high functionary would re-

commend the august body to appropriate a liberal
sum to compensate the British owners for the loss
sustained by the detention, and so on, of the *Sailor
Boy*; it being the fixed resolve of the Federal Government, whilst strictly enforcing their belligerent rights,
not to over-step them, or some such tall gammon. No
doubt the compensation would be liberal,—and under
instructions from Chuck, Stubbs might sell his stores
"by auction," the *Sailor Boy* also,—and the very devil
was in it if a thundering profit would not be realized.
A brig that had got safely across the Atlantic
would not be presumed to be unseaworthy, and the
munitions of war, Bob Richards said, would not,
under circumstances giving rise to no suspicion, be very
rigorously examined.   In his opinion the spec was a
first-rate one.   Of course there was the risk of going
to the bottom and feeding the fishes; but as Stubbs
was confident such a fate could not be his, it was not
worth taking into consideration.   As, however, that
immunity for the dangers of the deep might in the
book of destiny be restricted to Stubbses by blood, it
would be prudent that his (Richard's) sister, Mrs.
Stubbs junior, remained in England till she heard of
her father-in-law's safe arrival and success in Yankee-
land.   The introduction to Ezra Sidebotham might
next be improved; and if things in general wore a
promising aspect, he would himself accompany his
sister and her son to the New World, &c. &c.

The dodge was unquestionably a clever one, and

having the chance of not being heard of again, pretty sure to succeed. William Stubbs had the reputation of probity; but it's hard for an empty sack to stand upright, and tricks of the kind contemplated are never harshly judged by the world's opinion.

William Stubbs, at all events, lent himself to the project; the negotiation with Mr. Chuck was carried through by Richards : the *bonâ fide* of the shipment to Rio Janeiro was made capable of the clearest proof; Señor Rosas of that city being duly advised of the same, and a bill of lading forwarded to him by mail. The *Sailor Boy*, with full cargo, sailed from Plymouth, had fine weather throughout, and was captured in the latitude of New York by the *Roanoke*, Federal cruiser, and taken to the Empire City. Skipper Stubbs was much too ill at the time of the capture to give any explanation ; in fact, his confused, incoherent replies, satisfied the commander of the *Roanoke* that there could be no doubt of the legality of the seizure. So evident was this, that the President of the Prize Court —Captain Stubbs being incapacitated from illness to instruct counsel—ordered the *Sailor Boy* and cargo to be sold, upon the responsibility of the Government. This is not often done ; but, of course, *should* evidence be produced at the trial of the case, proving the illegality of the capture, ample compensation is awarded to the owners of the wrongfully seized ship and cargo. The munitions of war fetched a high price, and as if Fortune were determined to make William Stubbs amends for the calamities he had suffered during the previous years, the *Sailor Boy* accidentally caught fire in New York harbour, and was totally consumed! William Stubbs mended rapidly after that; the case of the *Sailor Boy* was pushed on in the Prize Court; the proof adduced that the brig was *bonâ fide* bound for Rio Janeiro was complete, irresistible; and William Stubbs was a better man by, at least, two thousand pounds than he ever had been. In the joy of his heart, he at once wrote home to his daughter-in-law and Robert Richards, inviting them out. From what he had already seen and heard there was a fortune to be had by running the blockade. Ezra Sidebotham bore a high character with those in New York who knew him; and the Bermudan schooner spoken of by Captain Crosbie would, no doubt, turn up trumps. He (Stubbs) would, however, delay his visit to Portland till after Richards, Mrs. Stubbs, and his grandson, arrived at New York.

He had not to wait long for Richards. That enterprising gentleman having heard from Stubbs, by first mail that left New York after the *Sailor Boy's* arrival there, how slick the affair was running off, lost not an hour in seeking to improve the success already substantially achieved. Discharging himself from his employer the attorney's service—with the drudgery of which employment he had long been disgusted—he went off to Birmingham, saw Mr. Chuck, had long and satisfactory conferences with that gentleman, with whom he matured a plan of operations which could hardly fail of a triumphant issue. Mr. Chuck, however, a cautious man, declined to go into the thing till the *Sailor Boy* business was definitely settled, and he had received the large sum of money for which he had a lien on the brig and brig's cargo. He would then assist heartily in the new scheme concocted by his clever young friend Richards. The ex-lawyer's clerk agreed that more could not be expected of a prudent man of business like Mr. Chuck, and himself returned to Falmouth in high glee. His first care was to see his sister, Mrs. Stubbs, explain to her that his presence was imperatively required in New York, for which city he purposed to immediately embark. As to her going out with the child, he thought that very unadvisable ; not only her womanly dread of the dangers inseparable from a voyage of three thousand miles was an objection, but there was no doubt, though he had talked of settling in America, that William Stubbs and himself would return together directly the affair of the *Sailor Boy* was disposed of. The young widow quite agreed with her brother ; had, indeed, never believed that her father-in-law, a Falmouth man—as the Stubbses had been for hundreds of years—would ever consent to end his days in a foreign country. Mr. Richards next paid a visit to a young woman he had long been courting, but whom he could not venture to marry upon a weekly wage of thirty shillings. Being strongly attached to the girl, and the vista of his future

16

being exceedingly bright in his lively imagination, he confided his hopes, expectations, and designs to her, so far as was needful, and Anne Dutton, an orphan girl, living with and drudging for a spinster aunt, whose barely-sufficient income would die with her, consented to accompany her lover, having first married him privately, by license, in Liverpool, where they were to embark.

The arrangements of Mr. Robert Richards were successfully carried out, and after an unusually rapid passage, Mr. and Mrs. Richards landed at New York, having but a few shillings in actual possession, but enormously rich by anticipation.

Richards had no difficulty of discovering the whereabout of the captain of the late *Sailor Boy*, by whom he was most cordially welcomed. He was not accompanied by his bride, nor did he allude to the trifling circumstance of his having married and brought out his wife with him—it might have damaged his reputation for prudence and sagacity in the estimation of William Stubbs ; and there were other reasons for silence.

The first move made by Richards, after thoroughly mastering the state of affairs, and dispatching the sum due to Mr. Chuck, with ample directions for that person's guidance as to the next and much more important venture, was to address a magniloquent letter signed William Stubbs, declarative of his high respect for the dignity and rigid impartiality of the American

Prize Courts, with respect to which so many scandalous reports had been circulated by baffled knaves :—as exemplified in the recent decision *in re* the *Sailor Boy* ;—and winding up with expressing his unbounded confidence that the dignified, if uncrowned chief of a great and glorious people would estimate with a large liberality the sum to be awarded the owner of the wrongfully captured brig, for the delay, inconvenience, and great loss he had sustained, taking into especial consideration he would be liable in heavy damages for not having delivered the military stores seized and sold— at an awful sacrifice, unfortunately—at the time stated by the charter-party at Rio Janeiro. A new con- signment had been ordered by the last mail from Eng- land, but it was highly probable that upon arriving at Rio Janeiro, it would be found that the Government there had provided themselves from some other quarter, and the stores be thrown upon the consigner's hands :—The illustrious President would no doubt give due weight to all the circumstances,—remember- ing, added Robert Richards, that *bis dat qui citò dat*, with which novel quotation the epistle terminated. The illustrious President was deaf to the voice of the charmer. The only notice taken at the White House of the buttered blarney published in the papers, forwarded to the President by William Stubbs, was a brief intimation from the Registrar of the Prize Court that any claim for compensa- tion beyond the paying over to William Stubbs of the proceeds of the *Sailor Boy's* cargo and the appraised value of the brig, which had already been done, must be preferred before and decided by the regular tribunal—a communication which excited Mr. Richards's unqualified disgust, and first shook his confidence in the superfine excellence of Republican government.

The letter in the newspapers would not, however, he trusted, prove to be labour in vain. Two or three copies were posted to Ezra Sidebotham, by the same mail which conveyed to that recently discomfited ship builder Captain Crosbie's letter of introduction, and a note intimating that William Stubbs and Mr. R. Richards, a young relative of his, would have the pleasure of visiting Mr. Sidebotham in Portland after the lapse of a very few days.

Mr. Richards was deeply concerned about Ezra Sidebotham. If that individual's active co-operation could not be obtained, the golden visions in which he had been indulging would melt to air like morning mist. Mr. Chuck would charter a ship for Halifax, pack her hold with the same kind of stores as the *Sailor Boy* had taken out, and consigned to the same merchant at Rio Janeiro. But a positive condition insisted upon by Mr. Chuck was that half the freight of the ship chartered to convey the stores, and half the invoice-price of those stores, should be paid in cash before his representative, who would go out with the said ship and cargo, delivered them over to William Stubbs.

Now, lucky as he had been, Stubbs was much short of
the required sum, owing to the illiberal behaviour of
the Federal authorities in the matter of compensatory
damages ; and unless Ezra Sidebotham would cast in
his lot with them, the clever combinations of Mr.
Richards would necessarily end in a ruinous failure.

The introduction of their proved friend Captain
Crosbie was potential with both Mr. and Mrs. Sidebotham. The most cordial civilities were lavished
upon William Stubbs and his relative Richards ; but
just as, says the proverb, a scalded child dreads *cold*
water, so did the Deacon and his wife shrink shud-
deringly from discussing business-ventures having
the slightest family resemblance to that dreadful Seth
Jones business. The Bermudan scheme mooted by
Captain Crosbie had long been dismissed from consideration. In addition to the awful risk, supposing
themselves to be associated with honest reliable
people, rebelliou, though but in a passive sense, against
the divine institution of Government, the Reverend
Caiaphas Boreham—cross-grained, snarled minister as
he might be and was in many respects—had convinced
them by sound Scripture texts, was a heinous sin.
That dogma met with the hearty assent of Robert
Richards,—it echoed the feelings of his own heart,
the settled convictions of his brain. The undertaking
to which he invited the limited co-operation of Mr.
Sidebotham was not in the slightest degree tainted by
the heinous sin of disloyalty. Mr. Richards referred

to the newspapers which gave an account of the unlawful seizure of *The Sailor Boy*,—and the subsequent
condemnation of that seizure pronounced by the New
York Prize Court, in proof that the immensely profitable ventures in which his friend Stubbs was engaged
were rigorously within the category of legitimate
commerce. Having for the hundredth time again
fluently set forth the brilliant results to be derived by
a very moderate investment in the venture under
consideration—Mr. Chuck, the wariest of men
and merchants, undertaking half the risk, Mr.
Richards, speaking for William Stubbs, declared upon
honour, from the bottom of his heart, that had it
not been for the sympathy excited in his bosom by
the excellent Captain Crosbie, for Mr. Sidebotham,—his
admirable wife,—promising family,—the most charming
girls, he might say, they not being present, he had ever
seen—he would have advised his relative and friend
to seek assistance in another quarter—Halifax namely,
—where the offer would be snapped at. Of course it
would. An investment of fifteen hundred pounds—
not one farthing more required—to realize at least
three thousand in less than three months! Mr.
Stubbs his relative would invest approaching to four
thousand ; Mr. Chuck quite double that sum. For
his own part, having experienced the warm hospitality
and kindness of Mr. and Mrs. Sidebotham, he should
grieve for their sake, for the sake of their amiable
family, that such an opportunity of recovering a con-

siderable portion of the large sum of which they had been so infamously swindled by infamous Seth Jones, should not be taken advantage of. Thus spake the tempter and his proem tuned. Into the heart both of Ezra and Esther Sidebotham his words made way. It seemed a feasible project, and if they could convert fifteen hundred pounds into three thousand, it would be a wonderful hit—a godsend for the girls. Ezra could no question raise such a sum upon his bond! And who shall say—worthy, serious people as were the Sidebothams—that the reflection did not glance through the minds of one or both, that if, which seemed scarcely possible, the fifteen hundred pounds should be lost,—it would not really be *their* money; whilst if the three thousand pounds so confidently promised should be really realized, the sun of an assured prosperity would illuminate their roof-tree. Briefly, the transaction was concluded; the fifteen hundred pounds was raised and banked, with William Stubbs' money, in Halifax. Stubbs, it would be unpardonable to omit saying, was an entirely passive instrument in the skilfully manipulating hands of Richards. He was dominated by a much keener intelligence than his own.

A telegram from Halifax informed Mr. Richards that the clipper-ship *Shannon*, Stephen Mace, master, from London to Rio Janeiro, but touching for special necessaries at Halifax, had arrived, and cast anchor in that port. William Stubbs, Ezra Sidebotham, and

Robert Richards, forthwith took train for that city. Esther Sidebotham, the barometer of whose mind with reference to the new venture was, as a rule, "variable," often "stormy," seldom "set-fair," or even "fair," ever insisting that Ezra should stick close to his fifteen hundred pounds, if the doing so should lead him to the world's end. Esther Sidebotham had unbounded confidence in the integrity of William Stubbs ; but as to Robert Richards——. Well, she hoped for the best ; but if a fellow that could talk down all the parsons in the State of Maine should turn out Seth Jones the second, it would not surprise her—not in the least ! However, God was above all !

Stubbs, Sidebotham, and Richards alighted in Halifax at the Crown Hotel, where they took up their quarters. The next day all three went on board the *Shannon*, which ship and her cargo, so far as they could judge of it from the manifest, and the contents of a few cases they had opened, pleased them greatly. Sidebotham, a remarkably considerate husband, wrote off immediately to his wife, assuring her that her suspicions, emphatically expressed at parting, of Richards, which he confessed had greatly disturbed him in a physical as much as in a moral sense (the brandy and ginger had, however, been of great service)—that her suspicions of Richards, so emphatically expressed at parting, were, he felt satisfied, entirely groundless. The *Shannon* was a noble ship, the cargo skilfully selected, and he (Ezra Sidebotham) nothing doubted, God willing, that he should be again in the bosom of his family within three months, with the three thousand pounds safe in his pocket.

Stephen Mace, commanding the *Shannon*, was a Falmouth man, who had been a wild slip, as Stubbs knew, in his youth. Stubbs had not seen him for years; but he had a first-class certificate as to competency from the proper authorities, and no objection could be taken to him on account of his having had more than an average quantity of wild oats to sow in his salad days. In truth, Stephen Mace was the half-brother of Richards's wife, and one of the conditions which the ex-clerk had insisted upon with Mr. Chuck was, that Stephen Mace should have the command of whatever ship he might charter, his credentials being unexceptionable.

The cash being ready, the agent of Mr. Chuck, in exchange for that cash, and the signing of certain documents, transferred the cargo and charter-party to William Stubbs and Robert Richards; all necessary papers for securing the several rights of the three partners were signed and sealed,—Richards's share, upon paper was one-sixteenth—and the luggage of those three partners was sent on board the *Shannon*, which, wind and weather permitting, would lift anchor on the following morning towards noon.

It would be only commonly courteous, Richards suggested, to liberally entertain Mr. Turner, the very gen-

tlemanly agent of Mr. Chuck. This was cheerfully agreed
to, and the small hours of the morning had struck
before the merry company separated and sought their
Crown-Hotel beds. Stubbs and Sidebotham slept in a
double-bedded room. Stubbs awoke first, with a splitting headache, and a hazy apprehension that he might
have overslept the hour at which he was to be on
board the *Shannon*. Upon consulting his watch he
found that was a groundless fear. It was half-past
ten; still there was not much time to spare. He
therefore aroused his friend Sidebotham, and as both
their throats felt like tanned leather, the bell was
rung, and soda-water, with a dash of brandy, for two,
ordered. The order obeyed, the attending waiter was
directed to have breakfast ready in two twos. They,
Stubbs and Sidebotham, would immediately get up and
dress, as they should be on board the *Shannon* in an
hour from thence at furthest.

"On board the *Shannon*, gentlemen," said the
waiter, with a mild expression of surprise—"on board
the *Shannon*, gentlemen, did you say?"

"Of course we said on board the *Shannon*," growled
both the gentlemen; "and please to look alive, will
you?"

"Beg pardon, gentlemen, but the *Shannon* sailed
at five this morning, with a rattling breeze; she must
now be at least forty miles away. Your luggage, gentlemen, has been sent here in a shore-boat; and there

is a letter in the bar for you. Mr. Turner directed me to ask if he should bring it up?"

The first phrase of the waiter's last speech had hardly passed the man's lips, when Stubbs and Side-bottom were bolt on end on their hams in bed, their terror-painted, cap-crowned figure-heads turned towards each other in dumb unutterable dismay. The waiter having repeated his question, and obtained no answer, took silence for consent, left the room, and presently Mr. Turner, who seemed much discomposed himself, made his appearance with a letter in his hand. The two victims were still silently staring at each other with dilated eyes. Mr. Turner, who pretty well comprehended the cause of the state of petrifaction into which Stubbs and Sidebotham had been thrown, and was himself nervously anxious to ascertain the contents of the letter, which he supposed would explain why the *Shannon* had sailed seven hours before the time she was expected to leave, and why the two gentlemen sitting up dumb and motionless in bed had been left behind, was impatient to open that letter.

"This letter," said Mr. Turner, "is addressed to Messrs. Stubbs and Sidebotham; it is from Mr. Richards, whose name is written in the left corner. As it probably concerns us all three, you will perhaps give me leave to open and read it aloud?"

Stubbs had sufficiently rallied to nod assent; Side-botham, who felt an instinctive, confused anxiousness that he was about to hear a *variorum* copy of a letter which had laid him upon a sick bed for nine weeks and three days, gave no sign. He could passively resign himself into the hands of the executioner, but was not going to draw the drop-bolt himself. Mr. Turner broke the seal, and read as follows :—

"On board the *Shannon*, 5 a.m., off Halifax, N.B.

"To my respected relative William Stubbs, and highly-respected friend, Ezra Sidebotham, conjointly :

"Gentlemen,

"I cannot doubt that this letter will inflict a severe shock of surprise, indignant surprise it may be, upon both of you. I grieve this should be so ; but the eternal necessities must be obeyed. Calm yourselves, therefore, respected relative and highly-valued friend ; do not permit passion to usurp more than momentarily the sovereign seat of reason. Listen with candour and indulgent consideration to the plain straightforward statement I am about to make.

"In the first place, I must remind my respected relative that it was never intended that highly-favoured *Sailor Boy* should sail to Rio Janeiro. Such an intention could never be entertained by any sane person ; *à fortiori*, he must have been convinced in his own mind, age not having totally and suddenly obscured his once clear intellect, that the destination of the *Shannon*, with her far more valuable cargo, could not be Rio Janeiro, or any similar or contiguous port. If, therefore, any deception has been practised upon my highly-valued friend Ezra Sidebotham, my respected relative is, if there be a pin to choose between us, more to blame than myself.

" With respect to Mr. Ezra Sidebotham, he and his exemplary wife took pains to leave no doubt upon my mind that they were profoundly convinced of the sinfulness, on their part, of attempting to run the blockade.

" These postulates stated, I hope, clearly, I proceed to justify my present course of action.

" The success achieved by the *Sailor Boy* was solely due to my advice ; in my brain that scheme was organized ; my respected relative was but the mechanical agent of its execution. Is it not reasonable, then, that I, the opportunity occurring, should avail myself of the capital gained by my genius to advance my own interest, my firm intention being to return that capital should I be successful,—probably by instalments at long dates ?   My defence, then, as regards my respected relative, is complete—unassailable.

" With respect to my highly-valued friend Ezra Sidebotham, my case is not perhaps so invulnerable ; yet it was indispensable to obtain his fifteen hundred pounds, and, as I have before said, the eternal necessities must be obeyed.   But for the conscientious scruples of Ezra and Esther Sidebotham, they would certainly have vested their fifteen hundred pounds in a vessel considered likely to run the blockade. Well, I borrow his money, and, as compensation, charge myself with the crime of the venture—take the risk upon my own shoulders—so that when he receives the three thousand pounds he has calculated upon, as a fair return for his borrowed capital, he will have made a tremendous haul without the slightest stain upon his conscience. That inestimable blessing he will owe to me. Of what evil significance is a compulsory loan of fifteen hundred pounds for a few months—say years—weighed against such a stupendous benefit as that ?

" Descending from principles to particulars, I assure my respected relative and highly-valued friend, that I am confident of running the blockade successfully, and than Stephen Mace no man is more fitted for such an enterprise. He is my brother-in-law ; his sister, my beloved wife, is with me on board the *Shannon*. It is a great happiness, when one is constantly liable to be exposed to the storms of adverse fortune, that the sunshine of domestic bliss will illuminate and cheer the darkest hour. My wife sends her kindest love to our respected relative, and although she has not the pleasure of the personal acquaintance of my valued friend, she includes him and his amiable family in her good wishes. In the full confidence that this frank explanation will be found entirely satisfactory, and prevent any unpleasantness from disturbing the intercourse of attached relatives and friends, I subscribe myself, dear Stubbs, dear Sidebotham,

" Your faithful well-wisher and servant,

" ROBERT RICHARDS."

The moment Mr. Turner ceased reading, Stubbs and Sidebotham, whose bodies would seem to have been kept in their erect position by the magnetic force of the reader's voice, fell back in their beds flat, rigid, and with closed eyes. The world was at an end, or if not, it ought to be! Mr. Turner stormed and raved like a madman; but of what avail were angriest words, the most contemptuous epithets?

The next day the silent sufferers crept out of bed, dressed themselves, paid the hotel bill, and left per rail, Sidebotham for Portland, Stubbs for New York, to ascertain if, by any chance, a tolerable sum in the way of compensation might, by hook or crook, be obtained from the American Government. It is stated that the two scarcely exchanged a single word till they parted at Portland, so completely were they stunned, knocked down, overwhelmed. Ezra Sidebotham, it being evening time when he reached home, crept into the house by a back way, and to bed by a side staircase, unheard by the family. This nearly occasioned a fresh catastrophe. Mrs. Sidebotham, having nodded till much later than usual by the fire, and her candle having gone out, ascended to her chamber without a light, and flopping into bed—she was a stout person—found, as she supposed, a strange man there, leaped out again screaming ten thousand murders, ran to the casement, threw it up, and broke the silence of the night and the repose of the neighbours by the wildest outcries. Unfortunate Ezra!

Not so unfortunate as he believed. Richards was far from being as black as he, in a spirit of rollicking banter, had painted himself. He had not the slightest intention of cheating his respected relative or highly valued friend out of a farthing. Confident that the calculated daring of Stephen Mace would enable him to successfully run the blockade, he wisely resolved to disembarrass himself for a time of his colleagues Stubbs and Sidebotham. They were in such ventures unreliable men ; and a divided command would almost necessarily produce fatal consequences. The result proved his wisdom. The *Shannon* successfully ran the blockade, at Norfolk, and though chased by a Federal cruiser, got safely away with a cargo of cotton. The ex-lawyer's clerk returned Stubbs and Sidebotham not only the capital he had " borrowed " of them, but handsome premiums over and above. Mr. Chuck was honourably paid ; and after that, Richards had a thumping sum for himself. He is still, I understand, actively engaged in running the blockade, though he himself does not quit Bermuda, where he has fixed his residence.

SPECULATION IN TEAS.

One hundred and fifty chests of tea of so inferior a quality that it would have been madness to have paid the duty on them, were sent by an eminent London tea-importing house to the island of Jersey, where no tea duty is leviable, with orders to sell them at any price. Now you can buy excellent tea by retail in the Channel Islands at about tenpence English money and English weight per pound. The price damaged or comparatively worthless teas might be expected to fetch would, therefore, be necessarily a very low one. These teas were, however, so inferior, that no offer at all could be obtained for them; and it was becoming a question with the owners whether it would not be better to pitch the teas into the sea, than to continue to pay warehouse-room for them. Before a decision was come to, a cash-customer presented himself, and after a good deal of haggling, bought the entire lot, at the rate of fifteen shillings per hundredweight, about three half-pence per pound; the agent of the London house gladly effecting the sale upon those terms

17

The purchaser was Captain Joly, a Guernsey seaman, and owner of a not very large coasting schooner, the *Guernsey Lily*. At a tavern in St. Peter's Port, he had read in the same paper two paragraphs which, taken in conjunction, excited his liveliest interest. One referred to the large quantity offered for sale in the neighbouring island for a mere song; the other, to the fact that tea had risen at Richmond, Virginia, to the fabulous price of from five to six dollars per pound. Captain Joly, calculating the average weight of the hundred and fifty chests, and the price he would probably get them for, and arguing that where teas, it should seem, were not in any quantity procurable at all, a very inferior article would be eagerly caught up at say, three dollars per pound : half the price of sound teas—slated the calculation and was perfectly dazzled by the row of figures which came out representing the profit of one hundred and fifty chests of tea bought at three half-pence, and sold at three dollars per pound. A Plymouth friend of his had only lately made a heap of money by running the blockade. The *Guernsey Lily*, a very fast vessel, could stow the hundred and fifty chests. The temptation was irresistible. Captain Joly took the next steamer to Jersey, made his bargain, returned to St. Peter's Port for the *Guernsey Lily*, and within three days had safely stored his speculative cargo, cleared for Gaspé, and was on his way to America. His crew numbered five men and a boy, his expences were trifling, and should he succeed, the foundation of a handsome fortune would have been laid. One of the crew, a new hand specially engaged for the occasion, had made several voyages to Charleston, and asserted that he could take a vessel as safely there as any pilot in the States. Captain Joly had, moreover, taken the precaution of purchasing two chests of really good tea, a clever move, judged by the Scripture axiom, that "the children of this world are wiser in their generation than the children of light."

"I had a capital run," usually begins Captain Joly when relating his American adventures; "a capital run till we were off Cape Hatteras. Then worries and troubles set in like a flood. Baffling, contrary winds, dead calms, sudden squalls keeping us knocking about for days and days, and not a bit the forwarder at the end. I was getting out of patience, especially as I had no rest day or night; if it wasn't a squall, or a calm, or a head wind, it was a Yankee cruiser heaving in sight, and the officers squinting at us through their glasses, till a man that had a little fortune at stake almost sweat blood and water at every pore. I had a clever chap serving as mate on board, John Lemaître of Jersey. 'Captain,' says he, 'if I was you, I'd just unbend them new sails, No. 1 canvas, as your'e proud on, fish up the old patched ones from the hold and bend *them* on.' 'What in the devil's name,' says I, 'will be the good of that?' 'Why this,' says he, 'the small size of the schooner has, I have no doubt, stood our friend up to the present time. 'Taint usual for vessels of our tonnage to come from England with intention to run the blockade. It wouldn't pay, except under particular circumstances, as tea at three half-pence a pound, selling at Richmond for twenty shillings. But if we bend on them old patched sails, the notion of a vessel so canvassed meaning to run the blockade, would be nonsense; and yet we shall get pretty near as many knots out of the *Lily* as with the No. 1 sails. We shall be taken for a coaster, or fishing-vessel, and them infernal cruisers will think us beneath their notice.' I felt there was gumption in that; and the thing was done as Lemaître proposed. It's a real fact that the *Guernsey Lily* would have been snapped up the very next day but for that simple dodge. A Yankee gun-boat who had paid us more attention than was pleasant, spoke us about noon. ‘Had we seen a schooner, about our build and tonnage, carrying the British flag?’ (With our patched canvas we had hoisted the stars and stripes)—‘Had we seen a schooner, about our build and tonnage, carrying the British flag, and spreading new white canvas?’ ‘Yes we had, at early morn; she was then steering sou-west, and couldn't be so very far off.' With that the gun-boat mizzled, steering sou-west. “*Sacré-re-re tonnerre,*” continued Joly—the reader may or not be aware that the Guernsey or Jersey people speak French as well as English; the fairly educated classes purely enough, the uneducated a patois curiously compounded of Norman-French and strange English, intelligible to neither Frenchmen nor Englishmen—"*Sacré tonnerre*," said Joly, "I was standing in towards James River, unwatched, unsuspected by the cruisers. We had deep-sea fishing lines out, and when night fell we should as certainly have run the blockade, the wind blowing steadily from the north-westward, and were not more than ten miles from the mouth of the river, when I was flung upon my back by a skulking rascal whom I had been obliged to ropes-end and put under stoppages for refusing to do his duty. That scamp, Jean Corbet, and, I am sorry to say, a Guernsey man, there being an English ship-of-war in sight, the *Rinaldo*, hung out his flannel-jacket on the fore-rattlings. The signal seen, away of course comes a boat from the frigate. Corbet complains of ill-usage, volunteers into the Queen's service, and being, as far as outside goes, a likely fellow enough, the officer demands the fellow's wages, his traps, and carries him off to the *Rinaldo*. That's, as we all knew, according to the rules of the Royal Navy, but it's a privilege often abused. It was in my case. The infernal scamp was determined to wreak his spite upon me for keeping him, the lazy hound, to collar ; and he knew very well that if once on board the *Rinaldo*, he should be able easily to com- municate in writing with one or other of the Yankee cruisers. Jean Corbet was cleverish at his pen, was loose of tongue, what we call a sea-lawyer. I guessed what would happen. So did Lemaître. 'We haven't a moment to lose,' said the mate. 'One of them

Yankee gun-boats will know what we are after, and what the *Lily's* cargo is, in just no time. Better top our boom at once.' I thought so too, and hauling in our sham deep-sea fishing lines, we stood away westward, close-hauled under about a four-knot breeze.

Not an instant too soon; but soon enough to escape the gunboat which was quickly after in chase of the *Guernsey Lily*. The veil of night fell between pursued and pursuer, and when day dawn lifted that veil there was nothing to be seen upon the broad waste of water but the sun-smile of God.

Joly and Lemaître held counsel together. The conference was brief, the decision unanimous. They both agreed that attempting to run the blockade in a sailing schooner was simply ridiculous, and that the best thing to be done was to make at once for Gaspé, and there endeavour to dispose of the teas in a legitimate way, and it might be hoped at no loss, if not with much gain.

The *Guernsey Lily* dropped her anchor in Gaspé Road, and some two or three hours afterwards, Joly and Lemaître were in the smoking-room of the Merchant Tavern, seeking (like a celebrated personage) whom they should devour. The *Guernsey Lily* had one hundred and fifty chests of prime tea on board, with which her owner and captain had intended, knowing what a tremendous price tea would fetch in Charleston and Richmond, to run the blockade. But his courage failed him now that the decisive moment was come, and he proposed selling both schooner and cargo at Gaspé to the highest bidder.

Amongst the company was one Ephraim Train, a Yankee, and, for aught I know, a relative of Tramway Train, at all events a speculative gentleman of the same sort, who listened with both his ears to Joly and Lemaître. Before the house closed it had been arranged between Train and Joly that the former should come on board the *Lily* at about eleven the next morning, and if the parties could agree, purchase schooner and cargo.

They did agree. The two chests of good tea purchased by Joly in Jersey had been broken by some accident—it was better to take test-samples from them. Ephraim found the tea excellent, and eagerly agreed to the price asked—sixpence per pound. The *Guernsey Lily* he moreover agreed to purchase at the price asked—four thousand dollars. The transaction was concluded, the money paid, and Joly and Lemaître, who were suddenly seized with an attack of the malady known as home sickness, left Gaspé by the next packet, and are now, I am told, getting on comfortably at Guernsey, Joly navigating a brig, Lemaître a cutter, of their own. They have a decided opinion that Yankees are not anything like such smart fellows as people suppose them to be. Are not by any means everybody.

Ephraim Train (following the story as it has been

told to me) Ephraim Train's suspicions, self-suggested
suspicions, it may be, induced him to more particularly
ascertain the value of his teas.   The result of that
ascertainment was a confidential visit to Mr. Crowther,
a highly-respectable gentleman, and a distinguished
member of the Society of Friends.   Ephraim had had
dealings with Mr. Crowther, and friend Crowther
rather envied the lucky hit Train had made in *re* the
Guernsey Lily and her cargo.   Ephraim Train had a
melancholy story to relate.   Mr. Crowther knew he
was a partner in the firm of Train and Company, New
York.   Well, that firm, though solvent in point of fact,
would be made bankrupt if a certain amount of money
were not immediately forthcoming.   Ephraim had
nothing but the teas and cargo which he could turn
into cash.   He had determined to make Mr. Crowther
the first offer, &c., &c.   Crowther, as I understand it,
ultimately accepted the offer; William Judkins—a
clever, dissolute seaman, well known in British North
America—having first undertaken to run the blockade with the *Guernsey Lily.*   Ephraim Train was
considerate.   He simply recouped himself for the
money he had paid for schooner and cargo.   This was
handsome, liberal.

Mr. Crowther, a gentleman of large sympathies,
embracing with equal good will both North and South,
arranged to travel over land to Charleston, which he
would find little difficulty in doing, so as to be there
as soon as, or before the *Guernsey Lily.*

He did arrive there some ten or twelve days before William Judkins succeeded, and he did succeed, in running the blockade with his precious cargo of teas. The rest of the story must be so familiar to the readers of Southern newspapers, that to them I shall be writing a thrice-told tale, vexing the dull ear of a drowsy man.

Judkins presented himself in full feather at the Constitution Hotel, in which Mr. Crowther had taken up his quarters, and was warmly congratulated on his success by his owner. The sale of the teas would take place on the day after the morrow, and four dollars per pound was the lowest figure it was expected they would make. Friend Crowther was rejoiced. God had blessed his basket and his store.

The sale was a highly successful one. The samples were taken from the two chests purchased by Joly in June. It does not appear that Crowther was cognisant of the fraud, nor Judkins. Most likely the two chests being broken, the samples were taken from them as of course. The average price realised, said the "Richmond Enquirer," was four dollars per pound. Friend Crowther had made a great hit.

He was very merry; had dined well, and was reclining in serene solitude upon a sofa, when the trampling of unrespective boots was heard upon the stairs, and presently eight fellows, looking in every one of their fierce faces revolvers and bowie knives, entered the apartment.

" I say, old feller ; you sold them teas, didn't you?"

Friend Crowther admitted that he *had* sold teas *ex* the *Guernsey Lily* and been paid for them.

" Yes, you rascally Yankee swindler, you have. Now, then, just hand back them dollars, and be smart about it!" Friend Crowther, though awfully frightened, decidedly objected to the disagreeable process of "paying back." A fierce altercation ensued, the ultimate result of which was the seizure and gagging of Mr. Crowther, and his transportation Heaven knows whither—he himself does not—by the eight brawny ruffians. One Charleston paper says he was conveyed out of the house in a slipper bath. However that may have been, John Crowther made his appearance at Boston about five weeks after his capture in a deplorable condition. He came unto his own and his own received him not ;—not, at least, till he was thoroughly scoured, and all remnants of tar and feathers had been completely removed.

Friend Crowther, though he had met with a most afflictive loss, was not quite ruined, and he was beginning to brighten up again—a wintry brightness—when a new and unsuspectable calamity befel him. William Judkins made his appearance at Boston, and fastened himself, like the unslakeable horse-leech that he is, upon the miserable Crowther. Judkins can prove at any moment that friend Crowther has been consorting with the "rebels," and holds, consequently, that venerable friend at his mercy. What will be the result I know not, but the gentleman to whom I am indebted for the foregoing particulars, says he is losing well-fed flesh rapidly, and has indistinct, hazy, intermittent ideas that emigration to Kaffraria or Timbuctoo would be a pleasant change. Joly and Lemaître have much to answer for.

L'HIRONDELLE.

I AM indebted for the following narrative to a French exile, who, with hundreds of fellow sufferers, supports with a noble patience the cruel sufferings of expatriation. I have not presumed, except in a few instances, to correct the Gallicisms which seem to be inseparable from the style of Frenchmen who have most successfully cultivated the English language :—

"I shall endeavour to speak without prejudice, without passion, of the dreadful struggle between the Northern and Southern States of America. That will be difficult, for my sympathies are entirely with the South. Yes, I confess to a fierce aversion for the Negro. *How* fierce, how well-formed is that aversion, the reader shall be able to judge by a full knowledge of its cause. I was a drummer-boy, ' un petit tambour,' in the army of General Le Clerq—the first Napoleon's brother-in-law,—sent to make Toussaint L'Ouverture listen to reason. To recognise, acknowledge the indisputable fact, and to act upon the conviction,—that 'the first of the blacks,' as Toussaint called himself, was, in the great attributes of man, inferior to the lowest white not stricken with idiocy. Ah, well, in the transport-ship were Madame Latouche and two daughters, Julie and Françoise, beautiful as what we imagine of angels both. It was my privilege to wait upon the Latouche family. I cannot even now with the experience of approaching to fourscore years to instruct and guide my pen, describe, analyse the sensation which possessed me whilst ministering to the wants,—humbly, oh, so humbly, ministering to the wants of those two earthly seraphs. They were very kind : the smiles which rewarded the small services I was able to render them, played like sunshine about my heart, sparkled in my veins with the golden glory of sunrise, drooped to sadness and gloom with regretful, farewell sunset. Madame Latouche and her daughters were going out at the invitation of her deceased husband's father, who had long since settled and prospered in Saint Domingo. He lived at a charming place about four leagues distant from the capital. He had a large plantation, had many negro servants, and was, I believe—let me be just even to those black fiends—a hard task-master. He received Madame Latouche and her daughters with cordial *empressement.* It had happened during the voyage that I had accidentally saved Madame Latouche from a possibly fatal accident. Our ship *La Révolution,* being a bad sailer, had dropped far behind during the night. One of the English frigates, which constantly

hovered about the fleet, endeavoured to cut off and capture *La Révolution*.   At daybreak she had not succeeded, but continued firing with vivacity.   The
French admiral sent a ship of the line to our assistance,
and the British frigate slowly withdrew from her enterprise, but her last shot broke the foremainyard.
Madame Latouche, always an early riser, was on
deck; she was a brave woman; the French blood
coursed hotly in her veins—that will be fully admitted presently.   A block was cut loose by the
cannon ball — I darted forward, but just in time.
I thrust Madame Latouche with violence out of
danger, and the block fell upon my own shoulder,
my left shoulder, of which I have never since recovered
the perfect use.   Madame Latouche was very grateful.
She and her daughters were ministering angels.   I
was still suffering acutely when the expedition reached
its destination, and, at the instance of Madame, the
colonel gave me permission to accompany her to the
mansion of her father-in-law, Etienne Latouche.   Convalescence was slow; and I was not desirous of getting well—fit for service, too soon.   St. Domingo was
on fire, as one may say.   There was parleying and
fighting, fighting and parleying, the end being that
Toussaint was made prisoner, and shipped off to France,
where he died.   That, however, is nothing to my story.
The blacks believed themselves able to expel the French.
There was general insubordination; local insurrections,
murdering of whites, which Toussaint's best troops made

but feeble efforts to suppress. Certainly they were not suppressed. I soon became much more anxious for the safety of Madame and Mesdemoiselles Latouche than for the recovery of my own health, except in so far that restored strength would enable me, a lad of fourteen, but of course a juvenile Achilles in my own estimation, to defend those ladies.

Etienne Latouche, as I soon discovered, held his property and his life at the mercy of the excited blacks. I have read a book written by Madame Martineau, a highly-respectable, eminent lady, called "Toussaint L'Ouverture." Talking over it with friends who have long dwelt in St. Domingo, who have practical knowledge of the disgustfulness of negro society, it was considered marvellous that so gifted a lady should have penned such miserable absurdities. This *en passant*.

There was a mulatto girl in the establishment who used to bring me meals—medicine. The name of this girl was Staffa; she was the daughter of a Frenchman, a small planter, who—eternal infamy to his memory!— sold Staffa with the rest of his stock when he left St. Domingo for France. Oh, yes—infamy of infamies! I have had the satisfaction of meeting with the *scélérat* in Paris, of reproaching him in the presence of a crowded audience with his scoundrelism, and in a meeting at the Bois de Boulogne of sending a bullet through one of his lungs, of which hurt I hope he died, though he did not sink to the silent land till about twenty years ago.

The sexes are precocious in St. Domingo. Staffa loved me. I was older by years. I respected Staffa; I did not love her. The shrine of my heart was occupied and crowned with one image—that of Julie Latouche. Even now I behold it beyond the abyss radiant, glorified. It beckons me—invites me with seraph-smile to the abode of bliss. A dream, it may be said. Ah, well, perhaps! Does not your glorious Shakspeare say this little life is rounded with sleep? I hope to die dreaming, if it be dreaming of that lustrous, beckoning vision. But no, there is no illusion. Julie awaits me in the other life. And Françoise, their mother, palm-wreathed and rainbow-crowned, will welcome me to the all-compensating land, where all tears will be wiped away, all wrongs, all griefs forgotten. Terrible, if this were indeed a dream: it would suppose that humanity is the creation of a malignant demon!

Staffa, with much hesitation, much reluctance, told me that a plot was hatching amongst the negroes to seize the Latouche family. A black devil, calling himself a "general" of Toussaint's army, had been mainly instrumental in organising the conspiracy. This was "General" Menoz. Action would soon be taken. She would warn me in time. I did not trust to the timeliness of that warning. I was still weak; but at my urgent request Staffa consented to procure me a horse—to steal it, ready accoutred, from the stables. The blacks were prepared; the soldiers of

Menor at hand to give the alarm. To notify Etienne
Latouche of the impending catastrophe, would be to
precipitate it. The French soldiers, brought to the
Château Blanc unexpectedly, were their hope of salvation. Not one of the family would be permitted to
leave. I, a mere insignificant boy, was not watched;
would not be missed.

Staffa was discreet and faithful. I mounted the
horse, unobserved as I believed, and rode *ventre à
terre* towards the French general's head-quarters.
This was about three in the morning—I mean the
time of starting. I was stopped by a negro picquet.
Confounded, I answered confusedly, contradicted
myself, and gave excuse to the negro officer to detain
me till he could communicate with Toussaint. My
horse was taken from me; but I was not very strictly
guarded. Devoured with impatience, believing I could
find my way easily on foot, I was again *en route* in less
than an hour after my arrest. I lost my way; it was
a wild country thereabout—was in those days, whatever
may be the case now. The blacks, as a rule, were
jealous—suspicious of whites. Murdering ruffians
most of them. I dared not ask for direction or suc-
cour from any of them. The mulattoes are always at
bitter feud with the niggers, *pur sang*. From a
mulatto family I procured not only needed sustenance,
but a faithful lad as guide. Late on the second day
after leaving Château Blanc, I reached the head-
quarters of the French general — ragged, travel-

stained—a miserable object.   Audience of the general
was not to be had ; the request was treated with
derision.   A singular circumstance, if I may so express
myself, relieved me from despair.   In our voyage out,
I had made the acquaintance of an individual who was
attached to the cuisine of General Le Clerq ; possibly
he was only a turnspit.   I am quite sure his *status* was
many degrees below that of the *chef*.   *Malgré çà*, he had
the ear of the *chef*, the *chef* had the ear of the general,
and I obtained an audience of the French Commander-
in-Chief.   My story interested him.   The general was a
more superior man than he has been represented to be—
what you English call a gentleman in its real sense.
Not, it may be, in manners.   No ; the general was
somewhat uncouth—vulgar, if you will ; but he was,
for all that, a brave, chivalrous Frenchman.   Captain
Dunoir, of the 12th Dragoons, was at once sent for.
" Take two companies, Dunoir," said the general ;
" this good fellow will guide you.   Hesitate at nothing
to secure the safety of the Latouche ladies."   For
Dunoir, as with all French officers, it was simply to
obey, and with alacrity and decision.   In less than a
quarter of an hour we were in saddle, and speeding
towards Château Blanc, as fast as was compatible with
the efficiency of the horses when the force should
arrive upon the scene of action.

Ah ! we were too late ; hotly as we pressed on.
The Château Blanc was a smoking ruin.   The body

of Etienne Latouche, the countenance stern, defiant as at the moment he met his death, was stretched by his own hearth-stone. The domestic negroes were nowhere to be seen. At last Staffa made her appearance. She was white as stone ; almost as dumb, petrified to a bronze statue. Ultimately I obtained information from her which set us on the trail of the murderers— the ravishers !

We came up with the infernal villains at about noon the next day. They were drawn up in a sort of enclosure—protected by a low abattis. They were all armed with muskets. When our *dragons* approached, a flag of truce came towards us, a white kerchief borne upon a tall stick. With the flag of truce came Madame Latouche and her two daughters. Ha ! the wife was bowed down, prostrated with unutterable agony. But the daughters !—but Julie, Francoise ! Theirs were faces cut in Parian marble—hard, inexorable, calm as despair, immobile as death. Menoz had surrendered them. He would answer for what had been done to Toussaint L'Ouverture. Etienne Latouche was a traitor to the native government. The ladies were questioned. Madame Latouche answered by sobs only. The girls spoke not, save by their eyes—a terrible *Judith* expression needing no commentary in words. Ha ! My heart was on fire ! Dunoir's dragoons were almost equally excited. Said Julie, as the Captain dressed his men preparatory to the charge : "Captain Dunoir, not

one of those fiends must be left alive !" "Not one,
Mademoiselle, assure yourself of that !" The bugle
sounded, and away our glorious soldiers bounded to
their prey. A feeble volley did not stay us for a
moment. We were upon them. It was a massacre.
All, all were slain ! Those once gentle girls—flowers
of heaven, fresh, lustrous with the pearled dew of
Paradise, surveyed the scene of carnage with hard,
tearless eyes. "Not one has escaped ?" asked Julie,
clasping and kissing my bloody hand ; I had done my
part in the work of vengeance, young as I was. "Not
one has escaped ; you are sure of that ?" "Positive.
Every devil amongst them has paid the forfeit of his
life—a too light penalty." Not many months afterwards, that heart-broken mother, those angel daughters, entered the Convent of Dominican Nuns in
Martinique. They all three died, and are buried
there.

My antipathy to negroes will now be understood. I
opposed, with all the energy of my soul, their emanci-
pation in the French colonies by the provisional
government inaugurated by the Revolution of 1848.
Victor Hugo's brilliant genius did not dazzle me. I
was too strong in right and truth. Yet right and
truth availed nothing to counteract the specious
theories which, despite physiological and psychological
science, proclaim an equality between the Caucasian
and the African races. Armand Marrast—I say it
boldly—shared my opinions, though he did not speak

upon the subject. So does Bethmont, and, I believe, Carnot.

Enough of this prologue to the tale I am to tell. I got back to Europe, served not without distinction in the great Emperor's armies, married late in life, and became the father of a noble son, whose adventures in *L'Hirondelle* (*The Swallow*), I am about to relate. Eugène Trouchet—my first son and only son—early manifested a decided *penchant* towards a sea life. Our domicile was in the vicinage of Saint Maleo, our family being of Bretagne origin. He entered the royal navy, and became, in process of time, Lieutenant de Corvette. He was enseigne in *La Belle Poule*, commanded by De Joinville, and forming one of the fleet under Admiral Baudin, which compelled the surrender of the Mexican fortress St. Juan d'Ulloa. The Prince twice mentioned him favourably in his despatches or reports—especially for his gallantry in the naval attack on Mogador.

All that has truly nothing to do with Running the Blockade, but a father's feelings *will* ooze out whether à *propos* or not of the subject immediately under consideration.

Eugène had a highly respectable, if not brilliant, career before him, when the Revolution of 1848, which seemed to disclose so dazzling a future for France, by placing her at the head of the great party of Progress scattered throughout Europe—at once its Mars and its Nestor—afforded an opening to the soaring ambition, the calculated daring of Louis Napoleon Bonaparte. How miserably blind we Republicans were! We died even as the fool dieth. The Adventurer of Strasbourg and Boulogne had been sedulously sounding France with the sword of Napoleon. Peasant France returned no uncertain sound, and we prepared not for the battle!

When the thunderbolt fell, both myself and son were thrust out of France. For awhile we resided at Brussels, but Belgian independence is but a very brittle affair; so we followed Victor Hugo, Pierre Leroux, and other celebrities to the island of Jersey;—not to dwell even in peace there. A stupid comment upon the Queen of England's visit to Napoleon the Third aroused the ire of the loyal Jersians, and we were ordered to quit ancient Cesarea. I, with my son and daughter, came to London. There for a certainty Pandemonium let loose could not harm us: so it has proved.

Our resources were mediocre; Eugène, after many fruitless efforts, was fortunate enough to obtain a commission in the Oriental Steam Navigation Company's service, his knowledge of the Turkish and Egyptian languages standing him in good stead. That was well, very well indeed. Eugène gained the esteem of his superiors. I, with my pen, scratched out a humble income in the stony, precarious path of literature.

We were thus plodding a weary way, though no' destitute of occasional flowers, towards the tomb, walking with more or less confidence in the shadow of death which stretches in unbroken blackness from the cradle to the grave, when the world-quake in America startled Europe.

Now, as before evidenced, I had a bitter, ineradicable dislike of the negro. Such a sentiment may be very unjust; perhaps it is so. I only know that fire will not burn it out of me. In my heart, and without reasoning at all upon the subject, I was one with the South.

It chanced that I had made the acquaintance, the intimate acquaintance, of a gentleman, whom I will call Mr. South. He was a man of wealth, an enthusiastic "states-man" from the old dominion (Virginia). He held numerous shares in the Hâvre de Grace and Paris Railway, and had married a French lady, a native of the thriving capital of maritime Normandy. My daughter Eulalie, whom the coup d'état proscription did not touch, more than once paid lengthened visits to Madame South, with whom and her charming family she was an immense favourite. Naturally Eulalie would talk of her brother Eugène; of his skill as a seaman, the bold adventurous turn of his mind; that he, too, like his father, was enthusiastic in the cause of the South. Mr. South listened with interest, and finding my son would be in London, and with me, on a not distant day, came from Hâvre especially to see us, and hazard a proposition.

"Messieurs Trouchet *père et fils*," said the worthy

gentleman, suddenly plunging *in media res*, as we sat
at our moderate dessert: "Messieurs Trouchet *père et
fils*, I have a matter of vast importance to discuss with
you. We Anglo-Saxons are practical people. An
ancestor of mine, in the great struggle from which re-
sulted the liberties of England, whilst others were
arguing, splitting straws about popular right and right
divine, advised and assisted Oliver Cromwell to seize
the plate of the Cambridge University, which was
about to be melted down for the King's use. Being
honest men, a receipt was given for the same. He
was also one of the soldiers who arrested the High
Sheriff of Hertfordshire at St. Alban's, whilst that
dignitary was haranguing a crowd of rustics in the
city of England's first martyr, and trundled him to
London. I am proud of that ancestor, and am a good
deal of his turn of mind. Now, the South in its agony
needs practical help. Words are but wind. I happen
to be the owner of *L'Hirondelle*, a large steamer now
lying in one of the Hâvre docks. I took her for a
bad debt. Now, with all respect to French seamen, it is certain that they are not, as a rule, individually enterprising men. They have a superstition
in favour of governmental organization. I have
thought, M. Eugène, that you, by your contact
with the British marine, have shaken those cramping
fetters. But no doubt Napoleon III. will not,
for a long time to come, interpose in the American
struggle. That is certain. Well, I offer you the

command of *L'Hirondelle*. I expect her in the Thames to-morrow. She will take in a full cargo of contraband stores, and will clear for the Cape de Verd Islands. No suspicion attaches to her, and the *Tricolor*, I am ashamed to say it,—but *fact* is *fact*,— commands more respect from the Northerners than St. George's Ensign. Never mind, St. George's flag will one day, depend upon it, signally vindicate itself. Meanwhile, I propose to run the blockade with *L'Hirondelle*, commanded by a Frenchman, manned by a French crew. What do you say?

Eugène hesitated. The proposition involved the throwing up of his lucrative appointment in the Oriental Steam Company's Service. Else, sharing as he did to the full my anti-African mania, if it be a mania, he would at once have leaped at and embraced the offer. It was not for himself that he drew back from the proposal to exchange certainty for uncertainty, positive competence for prospective, it might be illusory, riches. No, no : very far from that. But his father ! but Eulalie !

Our friend read his thoughts in the clear tablet, the open book of Eugène's honest countenance. "I have thought of all that," he said. "I am very rich. Neither your father nor Eulalie shall suffer in any event. That is part of the bargain. The details can be arranged. Are we agreed?" Sacred blue ! of course we were agreed ; and in less than a fortnight, *L'Hirondelle* left the Thames, *sensé* for the Cape de Verd Islands, really for New Orleans—with a heavy cargo of a highly valuable consignment of contraband stores.

The voyage was prosperous till *L'Hirondelle* rounded Cape Florida, and entered the Gulf. Then misfortune befel her. I shall state all the circumstances without reserve, being desirous of repelling, by the voice of simple truth, the scandalous calumnies invented by the New York and Boston presses. It may be that the infamous notoriety attained by Gordon Bennett and his worthy confrères renders it quite unnecessary, in the judgment of calm-minded, sensible persons, to refute any lies he and they may choose to publish. That is true, my friends, if only calm-minded, sensible persons read his and their infamous prints. Were that so, the proprietor of the *New York Herald* might count its subscribers upon his fingers ; but that is not so—very far, indeed, from being so—and filth flung upon you is not the less offensive because it is voided from an inexhaustible common-sewer ! This will be admitted, and I continue the narrative without fear of misconception.

The *Lone Star*, a large United States barque, bound for Vera Cruz with munitions of war purchased in Great Britain by Miramon's agents, had started a butt, and it was with great difficulty she was kept afloat till aid was rendered by *L'Hirondelle*. My son Eugène, with the actives of his equipage, went to the help of the *Lone Star*. Fortunately the weather was calm, and it was possible, by shifting heavy weights to, as one may say, careen the barque, enabling our men to get at the started butt. The disaster was remedied—the *Lone Star* continued her voyage. She was a fast vessel, faster than *L'Hirondelle*. Well, what happened? Some of our Frenchmen, in the gaiety of their hearts, and not for one moment able to conceive that people to whom they had just rendered a signal service, would, like the warmed serpent in the fable, turn round upon and sting their benefactors, talked openly of their intention to run the blockade. That was folly, imprudence in the last degree. The American captain, Philip Sangster, was a Unionist *enragé* — this may be some excuse for his doings. That, however, is not my opinion. The *Lone Star* and *L'Hirondelle* had not parted company two hours when a war-steamer, proudly bearing the Federal banner, was descried ahead a long distance off. She was standing away, crossing *L'Hirondelle's* sea-path almost at a right angle. Evidently the Federal steamer did not suspect or even notice *L'Hirondelle*.

The captain of the *Lone Star* decided that should not be long the case. He opened a pattering fire from two cannons of light calibre to attract the steamer's attention ; and having done that, bunting was run aloft, which told the Federal war-ship, as plainly as words could have done, the character and mission of *L'Hirondelle*. Immediately the *Iroquois'* bows were turned in the direction of my son's ship. Eugène understood it all, and at once resolved upon his course

of action. Night was near, the earlier stars were
glinting forth, and there was almost a dead calm. The
Iroquois is a wonderfully fast vessel; escape by flight
was hopeless. Calling his men aft, Eugène plainly
described the situation, and what he was resolved
upon attempting, if assured of the men's support.
The reply was a hurricane of cheers. Instant preparations were made : *L'Hirondelle's* boats were lowered,
plentifully stowed with provisions, spirits, water, and
abundance of small arms. In the darkness this operation would not be easily perceived by either the
Iroquois or the *Lone Star.* The boats, containing the
entire crew, pulled off; Eugène was the last to leave
the ship. It was afterwards known that the boats
leaving *L'Hirondelle* were seen by both the Federal
vessels : it was supposed they intended making for the
nearest land, a purpose which the Federal officer in
command had no desire to frustrate. He would be
quite satisfied with the capture of ship and cargo.

Eugène, I have said, was the last to leave the ship ;
he is a stickler for the British maritime maxim
in that particular. Before going over the side into
one of the boats, he fired with his own hand a slow
train of combustible matter. Ha! ha! In about ten
minutes tongues of flame shot up from *L'Hirondelle's*
hold ; in another ten minutes she blew up. The
coveted ship had escaped the secure captors. The
Iroquois, therefore, resumed her original course—was
soon lost in the dark distance. The sailing-barque,

Lone Star, was left alone upon the calmly-heaving sea : the wind did not rise—her sails hung idly from the masts and yards. *L'Hirondelle's* boats crept towards her with muffled oars. There was a slight struggle, in which Philip Sangster was wounded, not mortally as it proved. The *Lone Star* was a prize to the crew of *L'Hirondelle*—a legitimate prize I contend. No insult was offered to the captain or crew ; they were in the hands of generous Frenchmen—the lies in an adverse sense so industriously circulated are pure inventions. I *will* say, though my own son was the chief instrument in effecting it, that it was a bold, remarkable deed—the conception of genius, of ready resource, carried out with courage and decision.

L'Hirondelle did not run the blockade to New Orleans, but her *double*, the *Lone Star*, did. It was a good exchange. Mr. South was wonderfully pleased, and Eulalie's *dot*—she was married not many weeks since—was, having in view the modest requirements of herself and husband, a large, liberal one. The story of *L'Hirondelle* is now told for the first time, truly told, and I confidently claim for Eugène Trouchet the sympathizing brotherhood of the seamen of the sea nation *par excellence.*

ERNEST CARRUTHERS.

———

THE following " strange story" has been handed to me
by a highly respectable gentleman.   The sole reliance
for its authenticity is that high respectability of character.

Mr. Ernest Carruthers resided at Lymington, Hampshire.   He was an old man twelvemonths ago when
this strange story opens : so old, that if he himself
is to be believed, he was a midshipman in one of the
British ships which won the stubbornly fought battle
that gave Admiral Duncan his title of Earl of Cam-
perdown.

Ernest Carruthers was, what is usually termed, an
eccentric man.   He did not live, act, talk like other
people.   He had no visitors, and though rich in means,
lived penuriously.   A taciturn, almost savage man.
Occasionally, however, his pent up nature would over-
flow in a wild torrent.   When that occurred, the narrative was invariably the same. He repeated it so often
to his only visitor, the gentleman who furnishes this

paper, that my correspondent was able to repeat it ver-batim.

It seems that he had risen to the rank of lieutenant in the Royal Navy, in 1814, the year, as every body knows, before that which witnessed the crowning glory of Waterloo. He was present in that year at a court draw-ing-room held on behalf of the Regent by the Princess Augusta. There he saw Mrs. Colonel Farmer, subse-quently the first Lady Lyndhurst, and forthwith went mad about her, as it is said did Lord Dudley and Ward (first Earl Dudley). Carruthers was poor then, and the lady a married lady too, was to him only a bright particular star, which entranced, dazzled him, but to possess whom could only be the dream of a madman.

Waterloo was fought, and in that battle Colonel Farmer, the lady's husband, was killed. Now comes the to me incredible part of the story. Carruthers declared that, many weeks before Waterloo, he saw in the clear noontime, in day-dreams, I suppose, Mrs. Colonel Farmer, standing in a terrible battle-field, beside the ghastly corpse of her husband. He knew the corpse to be that of Colonel Farmer, though he had never seen that officer. Well, perhaps this may be accounted for. Carruthers knew that, Wellington's army being in Belgium, a sanguinary fight with Napoleon's legions was certain, imminent, and his wish, father to the thought, engendered the dream. The fruition of his hopes, should the enchantress be a widow, was no longer an impossibility, as he had become rich to the extent of seven thousand pounds per annum.

This leads us back to Carruther's youth : I am not constructing the facts furnished to me in a very artistic mode. This leads me back to Carruther's youth-time as depicted by himself. He was born at the mediæval, picturesque City of Chester. He was a posthumous child, and his mother died in giving him birth. He inherited nothing,—all was gone with his mother, who had a life-annuity. But his mother's sister had made what is called a fortunate marriage. That is, her great beauty had purchased her a very wealthy husband, and an ante-nuptial settlement by which, at her husband's death, she would possess his whole real and personal estate. We can all understand that such a settlement eagerly signed, sealed in the hot flush of desire, would, say after six months, a long stretch of moony time,—be looked upon by the husband as an intolerable burden,—a hateful clog. Why, he had no power,—his children would know he had no power—to will them one farthing. They could only turn to their mother ! Terribly exasperating that to a moody-minded man like Mr. Clifford, as I christen the Lancashire husband. Terribly exasperating ; and he spared no effort, even by cajolery, simulation of excessive fondness ; now by threats, ultimately by personal violence—to induce his wife to rescind in legal form the ante-nuptial contract. This went on for years, but the wife could not be bent to his

will. A daughter, Emily Clifford, gave her strength
of resistance. Before she married Clifford, the wife
had "kept company," as they say of humble courtship,
with a young man of the name of Bowdley. This
young man was the son of a sufficiently well-to-do
"statesman," as farmers cultivating their own ground
are called in the North of England. They were
strongly attached to each other, and Emily Proctor
had frankly confessed that truth to Clifford when he
offered her his hand, and all the wealth of which that
hand held the key—stated plainly that she yielded in
marrying him to the entreaties, the supplications of her
parents,—who, aged, terribly worsted in the battle of
life, besought her to marry the rich man. He would
settle upon them for life five hundred pounds per
annum, charged upon estates that at his death, should
she survive him, would be absolutely her own. Spite
of that frank avowal on the young beauty's part,
Clifford persisted in his suit, complied with all the
conditions insisted upon, and the espousals were so-
lemnized. Young Bowdley, on the very morn of the
wedding, was found dead in his father's threshing barn,
hanged by the neck to a beam by his own handkerchief
—stark, rigid, cold. He had probably been dead at least
twelve hours, the surgeon said. He had therefore destroyed himself at about eleven the previous evening
or night. One can understand that. And had Clifford
understood that self-slaughter in its full significance,

19

he would never, though his first-born Emily was a seven months' child, have been for ever engaged in a voyage of discovery over her tiny features. Such was, however, the case, and raging jealousy burned like consuming fire in his veins. His hatred of the child strengthened,—inflamed the mother's love. Clifford believed that Emily would be bequeathed all, or at any rate the major portion, of his property, by his wife, to the injury of his own, undoubtedly his own, children. Matters were in this state when Mrs. Carruthers died. Her rich sister was with her in defiance of Clifford's command that her relatives should be as strangers to her. Her father and mother had not enjoyed the pension obtained by their daughter's prostitution,—was it not prostitution?— legal, church-consecrated prostitution if you like,— more than about two years. Mrs. Carruthers commended the new-born babe to her sister's protection, —more by supplicating looks and gestures than by words,—she being almost incapable of speech. Mrs. Clifford understood that silent appeal, and weepingly responded to it, accepted the task, the responsibility, though at the moment not knowing how she could accomplish that task, fulfil that responsibility. Although nothing could deprive Mrs. Clifford, in the event of survivorship, of the Clifford estates,—she was almost penniless for the time ; one of her husband's modes of coercion being to stint her in money.

The exigency quickened her woman's wit. She ap-

plied to Mr. Hill, a legal gentleman, and as I am
told an uncle or other relative of the present Mr.
Recorder Hill, of Birmingham, for advice, and found
it would not be difficult to raise upon her ante-nuptial
settlement, a sufficient sum per annum to provide
decently for her nephew. This was done, and Ernest
Carruthers, kindly nurtured during infancy at a Yorkshire farm, was placed in a boarding school in Lan-
caster, fairly educated, and ultimately, through the
interest exerted by Mr. Hill, obtained the warrant of
Midshipman in the British Navy.

Before that the boy had become a visionary—a
dreamer of dreams. An idiosyncracy which had been
superinduced as it were upon his originally healthy
structure of mind by strange occurrences,—appalling
suspicions. The lad was seldom at Clifford Hall;
but often enough, as he grew in years and understanding, to perceive that between his aunt and her husband
there was deadly feud. There were four young Clif-
fords, including Emily the first-born. The three died
in one year: the hated girl—hated I mean of her
father—survived in robust health. Those untimely
deaths, that vigorous life, blew the fires of acrimony,
of hate, in the husband's bosom, consuming all of
manly, honest, human feeling. He did not suspect
that his wife had made a will; more than that, he
was advised that by the wording of the detested ante-
nuptial contract, she could only devise his property—
his property, that was the serpent-sting! in the event

19—2

of her outliving him. He was mistaken on both points. Mrs. Clifford had executed a will—having been assured by her faithful friend, Mr. Hill, that she had an undoubted right, according to the legal inter- pretation which a court of equity would give to the terms of settlement, to bequeath her contingent right to the Clifford realty and personals. The will was made in favour of her daughter Emily, who would in- herit all, with the exception of fifty pounds per annum charged upon the property, to William Carruthers. This niggardly provision for a favourite nephew was, as one may say, compensated for by a clause devising the entire property to him should the said Emily die unmarried —childless.

In one of the apartments at Clifford Hall was the framed portrait of a Lucy Clifford who had died on the morning of her marriage from, it would appear before unsuspected, disease of the heart. She was very beautiful, and her dark glossy hair, magnificent eyes, intimating, rather than revealing, unfathomable depths—her perfectly-moulded figure, suggested to my correspondent, as he listened to Mr. Carruthers' enthu- siastic word-painting, made bright, vivid, life-like by the fact that the describer, in part unconsciously, was describing the first Lady Lyndhurst, suggested to him the idea of Rebecca in Ivanhoe. Now, whenever the boy slept at Clifford Hall, that portrait left its frame, and, animate with seemingly substantial life, entered the

chamber, and gazed smilingly upon him. Mere dreaming there can be no doubt, though William Carruthers
would have gone to the stake in vindication of the
reality of the apparition ; that he saw Lucy Clifford
as she looked and moved upon earth, with his own
bodily eyes. Upon one occasion, a few weeks before
the midshipman's warrant was attained, and—the
reader will give the proper significance to this circumstance—and on the night, the evening of which had
been more strongly marked than usual by a frightful
quarrel between his aunt and her husband—that ani-
mated portrait, stepping as it were out of the frame, and
speaking to him, not by words, but by those bewilder-
ing, sad, immeasurable eyes, was accompanied by Mrs.
Clifford and her daughter Emily. A heavy snow-
storm had fallen, and Ernest Carruthers being wide
awake as he declared, and gazing outward through the
casement, the blind of which he had not drawn down,
saw those three figures pass the window, clearly discernible in the calm, moon and star-lit night, and
defined by a back-ground of snow. He could not be
mistaken. As they passed, all three turned prophetic,
melancholy glances upon Carruthers. Well, so far the
story is believable, in the sense that a dreaming man
might believe himself to have been awake, and have
really seen those passing figures—faces. But those three
figures, positively, according to Ernest Carruthers,
came into his room—through the street-door, and his

own chamber key-hole, I suppose—and, mystery of
mysteries! Mrs. Clifford had suddenly become transformed into a drowned lady,—death-white face, loose,
dripping hair, and other appearances of a woman having met with a watery death.   The apparitions gazed
earnestly upon the lad, and gradually dissolved from
view.   It is essential to mention, that in Clifford
Park there was a large sheet of water,—a miniature lake.
A fancy skiff floated upon that miniature lake, and
in that fancy skiff Ernest Carruthers had seen, on
that very eve-day, so to speak, Clifford and his wife.
It is easy to trace the lines of waking thought which
led to the suggested dream.

What is all that, it will be said, to do with Running the Blockade?   Much, you will find, though
in a roundabout way.   This curious vision, this
dream of William Carruthers, was in part strangely
realized, always supposing that the eccentric old man
residing in Lymington, Hampshire, did not confound
after, with preceding events, images, ideas—about
which I have my doubts.   It is, however, undoubtedly
true that Mrs. Clifford was drowned in the lake; that
her husband skulled the skiff at the time. He escaped
easily, being a fair swimmer.   Emily was rescued by
Francis Charlton of Wisbeach, who chanced to be in
the neighbourhood on a visit, and was fishing that day
(by leave) in the lake.   But where he sat with fisher-
quietude, beneath trees which glassed themselves in

the water, he would not be seen by Mr. Clifford. Charlton was a strong swimmer, but he could only save the girl. Francis Charlton never afterwards spoke with Clifford : told him openly he should consider it as a personal insult if he ever dared claim personal intercourse with him. At the inquest, Mr. George Day, a very intimate friend of Charlton's, a chum of his, as we say, who had been one with him in the fishing expedition, and who "happened" to be summoned as a juror by the constable of the Hundred, stoutly refused agreement to the verdict of "Accidentally drowned."

Now, these circumstances had a prodigious effect upon Ernest Carruthers. It does not seem to me that absolute *mania* was produced in his boy-mind, but that the mental texture was, so to speak, prepared to receive superstitions, fanciful impressions.

Yes, I feel sure that is the right conclusion. He obtained, as I have said, a midshipman's warrant in the royal service, and in old age was ever iterating that Duncan said he was one of the most promising youngsters in the service. Probably, if to be able to face the sudden uncovering of a masked battery without winking was the criterion of naval excellence. At all events, whatever moral flaw was to be found in his character, he was emphatically a *fighter*. He passed creditably, too, for a lieutenancy, attended the drawing-room in 1814, there saw, and was enslaved by—unconscious to herself, it being doubtful that any hint of his consuming passion ever reached her—the soon to be widowed Mrs. Colonel Farmer, subsequently the first Lady Lyndhurst. There is nothing very surprising in that, but the marvellous part of the story is that he really believed the lady to be the Lucy Clifford who, when he was a boy, stepped out from her gilt frame, and smiled benignly upon him. I need not say that this was not the first of the delusions by which William Carruthers was possessed. It is likely that Mrs. Colonel Farmer resembled the portrait of Lucy Clifford. But he himself, I am positively, sincerely assured, adopting a novel creed of metempsychosis, was convinced Mrs. Farmer was Lucy Clifford herself restored to life, and purposely inspiring him with frantic passion.

Still he could have had no hope of marrying the object of his maniacal idolatry, after Colonel Farmer had fallen at Waterloo, till, by the death of Emily Clifford, he came into possession of the Clifford estates. The acquisition was mainly important to him that he was thereby enabled to offer that property —encumbered by himself, of course—to the beautiful widow. He hurried to London for that purpose, and, palpitating with hope and fear, went to the lady's residence—her former residence, then no longer hers. He gave his card, telling the footman who received it that he wished to see Mrs. Colonel Farmer immediately.

"Mrs. Colonel Farmer," coolly replied the flunkey, "left here weeks agone; she is married to the Solicitor-General—Mr. Serjeant Copley!" The poor fellow was stricken down as by a thunderbolt, and the next eleven years of his life was, as far as concerned his own memory, a blank, or nearly so; he knew himself to be under restraint, and retained vague memories of stern keepers, punishments, and so on, but nothing definite, except that a radiant, lustrous figure—Lady Lyndhurst, of course—always interposed and saved him in moments of extremity. Reason at last resumed her throne—never more a firmly based one—he was pronounced capable of managing his own affairs, and liberated. Have I stated that Clifford committed suicide three or four years after his wife's death? The fact was so; he deliberately drowned himself in the lake. The *Nemesis* which pursues the man of crime is often strikingly dramatic in action. A "Receiver" of the rents had been appointed by the Lord Chancellor, *ex-officio* custodian of all lunatics, and, not at all a strange story, the proceeds had barely sufficed to defray the costs of management and the sustenance of the lunatic.

However, Ernest Carruthers was again his own master to the extent of God's permission, was possessed of an ample revenue, and fixed his hermit-residence near Lymington, a charming place, separated from the Wight by a mere ferry.

Time developed a new phase of insanity, intangible to "mad doctors"—but not the less insanity. The father of Serjeant Copley (Lord Lyndhurst) was an American—an American artist. I am told, and it may be, that the great and eloquent Nestor of the British House of Peers was born there. I do not say that is the fact. William Carruthers believed so, and an unappeasable, rancorous hatred of all Americans took and held possession of his infirm brain. The sudden death of Lady Lyndhurst, which he read in his morning newspaper as he was about to take breakfast, again smote him into positive idiocy. The servant found him on the floor apparently in an epileptic fit. Perhaps that really was the case. How the matter was managed my correspondent did not say—likely enough, did not know — but Ernest Carruthers was not on this second occasion placed under restraint ; he remained in his own house, and, after the lapse of two or three months, was again declared to be sane by his medical attendant, and this, notwithstanding that he obstinately associated the death of Lady Lyndhurst with that of Mrs. Clifford, who it may fairly be presumed was done to death by violence.

Thus moodily brooding on figments, unrealities, Ernest Carruthers brokenly lived on till the outburst of the present American war. That event inspired his feeble frame as with galvanic life. He, a sickly septuagenarian, when the affair of the *Trent* appeared to render a conflict between Great Britain and the Federal States inevitable, positively dispatched a formal tender of his service as lieutenant to serve against the detested Yankees, which magnanimous offer having been declined with thanks, the monomaniac tasked his eager, though flawed brain, to discover how he could best go into the conflict upon his own hook. Not a difficult problem to resolve. Supplying the foes of the Yankees with weapons necessary to sustain their great battle was obviously to render them vital aid. But how to do so most effectually was the question.

It was oddly resolved. Passing, as was his wont, dreamily along the High-street, Lymington, he was awakened, as it were, to the common-place realities of life by a public-house squabble. Some half-a-dozen rough fellows, all more or less drunk, issued from a tavern from which they were driven, good-humouredly enough, by the landlord and his friends, headed by a very formidable gentleman named Josiah White, but locally known as "Black White"—a dark, hairy fellow, of singular strength and iron-courage, some five and thirty years of age, who the gossip of the locality averred, perhaps believed, was a natural son of Sir Harry Neale, whose seat was in the neighbourhood of Lymington. Likely enough this was a calumny, and had its origin in a kind of blackened likeness which the man's features bore to those of that gallant officer. " Black White," moreover, being a seaman, and of unquestionable daring, might, by persons whose logical deductions seldom square with Archbishop Whately's rules or maxims, have added force in the popular mind to the assertion that "Black White" was really a sinister son— not, I fear, a correct phrase, but sufficiently expressive —of the gallant admiral. The landlord with the help of his friends, and notably of "Black White," was successful ; the obnoxious swillers were ignominiously ousted, and "Black White" and companions re-entered the tavern.

At once the conviction flashed upon the mind of William Carruthers, that "Black White" was the man for his money. Personally he knew something of the fellow, and that something was not to his disadvantage. He bore a ragged reputation; that is to say, was a known smuggler, night-poacher : ponds or game preserves within a radius of not a few miles extent were familiar haunts to him ; and he could, as a practical individual, have given sound hints, had he chosen to do so, upon the now much-vexed question of prison discipline. Nevertheless, " Black," as the old saying is, was not so black—nor "White," one is quite safe in remarking, so very white. He would not have needed to engage in running the blockade of the British Customs, nor have plundered fish and game preserves, had it not been that when returned home, after an exploit which made some noise at the time, with his pockets lined with cash, twelve or thirteen hundred pounds, he unhesitatingly disbursed every shilling to relieve the husband of his only sister, a noted smuggler, as he himself had since become, from the bilboes, in which he was lodged for an attempted fraud on the Customs in the article of tobacco upon quite a gigantic scale. Everybody knows that bankruptcy and insolvent courts have no power to sponge out debts to the Crown, and John Hayward might have remained for life in jail, but for the payment of the penalties in default of which he was incarcerated.

This circumstance, creditable as it was to Black White, had nothing, or at all events very little influence in pushing Ernest Carruthers to the conclusion that "Black White" was the man for his money. It was the recollection of how "Black White" obtained the twelve or thirteen hundred pounds which suggested that conviction. The received story or history of the very, or rather not all questionable exploit, was this: Black White was second mate of the *Lily*, a brig, owned by a highly-respected gentleman who firmly believed, with the late Prince Albert, that the black potentates of Africa—him of Dahomey inclusive—may be induced to give up their slave-hunts, the butchering or selling to slave-traders all of their neighbours that fall into their power, if it could be shown to them that the production of palm-oil, &c., would be a more profitable employment than chasing, capturing, and selling their captives to slave-traders. The *Lily* was dispatched to the African coast, taking with her a large quantity of the cheap and showy articles which excite the admiration and envy of the African, the return to be in palm oil, ivory, gold dust. The *Lily* was commanded by Joseph Smithers, a good seaman, but whose constitution had been fatally weakened by excess. He was killed by the African pestilence within a few days after the *Lily* reached the Bight of Benin. The first mate became captain, Black White second in command. Not very long afterwards the new captain followed his predecessor, and Black White was skipper *pro tem* of the *Lily*. Discipline could not have been very rigorously enforced, as a fire broke out in the *Lily* not many days after Black White assumed the command, caused by the ignition of a spirit cask by an uncovered candle carried by a drunken sailor, intent upon adding fuel to the flame raging in his veins.

The fire could not be arrested, but there was plenty of time to let fall and provision the boats. The small arms on board, with requisite ammunition, were also carefully placed in them, and the crew, about forty in number, left the burning ship at about midnight on the 14th November, 1850. Unfortunately a heavy gale from the westward blowing dead upon the iron coast, and which threatened to be of long continuance, had obliged Black White to obtain a wide offing as a matter of prudence, as quickly as possible. That was done by sailing east and by south as close to the wind as possible, so that when the *Lily* was abandoned she was fifty leagues or thereabout distant from any approachable shore, habited by what by comparison may be termed civilized savages. The storm, too, still raged, though the wind had greatly abated, and there was a heavy sea on. Not an agreeable position for men in open boats.

The morning, however, broke finely, that is to say, the sky was tolerably clear, the wind fast dying away; though the tumbling, swashing sea—not the long smooth heave of mid-atlantic, was still a great danger. However, there was plenty of provender, solid and liquid, and the men, by relays, pulled with a will towards the Loango river. Before long it was a dead calm; and at dawn on the following day the sea was smooth as glass.

Black White, anxiously sweeping the waters with his glass, having no mind to trust himself to the mercies of even semi-civilized Africans, observed, when the morning haze lifted sufficiently, a large brig, becalmed, motionless;—a painted ship upon a painted ocean. He was not very long in making up his mind as to her character; that she was the *Don Juan,* a Spanish slave ship, which the *Lily* had several times spoken with. He was sure of this, not only from the lines of the hull, and *set* of her foremast, which was peculiar, but that one of the mizen square-sails was quite new, substituted, no doubt, for one carried away, whilst all the rest of her

canvas was worn and patched. He was sure from
her position that she was full of negroes, and steering,
when arrested by the breathless calm, for Cuba. His
version of what followed, told by himself in half the
publics of Hampshire, was this, or nearly so.

"I saw at once that we might not only save our
own skins, get out of danger from both sea and savages,
but make a precious good thing of it. I am no
great shakes of a scholar, but I knew that by treaties
between Spain and England, Spain was bound, and
had been paid an enormous sum too for signing them,
to prohibit the slave-trade to her own subjects, and em-
power the British slave squadron to capture any
Spanish slave-ship that might be fallen in with. Now
this *Don Juan* had so far slipped through the fingers
of Her Majesty's officers; and surely any of the
Queen's subjects might carry out a duty which her
preventive squadron had failed to perform. That
stands to common sense. So getting the three boats'-
crews within ear-shot, I explained the thing. That we
were forty well armed fellows, that a fresh rising of
the storm which had gone down might send us to Davy
Jones at any moment, or at the best or worst drive us
upon some part of the African coast where we should
serve for breakfast, dinner, and supper,—luncheon also,
no doubt—white flesh being the favourite eating of
many of the African tribes. Well, in the ship about
a league away westward we should be quite safe—her

crew were not very numerous, and were Spaniards—
what, then, was to hinder us from having a shy—fulfilling a duty, and filling our pockets so full of gold
that we shouldn't be able to button them? The lads
understood me in a moment, gave a thundering cheer,
and away we pulled for the *Don Juan*. I was sure of
victory in any case, but as I did not wish any of our
Lilies to lose the number of their mess, I adopted the
stratagem of hoisting the Union Jack upside down,
in token of distress. All's fair in war, you know.
Well, that dodge puzzled the Don. Of course a full
slave-ship didn't want to receive forty foreign seamen
on board, but the Spanish captain, though commanding
a slave ship, was not a bad sort, and he fancied we
might only be in want of water or grub; of which it
happened he had plenty to spare, his ship not being
more than two-thirds full. That diddled him, or if he
had a gunner worth his salt, the two six-pounders he had
on board, which I did not suspect, might have done
mischief,—in fact, capsized the whole concern. As it
was, we were allowed to go close alongside. Up to the
deck we clambered like wild cats, and the *Don Juan*
was ours. No lives lost—no blood drawn, which is
always pleasant when a thing can be done without.
Well, gentlemen, we behaved as gentlemen to the
Dons—served them grub and grog plentiful—landed
them carefully at a part of the island of Cuba
where a few hours' walk would bring them to their

friends, leastways their countrymen ; then filled and
bore away under a lively breeze. Of course we painted
out the name on the stern, and as I was told by a clever
chap of ours that Don Juan is Spanish for Lord John,
I rechristened the brig Lord John Russell. We made
a tidy thing of it—very tidy thing of it, though I was
only allowed four shares to each man's one, which, considering that it was I that put our fellows up to the
thing, and was captain, cannot be considered otherwise than grossly unfair. However, as *mum* was the
word, it was of no use hollering. The niggers, a fine
ot, fetched good prices ; the *Lord John Russell* didn't
go off so well. Still, I should like to be in such another
game, and the sooner the quicker. Oh, as to where
we took and sold the ship and slaves ? There I must
be excused. I wouldn't whisper it to my nightcap.'

I am assured that this act of piracy actually occurred
as related by Black White ; and I suppose the only
reason he and his fellows have not been visited by
condign punishment is, that no legal evidence could
be obtained against them. Black White's tap-room
talk would, of course, weigh for just nothing in a
British court of law.

This, then, was the story which, flashing suddenly
upon the crazed brain of Ernest Carruthers, at the
sight of Black White in the High Street, Lymington,
determined that gentleman to engage his services in
Running the American Blockade.

An appointment was made for the next day, which Black White punctually attended, listened with eager interest to the scheme propounded by Mr. Carruthers, declared it could not fail of success, but before going the whole hog into it, he should like to consult his brother-in-law, John Hayward, an older and more experienced seaman than himself. He should like Hayward to be amongst them should the affair come off. Mr. Carruthers could have no objection to that, and at the next consultation Hayward was present. The two seamen-smugglers had no difficulty in convincing Mr. Carruthers that in order to be safe to win, it was necessary their ship should be a fast steamer, and manned with a crew of the right sort, whom *they* would select, being well acquainted with the genuine article. This was also agreed to, and full authority was given Black White and John Hayward to visit the Thames, the Mersey, the Clyde, or any other place where reliable building-yards were located, and treat for a suitable ship, though not to conclude the bargain.

A fine ship, just about to be launched on the Clyde, was finally pitched upon, paid for, and hurried with all haste to completion. Mr. Carruthers, consistent in his craze, had her named the *Lady Lyndhurst.* He then announced that he intended going in her himself; this was a new notion—not as captain, Black White would command her, but as a privileged passenger, for the fun of the thing. The announcement took the pair of rascals greatly aback. They remonstrated, spoke of the danger, hinted at the gentleman's age, but finding he was resolved, of course gave in.

The *Lady Lyndhurst* sailed in ballast, bound for Bermuda and Nassau, where it was proposed to purchase the required munitions of war. Not very long afterwards John Hayward's wife and family embarked for the Bahama in a Royal Mail steamer.

The destination of the ship was suspected, and before reaching Bermuda, she was twice brought to and overhauled by Federal cruisers. She could not, however, be detained, and without touching Bermuda went on to Nassau. There rifles, powder, and other military munitions were obtained, and a favourable opportunity of breaking through the first line of blockade was anxiously waited for. A swivel 12-pounder was also purchased and mounted amidships. The chief overwhelming anxiety of Black White and his comrogue John Hayward, was to successfully get *away* from Nassau. Once that effected, getting into a Southern port would, according to them, be mere child's play. That extreme anxiety occasioned weeks of delay, to the intense annoyance of Mr. Carruthers, in whose mind doubts of the good faith of the captain and chief mate of his ship began to arise. So early were these suspicions manifested, that the project of taking Hayward's wife and children on board upon some more or less plausible pretence, was abandoned. It was even carefully concealed from him that they were on the island.

It was, however, quite evident that the dread of being captured *going out* of Nassau, felt by Black White and his co-conspirator, was real. Ernest Carruthers himself could not doubt that. He imputed it to personal timidity, believed he had altogether mistaken his men, that that precious story of seizing the *Don Juan* was an audacious flam. Getting at last out of all patience, he sought to dismiss his two officers, but found he had no legal power to do so, so cunningly had the ship's papers, clearance, &c., been, with the aid of a Glasgow "writer," drawn up. During the voyage out from and return to the Clyde, Black White was commander, and could not be ousted of his post.

At last a furious gale, hurricane rather, blew the squadron of "Observation" far away to the westward, and then it was seen that want of physical daring had nothing to do with Black White and John Hayward's hesitation. Steam was immediately got up, and away dashed the *Lady Lyndhurst.* The fury of the tempest was at its height, the night black as Erebus, weather that would have induced the hardiest mariner to seek the shelter of the nearest port. The *Lady Lyndhurst* behaved nobly. When day dawned, and the violence of the tropical tempest had abated, nothing, it was found, had given way, nothing been strained or injured. The mask was then thrown aside.

Black White and John Hayward entered the cabin as Mr. Carruthers was turning out, said they must have a confab with him, and after some beating about the bush, told the aghast gentleman that before attempting to run the American Blockade, it had been determined by captain and mate to go into a scheme which would, twenty to one, with so fast a ship, make men of both for life, whether they afterwards succeeded in getting to Charleston, Mobile, or other Southern port or not. They would, however, stand word as to making a resolute attempt to do so, after their own turn had been served. "What, in the devil's name, are you talking about?" furiously demanded Mr. Carruthers. "What scheme, to make men whom I have for some time known to be two arrant scoundrels men for life, are you talking of?"

Black White mildly observed that, as the school copy-book said, civility gains esteem, and that it was no manner of use for the old gentleman to show his teeth, seeing that he could not possibly bite. Black White then coolly went on to explain what it was intended to do, and the fairness and reasonableness of the thing itself. He and Hayward were both poor men; he, Mr. Carruthers, was rich, and would be much richer should the *Lady Lyndhurst* at last succeed in breaking the blockade, whilst they, to whom success would be owing, would be not much better off than before. To remedy such an injustice they had made up their minds, before the steamer left the Clyde, to run along the African coast, picking up blacks in exchange for the muskets and ammunition on board. The ship would be filled in no time, big, roomy as she was. There were nine ship-carpenters amongst the crew, and all the necessary materials having been quietly shipped, water-casks and other requirements necessary to slave-ships would be speedily knocked up, so that there would be no time lost to speak of. In proof of the scrupulous honesty of their intentions towards the owner of the ship, they intended to buy in Cuba, where the negroes would be sold, an equal quantity of munitions of war to that then on board, and resolutely endeavour to run the Blockade. The business, if successful, and they had no misgiving about that, would leave them a very large sum, whilst Mr. Carruthers would have sustained no real wrong; all this, with a good deal more impudent rigmarole to the same effect, concluding with a significant hint, that if he acquiesced quietly, all would be well, whilst any attempt to excite insubordination amongst the crew would result badly for himself.

What could the entrapped monomaniac do—how help himself? There was really nothing for it but to submit, and he resigned himself to his fate with as much patience as he could command, and the *Lady Lynd-hurst* kept her swift course towards the African coast.

Black White was perfectly correct in saying there would be no difficulty in exchanging muskets and gunpowder for negroes. A full cargo of black "chattels" was rapidly obtained, and the *Lady Lyndhurst's* bows were pointed to Cuba.

No mischance occurred, the negroes were safely landed in prime condition, immediately disposed of at enormous prices, and the confederates, in fulfilment of their promise, began purchasing muskets, powder, &c. This was necessarily a matter to be discreetly carried out, as although there is a large depôt of arms in Cuba, intended for smuggling to Southern ports, the Spanish authorities are naturally very careful of avoiding any pretence for a quarrel with the Federal States.

Mr. Carruthers, if he believed Black White and Hayward were really buying military stores, had no doubt that a second African expedition was intended, and determined upon revenge. Black White never, he observed, by any chance left the ship, and remembering that, as the story went, the captain and crew of the *Don Juan* had been landed in Cuba, it was no difficulty to divine why the captain of the *Lady Lyndhurst* remained in strict concealment. Carruthers had been confined to his berth by illness since his ship's arrival at the Havannah, but rousing himself by a great effort, he determined to go on shore, and a servant was sent with a message to Black White, with whom he had ceased to hold personal intercourse since the announcement made to him of the African expedition, requesting that a boat might be got ready to convey him on shore, as he was anxious to visit the city and its environs. This had been foreseen, and his message was answered by Black White, by whom he was bluntly informed that he would not be permitted to go on shore. This raised his excitable spirit to frenzy, a violent scene ensued, and in an access of spasmodic rage he seized Black White by the throat, endeavouring to throttle him. Spite of the temporary strength given by his frenzy, he was as nothing in the sinewy grasp of Black White, who shook him off in a moment, and with such, we may presume unintentional, violence, that Carruthers fell, striking his head with great force against the edge of one of the lockers. He was immediately picked up, and carefully tended ; the exterior wound soon healed, but the unfortunate gentleman's shattered intellect was utterly destroyed. He was reduced to a condition of complete idiocy, a harmless idiocy, and when he again appeared on deck would invariably walk forward to the bows of the ship, gaze on the figure-head supposed to represent Lady Lyndhurst, for hours together, addressing it with wild passionate incoherence, in the evident belief that the lady of his love was before him in bodily presence.

"Black White" and Hayward kept their word as to running the blockade, which they did to Charleston, though exposed in doing so to the close fire of three American gunboats, during which poor Carruthers ceased not to gaze at and apostrophise the wooden image. He is now, or was lately, an inmate of a lunatic asylum in or near Charleston.

White and Hayward were unquestionably great scoundrels, but, as with all human nature, theirs was a mingled yarn of good and evil—the latter texture no doubt greatly predominating. At all events, they deposited in the chief bank at the now half-ruined city of Charleston the amplest funds to secure for poor Carruthers the best, most indulgent treatment which money could purchase ; they also proposed, and have perhaps carried out their promise, to invest the whole amount due, according to their mode of reckoning, to the unfortunate gentleman.

In breaking the blockade outwards, which, spite of friendly warnings, White and Hayward determinedly essayed, the *Lady Lyndhurst* nearly came to irreparable grief. Two sloops-of-war, in addition to gunboats, awaited her, through which she was compelled to pass the gauntlet. Her unrivalled speed sufficed to prevent her capture ; but the American cannon was this time much better pointed than usual. First one mast, then another, till all three had gone, were shot away, and "Black White" himself was knocked over, his dexter pin being shot away. Fortunately for the adventurers, the machinery was not struck, nor was the funnel; the loss of her masts rather accelerated her speed, and she made Nassau, where she is refitting for another, and possibly many more attempts at RUNNING THE BLOCKADE.

THE END.

www.ingramcontent.com/pod-product-compliance
Lightning Source LLC
Chambersburg PA
CBHW020953030726
47496CB00005B/1495